NOW YOU SEE HER

PAUL J. TEAGUE

Morecambe Bay Trilogy 1

Book 1 - Left For Dead

Book 2 - Circle of Lies

Book 3 - Truth Be Told

Morecambe Bay Trilogy 2

Book 4 - Trust Me Once

Book 5 - Fall From Grace

Book 6 - Bound By Blood

Morecambe Bay Trilogy 3

Book 7 - First To Die

Book 8 - Nothing To Lose

Book 9 - Last To Tell

Note: The Morecambe Bay trilogies are best read in the order shown above.

Don't Tell Meg Trilogy

Features DCI Kate Summers and Steven Terry.

Book 1 - Don't Tell Meg

Book 2 - The Murder Place

Book 3 - The Forgotten Children

Standalone Thrillers

Dead of Night

One Last Chance

No More Secrets

So Many Lies

Two Years After

Friends Who Lie

ONE

Monday—Day 1

REECE TURNED the key in the ignition for the third time, fearing that it would finally flood the engine. There was no auto-choke option for her—it was a miracle that the four wheels stayed on. The engine turned with the bad attitude of a churlish teenager reluctant to get out of bed in the morning. If it could, it would have groaned *Leave me alone.*

'Start, goddammit,' she shouted, pounding her hands on the steering wheel. She was late, and the school principal had already had words with her about cutting it close at school pickup.

'We simply can't leave children unattended at the school gates, Mrs... Ms... Miss Norman,' she'd faltered. 'The teachers make themselves available as supervisors, but last week you were ten minutes late. That's simply unacceptable.'

Reece knew it was unacceptable, but try telling that to her dick of a boss at the local gas station. He wouldn't let her finish her shift until the guy who was due to take over turned up to relieve her. She stood there looking at the digital counter on the register, counting down the minutes before she became an unfit parent. If she walked, she'd lose the job, and she simply couldn't afford to do that. Welfare had already caught her scent and she could hear the barking of their hungry dogs far off in the distance.

Reece tried the key one more time. She'd done it before, and she'd do it again if she had to. It wouldn't be the first time she'd run from the gas station to the school gates and she was sure it wouldn't be the last. Up to now, the school principal hadn't bothered to ask her why she was late. She assumed it was because she was Reece Norman and... well, a woman like her would be late, wouldn't she? Having three kids by three different fathers—what more did the school principal expect?

Reece placed her hand on the key once again and held it there, hardly daring to turn it. She loved her three kids. It was their fathers that she didn't like so much. She'd do anything for her children. It was just a shame that the men who'd helped her bring them into the world didn't feel the same way. There was not a lot she could do about that, other than carry on doing what she was doing. And that meant taking any shift she could get her hands on at Curly's gas station and bringing up her kids as best she could. It was a job that paid, and it didn't matter that she couldn't read.

The engine turned on begrudgingly. Reece had almost given up all hope when something sparked somewhere and kicked the engine into life. The running motor was the only positive thing that had happened to her that day. That's as good as it got for Reece Norman. The entire car shook and rattled and a blast of dense, black fumes shot out of the exhaust as she moved the gearshift out of the park position to start the journey to the school.

The school run was a finely-timed cross between The Hunger Games and an elite sport. It was a fight to the death to grab a parking place somewhere in the vicinity of the school gate. The stay-at-home moms with cleaners and gardeners were always first in line, fragrant and calm, ready to greet their little darlings with gifts of candy and promises of after-school treats. Next in line were the walkers, the moms and pops lucky enough to be able to walk there and back. Then there were the working parents, those who had to balance a working life with bringing up a family, no small feat and a constant challenge and pressure.

Finally, there was Reece, who barely earned enough to keep the show on the road, with no stake in life great enough to control any of the mayhem around her. When she did finally arrive at the school gate, she was forced to drive around the block until she could find some space big enough to be able to abandon her car for the five minutes required to pick up the kids.

That's how it all played out on the day Poppy disappeared. For Reece Norman, what was one more day when the car was acting up, her boss was using controlling behavior, she had to cook for four on a budget of just over four dollars until she got paid, and all she wanted to do was go to bed and cry for the rest of the day?

The car shuddered as the automatic transmission engaged and took a small lurch forward. Even that was a small victory. Sometimes it missed the gear—another problem Reece was thrusting to the back of her mind. Something else to deal with later.

By the time she reached the school, some of the moms were leaving. Shallow Falls Elementary even boasted pickup dads, ripped guys in shirts that were opened two buttons down, holding the hands of their kids and chatting about their school day like it was the most natural thing on earth. It was, of course, but the men in Reece's life hadn't quite managed to get the hang of the twenty-first century. It was a mystery to them, as bemusing as building a piece of IKEA furniture and as challenging as seeking a profound moment in an episode of The Kardashians. Reece envied their lives, seemingly so simple and carefree. What she'd do for just one day of that.

She bumped the tire as she hurriedly swung the vehicle off the road into a space that had become available, thanks to a very slow-driving retiree who was in the process of vacating it. Reece set the emergency brake and hesitated before turning off the engine. If she'd been able to leave work on time, she might have gotten closer to the school gate. Then the kids would have run up to her, so she wouldn't have to risk turning it off.

She was too far from the gate for that, so she reluctantly turned the key and switched off the engine. If it didn't start again, it wouldn't be the first time she'd had to walk the kids all the way through the town, right to the far end where fields and woodland met concrete and brick, on the far boundary of Shallow Falls where their trailer was located.

Reece didn't bother locking the car. If anybody tried to steal it, at least they'd get it started for her. They'd be doing her a favor. She wasn't even sure if she'd renewed the insurance; she just prayed that she never hit anything. A bill like that could break her. If she was insured, it would only pay the price of towing to the junkyard anyway. Nobody in their right mind would want to take that heap off her hands as a going concern.

She stepped onto the sidewalk and began to run as fast

as she could through the stream of parents and children who'd managed to leave the school on time. Nobody acknowledged her or gave her a cheerful hello; she might as well have been invisible as she made her way to the gate.

Toni and Megan were waiting by the large concrete pillars which formed the grand entrance to the school, over which were carved the words *Shallow Falls Elementary School*. They were used to seeing their mom flying around one of the two corners available to her, always recognizable by her red face, her gaunt, tired look, and her threadbare jeans.

'Hey, girls, where's Poppy?' she asked, kissing them both on the head, then kneeling to give them a hug. It was this feeling that made her do everything that she did. The sight of her kids at the end of the day, and the tight, loving hugs they gave her because they were pleased to see her, all made it worthwhile.

'No sign of her yet,' Toni replied, shrugging.

'Maybe she's still in class?' Megan suggested.

Reece held back from scolding them, not wanting to spoil such a lovely welcome.

'Girls, I've told you, we have to take more care of Poppy. You must try to look out for her. The world's not as straight-forward for her as it is for you.'

She was as gentle as she could be. She'd asked them before to look out for Poppy, to make sure she was waiting with them when she arrived.

'We did go looking for her, Mom,' Megan said, 'but we couldn't see her.'

'Wait here a moment,' Reece said. 'I'm just going to check with the teacher on duty. What's her name? Mrs. Willoughby, isn't it?'

The girls nodded. She could see guilt in their eyes, knowing they'd let her down.

'It's okay, girls, she'll be around somewhere,' Reece reassured them.

Mrs. Willoughby was just turning to leave her post, having assessed that all children were accounted for and her teaching duties were done for the day.

'Mrs. Willoughby... Mrs. Willoughby,' Reece called. The teacher had her hand on the entrance door to the school. There was something about crossing the threshold to that place that gave Reece the shivers. Maybe it was the fact they'd failed to teach her to read there, dismissing her dyslexia as pure stubbornness and a general lack of intelligence and application. Those were the precise words used on the report card. Walking through those doors was like stepping through the fiery gates of Hell for Reece, and the judgment she received in there was equally harsh.

Mrs. Willoughby turned and looked her up and down, making every assumption that was needed before giving her dismissive response. Reece saw how she observed the faded, overwashed T-shirt, the threadbare jeans going through at the knees—not as some trendy fashion statement, but because they'd worn out the good, old-fashioned way—and the fatigued, unbranded sneakers whose soles were partly detached. The teacher took it all in in an instant and asked pompously: 'How may I help you, Ms Norman? Don't tell me you've lost Poppy again?'

In that moment Reece felt like the same six-year-old school child who'd tried to tell her teacher that she simply couldn't make any sense of the words on the page, because they all looked jumbled.

'She's not with Megan and Toni, and I wondered if she was still in the classroom.'

'Ms Norman, I believe Principal Murphy has already had a conversation with you about coming so late to pick up your children.'

'Yes, but please, you know Poppy's deafness means she sees the world differently to the other kids, sometimes it's hard to...'

'Ms Norman, you and Poppy both know the rules about end of school. She knows to wait in the playground until a parent or caregiver arrives. She's not here now; she must have gone.'

'Please, Mrs. Willoughby, please will you check in the school?'

The teacher paused for a moment and looked at Reece. They all knew Poppy had special needs. It didn't make a lot of difference in the school day, not at her age. She was still happy to run around and play all day, and she and her little friends seemed to communicate just fine.

'I'll check inside,' she said, softening at last. 'I'll be out in one moment. Can you and the girls walk around the block and make sure she's not wandered off somewhere?'

Reece nodded and ran back to Megan and Toni. As she did so, she felt a churn in her stomach, not unlike the uncomfortable grinding of the car engine. Poppy hadn't done this before. She was prone to wandering off in the playground, in a world of her own, but she knew the drill, and was sensible enough not to walk off down the street.

'Megan, check the sidewalk on that side of the school. I'll take the other side. Toni, check the playground, and make sure she's not in the nature area or somewhere like that. When you're done, come back to the entrance and wait for Mrs. Willoughby.'

Megan headed off as instructed, and Toni ran off into the playground. Reece walked around the opposite corner, anxious, a rising panic welling within her. Some parents were still standing chatting before they got into their cars. More desperate now, Reece ran up to them, interrupting, asking if they'd seen a little girl with a patchwork dress and hearing aids. Each time, they looked at her as if she were some druggie asking for money. They glared dismissively at her, shrugging their shoulders, anxious to get rid of her and continue their chattering.

It was another half-hour before the first call went into the police; half an hour to determine that Poppy Norman had gone missing. She wasn't in the school building, she wasn't hiding in the grounds, and she hadn't wandered off along the sidewalk. She had just disappeared, and it seemed that nobody had seen anything. Reece Norman's bad day had just gotten a whole lot worse.

TWO

'How are those calls going?' Cory asked, taking the final sip of his cold coffee. He was half asleep, having just typed up an uninspiring news story about a plant pot that had been pushed off the wall at the town's bus station, smashing the clay container and damaging the plants. It was the third time that month, and it was getting a bit wearing trying to find a new angle on an item whose presence on the front page had been hard enough to justify the first time around. But that's how things were at The Shallow Falls Tribune these days.

'All three dogs have been reunited with their owners,' Bianca announced. 'One of the owners even picked up a new cat, as well.'

She smiled at Cory with the youthful enthusiasm of a first-day intern. At least she spoke to him. The previous intern had barely uttered a full sentence to him all week. And his application letter had claimed that he coveted a career in the communications industry. Cory had chuckled at the irony.

He was grateful for the distraction that Bianca had

created in the office. Before she'd arrived, Mitchell Kane, the paper's owner and patriarch, had called them all into the main office to deliver the bad news.

It was straightforward and simple: the population of Shallow Falls had gotten web-savvy. Even the older population were permanently connected to their mobile devices these days. That meant a plummeting circulation for the local paper, as their readership turned in droves to the online world. And although the paper was available online, it simply couldn't pay the bills. The writing was on the wall; Mitchell would have to stop the press and downscale the entire operation to run on a shoestring if something didn't change soon.

It was a glum start to a quiet day. The distraction of having to meet and greet Bianca Williams was a welcome one, discouraging Cory from dwelling too much on how things might pan out if he were to lose his job. In the hierarchy of attractive salaries, local newspaper hack was somewhere between supervisor at the local fast food outlet and clerk for a medium-sized builder's store. It was still a respected job, but it didn't pay very much, in spite of the training it required, along with the skill and legal knowledge to keep the publication out of the courts.

It was the only job Cory had ever wanted to do. Even though he could make no promises to Bianca of worldwide fame or industrywide respect, he could still guarantee her a challenging job which would take her to the heartbeat of the community and allow the sharing of essential news and information. It was satisfying, even if you occasionally had to deploy your considerable writing talent on a story about a vandalized plant pot in a dramatic style which wouldn't be out of place if Godzilla had arrived in Shallow Falls and trampled it underfoot.

He'd warmed to Bianca immediately. She was eighteen or nineteen—old enough not to be a kid and sensible enough to be able to hold a conversation which did not, by default, include the words *Fortnite, Love Island* or *whatevs*. That seemed to Cory like a great start, bearing in mind the previous candidates from the local high school. Some of them had made him shudder.

Bianca seemed genuinely interested in how things worked around Shallow Falls. She understood how the town council operated, and even grasped how that all related to the wider influence of national government. She had a firm grip on the local issues in the town: threats to the few manufacturing plants that still remained, the pressures on farmers, the crumbling infrastructure, and the relentless march of progress. And, even better, she understood that reuniting lost dogs with their owners was as important to the people of Shallow Falls as the quality of their drinking water, the safety of their roads, and the price of parking in the town center.

He looked at the list he'd made on his notepad. Officially, Bianca was entitled to the same induction process as any other employee. But it was a long time since someone new had joined the ranks of The Shallow Falls Tribune. It was mostly an exit-only establishment these days. As staff retired or left, they weren't replaced.

The paper had been reduced from a broadsheet to a tabloid, the fonts changed *to jazz them up and make the paper more edgy*, as Mitchell had explained it. The number of pages had been reduced to a level which could be sustained week-in, week-out by a small team of three reporters, two freelance photographers, one sports writer, two ads reps and a receptionist. Such was the diminished importance of a journal which had once won awards for its coverage of a huge political scandal in the sixties and had been bought religiously by readers within a radius of thirty miles of Shallow Falls.

Cory took the job as seriously as if he was still working in those halcyon days—lost dogs, broken plant pots, and all.

Bianca had been particularly impressed by the printing press.

'You still print on the premises?' she'd asked.

It was a pertinent question. Most printing was now outsourced, and traditional printing presses were in greater demand in countries like India. Mitchell Kane was old-school enough to want to hang onto the press, in case they might generate more income by printing third-party publications.

He'd separated the press from the newspaper, to make it easier to sell off, should the need arise. The need had arisen, sooner than he'd expected. The press was up for sale; it had received interest from around the world, and the staff who operated it knew they were on borrowed time. Not only were their jobs at threat, they had no transferable skills to take into the modern world.

'If worse comes to the worst, I'll start a blog,' Cory would joke with the other reporters. 'Or maybe even a YouTube channel.'

'I can just see you as the next Zoella,' Oliver Vasey quipped.

Oliver Vasey was the man who'd published *Vasey's People* column in Shallow Falls for nearly thirty years. When he retired, he'd take the Tribune's history with him. After Mitchell, he was the longest remaining member of staff.

It was four o' clock; not much more was likely to happen that day. For a moment, Cory wondered if he should send

Bianca home. She'd had the grand tour—that had used up ten minutes of the day. She'd been introduced to the other staff—that was another five minutes. The press had burned up almost half an hour and the canine population at Shallow Falls was all present and accounted for, in readiness for that week's *Missing Mutts* column. He ticked off the items on his list. That was it—nothing else to show her.

'Anything else you want to ask me, Bianca?' Cory said. 'Or have I covered all the basics now? Hopefully I'll be able to take you out on a story tomorrow.'

The phone began to ring in the office. Cory looked over to see that Oliver was picking it up, so he carried on his conversation with Bianca.

'I think that's pretty well it.' She smiled, still looking as fresh as she did when she'd walked through the door at ten o'clock that morning. 'I can't wait to do some reporting, and I'll read these style guide documents when I get home tonight.'

'Cory.'

Oliver Vasey called across the office.

'One moment, Oliver, I just need to finish up here with Bianca...'

'It won't wait,' Vasey replied.

Cory stopped, raising his eyebrows at Bianca to convey as much of a sense of intrigue as he could muster. He suspected he'd just made himself look constipated, but hopefully Bianca would get the gist of what he was trying to achieve.

'There's a big story kicking off in town. You'll want to take this—what extension do you want it on?'

'Put it through to 205,' Cory replied. 'This is promising,' he said to Bianca.

The phone rang at his side and he picked it up.

'Got it,' he said, initiating the baton transfer in the daily version of a phone call relay that punctuated office life. The calls never seemed to come to the right person.

'Hello, Cory Miles speaking. How can I help?'

He noticed how Bianca was watching him, sensing that something important was about to kick off.

'Uh-huh, yes, where? Shallow Falls Elementary. What time? Over an hour now? Poppy, age four. Damn, that's not good. Hearing impaired. Damn, that's really not good. Okay, got it. Thanks for the tip—I'll be over right away.'

Cory replaced the receiver and took a beat to gather his thoughts.

'What is it?' Bianca asked. 'A news story?'

'Yes, it's what we call a breaking story in the reporting business,' Cory replied. 'We've got a missing child at the elementary school. The police are already there. They think she might have been snatched. I hope you weren't in a rush to get home. It looks like it's going to be a long evening.'

THREE

'Are you sure you want to come inside? Police stations are best avoided, in my experience.'

Bianca had unbuckled her seat belt already. Cory took that as a *yes*.

The Shallow Falls Police station was nothing like the well-oiled, law enforcing machines seen on TV. Its drab appearance reflected the lack of crime in the area, as if it had given up all hope of anything more significant than a parking ticket. The peeling paint of its window frames and the weed-scattered asphalt of the parking lot gave every indication that the building was longing for retirement, even if the local criminal fraternity were not.

Like it or not, though, this was one of the most important buildings in Cory's job. The relationships and connections that were forged here were what oiled the wheels for a successful local journalist.

'Why are we going to the station first, rather than the school?' Bianca asked.

It was a very good question, and it was encouraging that Bianca had thought to ask it.

'When a news story breaks, the press guys know as little as everybody else does—at least at first,' he'd explained as they drove through the town. Two police cars had passed them already, traveling in the opposite direction. It still felt counterintuitive to him to be going to the place they'd just rushed from.

'It's the same for the police; they know nothing at first, not until they've had some time to gather information and get on top of the basic facts.'

"But isn't the school where all the action is?'

'Yes, and we dispatched our photographer before you and I left the office. Did you see Oliver doing that the moment he transferred the call to me? The photographer needs to be getting pictures as soon as possible. But I can't report the story on the basis of a tip from the store opposite the elementary school, especially if a child is involved. I have to get the facts right, which means I need to validate the information before we publish anything. Imagine if I got the name of the child wrong? It could cause all sorts of problems.'

Bianca nodded.

'I'd never thought of it like that. I just assume the press knows everything.'

'No, the police and then the press get on top of the story before anyone else, then we become the main sources of information. The police know most, of course, and sometimes they won't share everything. That's when we have to use our skills to extract the information from them. And sometimes we end up discovering something even the police don't know. Then we have to decide if we're going to share information with them. We can't ever put our sources at risk, or else they might dry up.'

Bianca nodded again. She took out a small notebook

that she'd concealed in her pocket, then pulled a pen out of her shirt pocket and jotted down some notes.

'You're making a great start as a journalist, Bianca. A reporter is never fully dressed without a notebook.'

She smiled at him, clearly pleased that she was passing as a professional already.

'I'm going to leave you in reception for now. It's best if I speak to Chief Tarrant on my own at first. I don't want to spook him with an unfamiliar face.'

Cory walked over to the desk and introduced himself to the officer in charge. He was a well-known presence in the offices, so he was shown through immediately. Cory walked through the open-plan office space, noting the gray tape that was holding the torn carpet together and the brown staining on the ceiling tiles which suggested there was a leak in the roof that somebody probably needed to attend to. He arrived at a dark wood office door and knocked. Its occupant was on the phone.

'Come in,' came a sharp and snappy voice, already stretched for patience.

If chewed pens could be people, that would be Chief Lance Tarrant, the man in charge of Shallow Falls Police Department. He looked gnarled and weathered, as if his whole life he'd been battered by unrelenting storms. His thinning gray hair was hanging onto his scalp for dear life, as if at any moment it might give up all hope and slide off his head into the metal trash can at his feet, tired of the world and eager to end the struggle.

His portly frame suggested it was some years since he'd had to give pursuit in the field of duty. Chief Tarrant was in management, and his policing duties these days involved the hot pursuit of purchase order numbers and requisition slips. As his waist expanded, so did his worries.

As Cory entered the room, Tarrant waved him over to a chair at the side of his desk while he concluded his call.

'So, you want to know about the child?' Tarrant asked, slamming the phone down and clearly irritated by whoever he'd just been talking to. Cory was used to this dismissive attitude; it was water off a duck's back to a reporter.

Cory ran through the information he'd gotten from the tip. Although it was always a brief experience speaking to the chief, it would at least confirm the basic facts and allow him to publish the bones of the story online. He'd typed up a holding headline and published it before he left the office. He'd need to add to it as soon as possible. If not, the Twitter machine would get ahead of him and start spreading all sorts of misinformation.

'Here's what we've got,' Tarrant began. 'School ended at 3pm, and the child was reported to us as missing at 15:42...'

Cory watched as Tarrant checked his notes. The call time would be in twenty-four-hour-clock format and to the precise minute. The press would accept nothing less, and the chief knew it.

It was tempting to jump in and ask questions, but he knew better than to interrupt Tarrant in briefing mode.

'Age and name of child unconfirmed at present. My officers will release that information as soon as we clarify if this is a missing child rather than a lost child...'

Cory ventured a question.

'What's your gut reaction?'

'The truth? And off the record?'

Cory nodded and lifted his pen away from his notebook to confirm it.

'The mother is Reece Norman. Do you know her?'

'Maybe,' Cory replied. 'Should I?'

'Not particularly, but I'll bet you know her place. She

lives in that ugly trailer right at the edge of town, just on the boundary by the Shallow Falls sign.'

'Yes, I know the one. I don't know who she is, but I know where you mean.'

'Well, I think it's fair to say that her mothering skills are to be questioned by the local population. She's got three kids, all by different fathers. None of them are still on the scene. If you ask the locals, they'll say she looks like she's on drugs all the time or that she's got some new man in tow. Either way, she turned up late at the school gates and one of her kids was missing. We need to confirm the age of the child and her name before we release it to the press.'

'Can you give me anything off the record?'

'It's a child, Cory, you know that. We can't scare the locals and we have to get it right. These are vital minutes after a child goes missing. She'll probably turn up somewhere stupid or at a friend's house. But until we know for sure, we treat her like a missing person, and we follow the drill.'

Cory knew that, but as a reporter, he always had to push. There was a constant love-hate relationship between the police and the newspaper, like a bickering couple, never completely happy with what the other was doing, but knowing that they depended on each other entirely.

'When will you escalate to missing person status?' Cory asked.

'Already have,' Tarrant replied. 'Reece Norman's credentials as a mom might be a subject for debate, but the welfare of a child is not. I've dispatched as many officers as I can spare already, and they're scouring the town looking for her. It'll be getting dark soon; hopefully we'll find her by then. In the meantime, that's all I've got. Scribble your number down on this pad. I'll let you know ASAP if there's a breakthrough.'

Cory thought the chief would just throw the sheet of paper in the trash the moment he left, but he went through the motions anyway and left his cell phone number.

Tarrant's phone rang, as if perfectly timed to dismiss Cory from the room.

Cory stood up, gave a wave of thanks to the chief, and made his way out into the office. Tarrant was right—the office was all but empty. At least he'd got straight onto it; any parent would insist on the same response if it was their child who'd gone missing. If it was his own son, he'd be going out of his mind until he'd been located.

Bianca stood up as soon as she saw him walk through the connecting door from the main office. She still had her notebook in her hand, looking pleased with herself.

'What did Chief Tarrant say?' she asked. 'Have you confirmed that the child is missing?'

'Not necessarily missing—they're hoping she may just have wandered off. I have a name, though. Do you know Reece Norman, who lives in the trailer at the far end of town?'

'I know her a bit, only from saying *Hi* in the store. I used to work there before I... before I left school.'

'It's one of Reece's children. Tarrant won't give me any names, not until it's all confirmed.'

They stepped through the double doors into the parking lot of the police department. The light was beginning to fade; Cory knew this was a crucial time in the search.

Bianca stopped and studied her notepad.

'I think I can help you there,' she grinned. 'I got talking to the officer at the reception desk. It seems she's not quite as cagey as Chief Tarrant. Apparently, it's Poppy Norman, the youngest child. She's four years old—just started school recently. She has a severe hearing impairment, too; she wears hearing aids in both ears. I've seen her, she's a cute little kid, but lives in a world of her own, I think.'

Cory looked at Bianca, astonished that in less than one day on the job she'd succeeded in finding out more information than he'd managed to secure from his most senior source.

'Wow, great work, Bianca—well done. Let's get down to the school now, and see what else we can find out about Poppy Norman.'

FOUR

'I know you've only seen her in the store, but how would you describe Reece Norman?'

Bianca waited until she'd clicked the seatbelt buckle into place before she answered.

'I felt sorry for her and the girls, if I'm honest with you,' she began. 'I don't like to use the p-word, but if you pushed me, I'd say they looked poor.'

'That's the impression I'm getting so far. Is there a father on the scene or is she on her own with the kids?'

'I saw her with some guy a couple of months ago, but I haven't seen him around recently. She seems to keep herself to herself. The kids are nice—you never hear her screaming at them or anything like that. And there's something really different about them...'

She paused a moment.

'What?' Cory probed.

'The kids never asked for stuff in the store. I used to see the other children rushing straight for the candy, demanding that their parents buy this or that for them. I never saw that with Reece's kids, or I didn't ever notice it if they did. They seemed to understand that they couldn't have stuff. It was sad, really, like they'd had that expectation knocked out of them so young.'

'I need to call home.' Cory changed the subject, glancing at the clock on the dash. 'Will you excuse me one moment? I must check in with my own son before we head over to the school.'

'Sure,' Bianca said. 'I'd better let my mom know where I am. I may be eighteen now, but that doesn't stop her worrying.'

Cory stepped out of the car to make his call, not yet ready to let Bianca into the details of his personal life. He called the number at the top of his contacts, one with a hashtag added to make sure it always rose to the top. It used to be labeled with the name of his wife—Nadia—but it had become less painful to edit the entry in his phone to display the name of his son, Zach.

He always felt trepidation when he listened to the dial tone, not because he didn't want to talk to his son, but because he felt an impending sense of crisis with his wife. It was like the faraway drums in a Tarzan movie, a distant beat that never resulted in good news.

'Hey, Cory, nice of you to call.'

He was on the defensive already. He'd only wanted to check in on his son.

'Hi, Nadia, I hope it's not a bad time?'

'It's never a good time for you to call, Cory. I'm busy, what do you want?'

Cory couldn't quite put his finger on when things had started to go off in the marriage. One minute they'd been a tight little family unit, and the next they seemed to be arguing all the time and were now separated. It didn't help that Nadia had been promoted in her law firm. Sure, the money was very useful, but the stress it placed her under didn't appear to suit her. She started to take it out on Cory, telling him if he was more ambitious, she wouldn't have to work such long hours. But Cory's passion was in providing local news; he had no aspirations to move any distance away from Shallow Falls.

'I'm happy to take Zach more regularly, if that will help?' he ventured.

There was an ominous silence from Nadia. Cory figured they'd been doing okay for money before she took the promotion, and Nadia had seemed much happier before she took on the burden of management. He didn't really know why she'd accepted the offer in the first place. Though if he was really honest with himself, he did know the reason. Her parents. As a successful judge, Nadia's father had leaned on her since she was a teenager. Her career in the law was a foregone conclusion. Pressure like that was hard to resist, and it had broken up their marriage.

Cory didn't want a fight. He never wanted to fight—he'd rather they were a family again. So he didn't rise to the bait, but asked to speak to Zach instead. He was the one remarkable thing to have come out of their marriage; even if they didn't succeed in patching things up, he'd always be proud of the child that they created together.

'Hi, Zach, how's it going?'

'Hi, Dad, can I see you again soon? I miss you.'

It broke his heart to hear those words coming from the mouth of a five-year-old. He was one year older than Poppy Norman. A chill moved through his body as he realized for the first time what Reece Norman must be experiencing.

Even if Poppy had just wandered off somewhere, and was perfectly safe, Reece must be out of her mind with panic.

'I'll be around after soccer practice this week and we'll go out for pizza. Or would you prefer a burger?'

His relationship with his child was parceled out like portions of a meal, never too much and always too little. An hour here, a half-day there. Why was Nadia being so difficult? He was reluctant to set up a formal arrangement, which might mean him losing out on the precious time they already had together. Cory was still hoping they'd sort it out and get the marriage back on track.

'I don't really mind, Dad, I'm just looking forward to seeing you again. I miss you.'

Cory felt his eyes welling up with tears. He hated what they were putting their son through. If he'd told Nadia not to take the promotion, would that have made a difference?

'Zach, your meal is ready. Finish the call, please.'

Nadia's voice could be heard calling from the kitchen. He could picture it in every detail. After all, it had been *their* house before the separation. The large, metallic fridge from which he'd collect a chilled beer after work. The Bosch dishwasher which held all the plates from their family meals. The granite worktop he didn't really like, but which he'd agreed to have fitted because Nadia loved it so much. All bought with help from her parents. No wonder Nadia felt so imprisoned by her own family.

'Sorry, Dad, I've gotta go.' Zach said. 'Love you, Dad, see you soon.'

'Bye, Zach. I love you, too.'

The call ended. Less than one minute speaking to his own son, the time like a priceless gift, one to be stored away in a secure box and coveted for the rest of his life. He wiped his right eye to remove a tear and got back into the car.

'I'm all good,' Bianca said, 'No problems about when I get home. Are you okay?'

Cory sniffed and wiped his eye again.

'Sure, just an allergic reaction,' he replied. 'Nothing to worry about.'

He fastened his seat belt, placed his hand on the key which he'd left in the ignition, then pressed the start button. There was silence. He tried again.

'Sorry, Bianca. I need a spare part, but I haven't had time to pick it up yet. It shouldn't be a problem, but I'll need to lift the hood and give the starter motor a tap with a wrench.'

He bent to release the hood and got out. After some fiddling in the engine compartment, he shouted through the window at Bianca.

'Can you turn the key?'

She leaned over and did as he asked, and the car fired into life. Cory released the hood from its support and shut it firmly, then climbed back into the car.

'Sorry about that. I've been meaning to get over to the junkyard to see if Kelsey Baker has the part I need. I don't think it's anything serious, but I don't want to buy one new if I can avoid it—they're very expensive. Do you drive?'

'I passed my test, but I can't afford a car yet. Sometimes I get to drive Mom's car, but I'm a long way from having my own. It's why I worked in the store, to pay off my lessons.'

Cory was relieved that the car was now cooperating. If he didn't get the part replaced quickly, it might start causing problems with the job.

Shallow Falls Elementary School was just a short distance away. It was clear when they arrived that something very serious was happening. For a start, they couldn't park anywhere near the school gate, and the surrounding streets were jammed with police vehicles and other cars.

There was no sign of any TV crews, which suggested this was still a local story. Chief Tarrant and his team clearly believed this was lost child territory, rather than a missing child.

Cory parked as close as he could get to the school, locked up, and led Bianca to the main entrance. Police tape had been used to create four areas within the playground. Deputy Freddie Cabera was clearly the officer in charge, coordinating events and making sure everybody knew what they were doing.

'Hey, Freddie, how's it going?' Cory asked, shaking Cabera's hand warmly. The two men had a good working relationship.

'This is Bianca Williams—she's just started working with me as an intern. What can I report?'

'We're just about to organize the officers and volunteers into search parties,' Cabera began.

'There's been no search yet?' Cory questioned.

'That's right. We've had officers working the streets, but they haven't come up with anything. Confidentially, we're on the verge of saying she's missing—we'll know that in the next hour. Can you get something out on the paper's social media channels, Cory? We need people down here—the more the better. I want us to scour every inch of this town to find the child.'

'Can you confirm the name of the child yet?' Cory asked. 'Is it Poppy Norman?'

'How'd you know that? I just confirmed that information two minutes ago to the chief.'

Cory gave Bianca a small smile; she looked rightly pleased with herself.

'I know you need to get reporting the story,' Cabera continued, 'but we could do with all hands on deck here. Would you and Bianca be willing to join the search parties?'

'No problem,' said Cory. 'I'll get the word out on social media, file the name of the missing child, and we'll be happy to help you find her.'

FIVE

The briefing was over, and Cory and Bianca were assigned to the search party covering the east side of the town. A decent number of local residents had already gathered to join the hunt for Poppy. Word had gotten around quickly. If she'd wandered off, they'd locate her quickly.

'I suggest we stay close, Bianca,' Cory advised. 'If you pick up any useful info as we're going along, let me know, and I'll tweet it out.'

They'd done as much as they could to get the story reported. Nate O'Brien had been taking pictures since well before Cory arrived on the scene, and Mitchell Kane had told them to prepare for a big splash in that week's edition. If Poppy Norman was missing, the newspaper would be all over it.

Cory had updated the social channels and shared every scrap of information that he'd managed to confirm with the police department. Truth was, from a reporting point of view, there still wasn't much to say. Poppy was missing, but probably lost. Nothing had been unearthed by calls to the hospital, so she hadn't been in an accident. Nobody had reported seeing anything, so it didn't appear to be a snatch or anything like that. The simple truth was, less than two hours after she'd disappeared, it was still most likely that Poppy Norman would turn up safe—even though the Shallow Falls Police Department had to treat it like a chase scene in The Fugitive.

'Any chance I can speak to Reece Norman or one of the teachers?' Cory asked.

'Come on, Cory, you know how it is. The mother is out of her mind with worry and being comforted by a female officer. The teachers are being questioned as I speak, to see if we can get a sense of what happened after Poppy left her classroom. The earliest you're getting a full briefing is tomorrow morning, and that's if the child doesn't turn up. Sorry, but the most important thing right now is to search the town top to bottom to see if we can find this poor kid.'

Cory knew that's how the land would lie, but it was always worth a try.

'Okay, Bianca, you heard what the deputy said. I suggest you and I keep up with our group. We're on the lookout for Poppy and for anything that can give us a clue to where she's gone. Did you get one of those photos they were handing out?'

Bianca had two of them. The school had allowed the police to use their photocopier to hastily print out a pile of pictures of Poppy from her class photo. The ink cartridges looked like they were on their last legs, but the picture gave a sense of who they were looking for. A blonde girl, wearing pink glasses, a shy smile on her face and with gaps between her teeth. Cory was just able to see the hearing aid in the ear. He wouldn't have noticed if he wasn't looking for it specifically.

He and Bianca walked fast to catch up with their group.

The numbers were growing all the time, with dog-walkers and people heading home from work asking if they could help and joining in. It seemed that word had gotten around already, one of the many reasons Cory loved Shallow Falls and would love to bring Zach up here. Pennsylvania had always been the state to beat as far as he was concerned, and the town had a strong sense of history and community. Why else would they all be turning out like this to support Reece Norman?

'Have you heard? It's the trailer girl's kid,' Jed Walters muttered as Cory and Bianca caught up to him. 'That ugly shack's been blighting the entrance to the town for years. High time somebody pulled it down, if ya ask me.'

Cory knew better than to venture an opinion on a topic like this. The newspaper boasted on its masthead that it was *Proudly independent since 1920* and he firmly believed in those values. It was his job to report the facts, not the gossip. If gossip were sufficient, Shallow Falls could have disposed of its local paper many decades ago. In the meantime, idle chatter flourished, the townsfolk felt free to express their opinions—whether based upon fact or not—and they all turned to the website or newspaper to get the truth.

'Reece Norman is missing one of her children, Mr. Walters,' Bianca interjected. 'I'd have thought you'd be more concerned about that than the state of her trailer.'

Cory stopped for a moment and looked at Bianca. Sure, that's what he was thinking, but he hadn't said it out loud.

Jed Walters was immediately chastened by her remark.

'You're right, Bianca. I'm just an old man moaning about something that doesn't really matter. If that was my kid, I'd be going crazy right now. Forget I ever said it—it's just me and my big mouth shooting off again.'

Jed sped up and moved away from Cory and Bianca.

'That was a surprise,' Cory said. 'I hadn't expected you to say that.'

'I've known Jed Walters for a while,' Bianca replied. 'I've told him off before; it's like he can't help himself sometimes. He's not a bad man, but his default is to moan and bitch. He soon sees sense if you give him a little push in the right direction.'

'Well, you certainly did that,' Cory laughed. 'Good for you, sticking up for Reece and her family.'

'I should learn to do it for myself sometimes...' Bianca began.

'That sounds ominous.'

'Oh, it's nothing. Just thinking aloud. We're here now. I'd have thought the main street was a good place to look for her. I hope we find her.'

Shallow Falls' Main Street looked like it had been built for a cowboy film. If it had boasted a saloon and a casino, visitors to the town might have expected Clint Eastwood or Yul Brynner to step outside at any moment, six-shooter in hand, on the hunt for some bad guy from a Wanted poster. Straight rows of shops lined either side of the street, many of them of wood and brick construction. Their signage was traditional in nature, mainly hand-painted. The neon variety had been resisted by the town council, but the residents knew it was only a matter of time.

Shallow Falls had its bank, a hardware store, two family-run food stores, and an array of other services: a florist, a stationery and card shop, a small toy shop, a bakery, and a candy store. It was like any other American small-town main street, except for the cowboy bit. Even the asphalt-covered road and beautifully planted plant pots couldn't hide it. If John Wayne himself had stepped out of the bank, Cory truly believed he wouldn't have looked out of place.

Many of the shops were already closed or closing for the evening. Poppy had gone missing at an awkward time of day for the police investigation. The owner of the candy store was just locking up. Cory walked over to her to ask if she'd seen anything.

'Hi, are you the proprietor of the store?' he asked. 'I'm Cory Miles. Have you heard about the child who's gone missing?'

Cory didn't know the woman, though he was certain he'd seen her around somewhere. It was hard not to recognize people in a community like this, but it was still sizable enough not to know everybody, even in his line of work.

'Yes, it's terrible what happened to that poor child,' she began. 'I'm going to join the search myself once I've had something to eat. It's a terrible business. Have they said who it is yet?'

Bianca answered.

'It's Poppy Norman, Reece Norman's youngest child.'

Cory wondered if there was anybody Bianca hadn't met while working at the store. They all seemed to like her; she had that quality about her.

'Reece Norman, you say?'

Cory and Bianca nodded.

'Isn't she the one who has men coming and going like they're passing through a revolving door?'

Bianca looked at Cory, obviously horrified by what she'd just heard.

The candy store owner didn't let it go. 'She's got three children by just as many fathers. That's no way to raise a decent family. Those poor children of hers must be confused. And that last man she had—what was he, a soldier or something? He stuck at that as long as he did caring for his kid.'

Cory had taken an instant dislike to this woman, but his journalistic antennae had just started twitching, like a water diviner suddenly surprised by the jolt of a Y-shaped twig. He hoped Bianca would resist admonishing her in the way she'd tackled Jed Walters. Instead, she appeared to be distracted by something she'd seen in the road and she was going over to investigate.

'What's that about Reece's partner?' Cory asked. 'Is he still on the scene?'

'Depends who you ask,' the woman replied. 'He's a new recruit in the Army, just upped and left Reece, by all accounts. Only he went AWOL. Not a trace of him. If the Army can't find him, nobody else is likely to be able to. But that's Reece Norman for you. Terrible taste in men.'

Cory was intrigued by what she was saying, but became distracted by Bianca, who seemed very excited at something that she'd found at the roadside.

'Is that all confirmed to be true, or just town gossip?' Cory asked.

'I'm sure it's true, but I can't confirm it,' the shopkeeper replied.

Bianca was running towards them. It was time to finish off the conversation.

'Well, thanks so much for your help. Be sure to let Deputy Cabera know if you see anything that might help.'

The candy store owner was on her way, keen to get her priorities right. Evening meal first, then a lost child.

'What is it, Bianca? You look like you just won twenty dollars on a scratch card.'

She held up a pink rabbit with a dirty brown tire mark running straight across it.

'This is Poppy Norman's' she said, holding it up so that Cory could take a closer look. 'She carried it with her wherever she went.'

'Are you certain, Bianca?' Cory asked. This was important; Cabera would need to know as soon as possible. They couldn't mess it up.

'Totally sure,' Bianca replied. 'She had it every time they came in the store. She was always dropping it—I had to shout after them down the street more than once. Besides, look...'

She held up the white tab on which the washing instructions were printed. Written there in black ink were the words *Poppy Norman*.

SIX

'I have to get this story update filed, or I'll have Mitchell Kane breathing down my neck,' said Cory as the search volunteers were called back to the schoolyard. 'Do you want to take off, or can I buy you something at the diner? It's the least I can do after such a long day.'

'I'm good,' Bianca replied. 'I'd like to see how you do it. I don't mind the long day—I'm here to learn, after all.'

Deputy Cabera had been delighted with Bianca's find. Cory felt sorry for him, now the light was failing and the search parties had returned empty-handed. Poppy was no longer regarded as lost; she was now confirmed as missing. That meant she hadn't wandered off on her own, she hadn't walked home alone, she hadn't gone to play with a friend, and she wasn't curled up fast asleep in the classroom in some hidden alcove.

The seriousness of the situation—if it wasn't bad enough —was now ramped up considerably. Poppy had either been snatched by somebody or was hurt after wandering off and having a fall or some other accident. The scenarios became graver, not helped by the impending darkness.

It looked like Cabera was ready to kiss Cory when he handed over the toy rabbit that Bianca had found. He'd taken plenty of pictures with his own smartphone first. If this became a crucial piece of evidence, it would be a massive scoop for the paper.

Cabera was full of questions, which he put to Bianca at machine gun speed.

'Where did you find it? Was there anything else nearby? Are you certain it's Poppy's? Could you show us the precise location? Was this mud there when you found it?'

Bianca answered calmly and confidently, like she was an old hand at being interrogated by the police.

When Cabera saw the name marked on the label, he called over a couple of officers and got the toy bagged and taken into the school.

'Ask the mother about the toy,' he said. 'I want to know everything about it. Did the kid have it at school today? Did she leave school with it, or did someone steal it? I need to know everything about that toy. Ask the teachers, too.'

Cory watched as a pizza delivery guy handed over several flat boxes to another officer who was standing at the doors at the school entrance. He guessed Reece was still in there, along with the teachers. It was a long, hard day for all of them.

'You did well, Bianca,' Cabera said. 'A tip for next time, though. Try to leave anything you find where it is. There may be evidence around it that we can use. But don't worry, this is good—it helps us big time.'

Cory could tell Bianca wasn't sure how to respond to what the deputy had just said. Cabera walked off to grab himself a slice of pizza before it made its way into the school.

'It's okay, you did well,' Cory reassured her. 'That toy

would still be sitting in a puddle if you hadn't found it. If Poppy has been taken, it will help the police figure out which way she was driven.'

Bianca perked up.

'Come on, let's get this story filed and find something to eat. The smell of that pizza is reminding me how long it's been since we both ate.'

Cory was relieved when his car started the first time. He was so hungry that he didn't have the energy left to mess around with the engine.

'Lacey's Diner okay?' Cory asked.

Bianca nodded, so he pulled over and parked farther down the road.

There were two diners in Shallow Falls, and Lacey's was the most popular. It was a traditional diner, just the way the local residents liked it. Need 24/7 coffee on tap and a burger that'll destroy your heart but blow your mind for taste? Lacey's was the place to go.

There were a few people dotted about the place. As he walked in, Cory gave a noncommittal wave to Spencer Jones, who was at the far side of the premises, emptying one beer, with the next bottle already delivered to his side.

'Who's that?' Bianca asked.

'Spencer Jones—retired magistrate, Shallow Falls busybody, and occasional drunkard. Scratch that—frequent drunkard. It seems he hasn't taken too well to retirement. Or some might say it suits him very well, particularly when he likes a beer.'

They placed their orders and Cory steered her to a table that was well away from Spencer and separate from the other diners.

'I don't want anybody listening in to our conversation.

They have to buy the paper to read this information,' he said with a smile.

He took out his laptop from the bag at his side, fired it up, and connected to the diner's Wi-Fi. Within minutes, he was tapping at the keyboard, updating the breaking news story online, writing the first few lines of the newspaper version for that week's printed edition, and transferring images of Poppy's toy to the office system so that his colleagues could access them the next day. Sometimes Cory wondered how reporters managed in the old days, before the internet.

He became aware of somebody approaching from behind. Thinking it was their server, he tilted the top of the laptop downward so as to conceal the image of Poppy's toy.

'If ya ask me, that woman got what she deserves.'

It was Spencer Jones. Sitting well away from him hadn't been a sufficient deterrent; he was intent on making conversation. Cory could smell the beer on his breath.

Spencer sat down next to Bianca, pushing her out of the way as he dropped down unceremoniously at her side. She made a face at Cory.

'How can I help you, Spencer? I'm a bit busy writing up this story at the moment, to be honest with you.'

'That young girl—her trailer is nothing short of a whorehouse, what with all those men coming in an' out all the time.'

'Easy, Spencer—that's a bit much,' Cory tried to protest.

Bianca's body language said it all.

Spencer took a long swig from his bottle.

'She got what she asked for, if ya ask me. All those children, all those fathers, it's a right ol' mess. And that ol' trailer of hers, that piece of junk cluttering up the town. I guess you get what's comin' to ya, that's all I can say.'

Cory could see Bianca was about to lay into him. He held up his hand slightly to give her a gentle warning. He knew Spencer Jones from way back. He might be retired, but he still had influence in the town. Bianca would do well not to cross him if she wanted to keep a low profile.

'That poor kiddie of hers is probably better off. She probably found some responsible adult who knows how to take care of her.'

Bianca could stay silent no longer.

'You do know that what you're saying is highly slanderous, don't you, Mr. Jones? As a former magistrate, you of all people should know that Reece Norman has the same rights as everybody else in this country, whatever you think about her lifestyle.'

'Aren't you the Williams girl?' Spencer asked, looking at her closely now. Bianca drew back at the smell of his breath and flinched as he leaned in uncomfortably close.

'Yes, what of it?' she answered, more defensively than Cory had expected.

'You're the one who caused all that trouble at the high school, ain't ya?'

Bianca's face reddened and, not for the first time that day, Cory's finely-tuned antennae detected an incoming signal.

'Yeah, I know ya. Real piece of work. You're the one who got banned from the school prom and left out of the year book because of what you did. First time ever in Shallow Falls' history. Nope, it never ever happened before. Sounds to me like you're defending Reece Norman because you're a pair of peas in a pod.'

It took Cory some time to get Spencer Jones to move on from their table, but he saw the relief on Bianca's face the moment he finally stood up and headed back to his spot at the other side of the diner.

'I'm sorry you had to sit through that,' he said. 'Are you all right?'

She didn't look all right, but she nodded anyway.

'Do you want to talk about it, or would you rather I leave well enough alone? None of it makes any difference to me—Spencer Jones stopped making sense a long time ago.'

Bianca shuffled in her seat and looked out the window into the parking lot.

'It's almost fully dark now. That poor child. Reece Norman must be out of her mind with worry.'

Cory followed her gaze. It was starting to rain, too. Large drops began to pound against the diner's windows.

'It was just something that happened at school,' Bianca began. 'I had some problems with... some people in my year at school. They made life difficult for me. The school blamed me about an incident there. It's difficult to recover from something like that at my age. The principal agreed to write me a clean set of references if I took the rap. The penalty was writing me out of school history. No prom, no yearbook—that was the deal. I had to take it; mom and dad said it could mess up my life if I didn't.'

Cory had covered enough news stories to know that there were always many points of view when it came to a sensitive issue. For every proposed new building, there was always the builder who'd make a profit and provide employment with it, the landowner who stood to make good money from it, and the people who lived in the surrounding area who'd be concerned about road access, views disappearing, property values, and so on. Every dispute was a tight knot that had to be picked apart. Either way, he liked Bianca, so he decided to go with his gut on this one.

The sound of a voice at the counter distracted him.

'I think that's the last beer now, don't you, Mr. Jones?'

Spencer Jones was demanding another bottle, but the waitress was having none of it. If Spencer hadn't drunk enough when he joined Cory and Bianca at their table, he had now; he was growing belligerent and aggressive. Cory watched, wondering if he should step in and help the waitress. Two men, a couple of tables away, were obviously thinking the same thing.

'A man can't even get a beer in this town no more,' Spencer slurred. 'I spent my working life looking after everybody round here, and what do I get in return? Let me tell you, there are things in this town that would make the hairs on your neck stand up on end...'

'That's enough now, Mr. Jones. It's time for you to be leaving.'

Tom Lacey, the owner of the diner, had seen fit to come down and intervene, alerted by another of the waitresses.

He was wearing slippers and a cardigan, evidently interrupted while watching television. He seemed annoyed, but showed Spencer Jones polite respect.

Cory wondered how many drunks Lacey had had to throw out over the years. He was probably quite an expert at it by now, considering he looked close to retirement age, if not past it already. Some people in Shallow Falls never seemed to retire. If Tom Lacey wasn't careful, he'd become one of them.

'He's going,' Cory said to Bianca. 'Thank heavens Tom came down to sort it out. I thought I was going to have to get involved there.'

The rain was coming down heavily now, beating down like tiny pebbles on the wooden roof above their heads.

'What do you think he meant by that?' Bianca asked. 'The bit about things going on in the town?'

'He's drunk, Bianca—ignore him. People can say some stupid things when they've had one too many beers. Besides, remember what I said about journalistic work? You need to listen to everything but always reserve judgment; most things are not what they seem. A reporter's job is to listen to all sides of the story, then weave it together to get to the truth. It's not unlike being in the police, except we just write the story—the cops have to do all the hard work and dangerous stuff.'

'Look at that rain. Do you think they'll call the search off now?' Bianca asked.

'It won't help matters, that's for sure. Tomorrow morning, I'm going to try to get an interview with Reece Norman. We could do with a decent picture of Poppy for the newspaper, to help get the word out.'

Cory noticed Bianca tensed.

'What is it?' he asked.

'It feels a bit insensitive calling on Reece when she must be going crazy with worry.'

'People complain about the press sometimes,' Cory began. 'But if we get the word out about that little girl, it's going to help Reece in the long term. Sure, it'll be hard for her. But we're here to help, not to hinder.'

Cory continued typing up his news story, then tilted his laptop so that Bianca could take a look.

'I'm going to file that now—it'll go live on the website right away and sit in the template we use for the weekly edition of the newspaper. This is now a missing child news story, whatever the police are saying officially. We'll splash it all over the paper on Friday. Most importantly, we need pictures of the child. We'll have to ask Reece for those tomorrow.'

Two police officers stepped into the diner, shaking themselves like wet dogs on the huge doormat at the entrance to avoid dripping all over the tiled floor. Cory didn't recognize them; they must have come from the next town.

'Good evening, officers. Have you been involved in the search for Poppy Norman?' Cory asked. 'I'm local press, from the Tribune. Cory Miles.'

'Hey, Cory,' the first officer replied, 'I've read your stuff. It's good to meet you. We've been up by the woods and falls at the edge of town. The chief has spread the search area. It's hellish out there—the ground is wet and deadly slippery. If that poor kid has wandered off the roads, she's in for a hard night.'

'Are they out there now?' Cory asked. 'By the falls?'

The second officer nodded.

'They're probably going to call it off until daylight—it's too dark and dangerous now.'

'Sherri,' Cory called over to the waitress, 'I'd like to settle my bill. And please would you get these officers whatever they'd like to drink? Two coffees, I'm guessing?'

'You bet! And strong ones, too. Thanks, Cory, it's appreciated.'

'You're doing valuable work out there, officers—it's the least I can do.'

With the two officers served, the story filed, and the bill settled, Cory nodded to Bianca, indicating it was time to leave. They ran out to the car and got in as quickly as possible, still getting drenched over the short distance from the diner.

'Okay if I take a run out to the falls and just see what's going on? Then I'll drop you off at home, I promise.'

'Fine by me,' Bianca said. 'It's interesting.'

Cory felt himself making a wish before starting the car. He had to get that part replaced; it was getting ridiculous. The car started and he felt himself relaxing.

The drive to Shallow Falls took them past Reece Norman's trailer at the edge of town. He'd passed it a thousand times, but had thought nothing of it—as if it was part of the town's furnishings. There was a police car parked outside and he could see that the lights were on inside the trailer. He couldn't help but feel for Reece, thinking about what she was going through.

The moment he passed the trailer, they were into woodland. He switched on his high beams as they left behind the streetlights and drove into the wet, dismal darkness of a rain-saturated woodland. At Devil's Corner, he slowed right down and took the car around it gently.

'You can never be too careful right there,' he said to Bianca. 'When you start driving for real, be really careful on that stretch of road—it can be deadly.'

As they came around the curve of Devil's Corner, they were immediately greeted by a cluster of police cars, flashlights, and generator-powered floodlights. Cory pulled up by a small group of police officers who were huddled under the branches of a large tree, keeping the rain off as best they could. Cory lowered his window.

'How's it going?' he asked.

'Hey, Cory, that's it for the night—the chief has called it off until first light. It's far too dangerous in this weather. We're back at six o'clock tomorrow morning. There'll be officers posted out here all night, but that's it for now.'

Cory nodded and closed the car window. The rain had driven in as they were speaking, and his pant leg was wet.

'Is there anybody you don't know in this town?' Bianca asked.

'Yes, lots of residents,' Cory said with a smile. 'It's just that, as a reporter, you get to know certain people. It helps with the job—the more of them that are happy to speak to you, the better.'

Cory turned the car around, making the most of the large parking area at the side of Shallow Falls. He was calling it a night; the next day would be long and possibly very difficult. If they found Poppy, all well and good. If they found a body—God forbid—it would be a dark and terrible day for the entire town.

Bianca directed Cory back through the streets to her home, where he dropped her off and waited until she was safely through the door before moving away. She lived in a nice part of town: pleasant detached houses, wide roads, two-car garages and well-tended gardens. He wondered what had happened to get her kicked out of school like that.

He was still churning it over in his mind when he pulled up outside his own apartment. Luckily, there was a parking space on the street outside his house. He sensed there was something not right before he saw it. As he locked up the car and walked towards his door, he spotted something on the pathway. Moving closer, he realized it was a brick. The small glass pane at the top of the door was untouched, so he checked the windows to the side. His bedroom window had been cracked.

There was no sign of a break-in; the damage was superficial, as if the brick had been thrown from a passing vehicle. His immediate guess was an attempted burglary or kids causing trouble. But there was something about the timing of it, on the night of Poppy's abduction, that made every journalistic bone in his body scream out that there was something much more to it than that.

EIGHT

Tuesday—Day 2

CORY NEARLY SLEPT in the following morning, thanks to the boarded-up window blacking out his bedroom and preventing the light from waking him. He automatically reached out his arm for Nadia. It was force of habit; he wondered when he'd stop doing that.

He'd been up late waiting for the glazing team to arrive. They were as reluctant to be out so late as he was to be there waiting for them to finish the job. But there was no way he was leaving it wide open. The landlord said he'd get it fixed properly the next day.

It was six o'clock. The moment Cory opened the door of his small bedroom, the dim, early-morning light spilled in from the rest of the apartment, revealing a lovely day, the complete opposite of the torrential rain the night before. Any town with water figuring in its name is bound to get its fair share of rain, and Shallow Falls was no exception.

Cory decided to skip breakfast in favor of getting in an

early run. He knew which route he would take to make an early call at Shallow Falls. He pulled on his shorts and t-shirt, tied up the laces on his running shoes, and left the house, checking carefully to make sure the door was locked properly.

Cory liked jogging; it helped him get things sorted in his head. It often helped him make connections in news stories, too. There was something about the rhythmic motion and the mindlessness of it which enabled him to take a detached view of things. He started at a slow trot, feeling the bright sunshine on his face and squinting from its glare as he turned onto the main street. The sidewalk was completely dry, as if the rain of the previous night had never happened.

The Shallow Falls road was not Cory's normal route. It could be a bit winding for his tastes, but he'd done it a couple of times before and it was a decent enough circuit. To the falls and back would be roughly three miles, so he'd be back, fed, and showered well before half-past seven, in plenty of time to pick up Bianca at eight o' clock.

As he sped up to a steady pace, Cory thought through the events of the night before. If Reece Norman had gotten lucky, Poppy would have turned up overnight while they were all sleeping, and it would all be over by now. That outcome was unlikely; the town had been searched thoroughly the night before, so it was looking increasingly as if she'd wandered off somewhere more remote or dangerous. Or perhaps she *had* been taken.

Cory felt a surge of panic wash over him as he thought of his own son disappearing like that. It was difficult enough being separated from his son and knowing that he was safe, but he couldn't imagine how frantic Reece Norman must be.

Now he was reaching the outer edges of the town,

where the houses became less frequent and the plots of land bigger, until they were replaced by woodland. He ran by the Griffens' large house and noticed up close how worn it was. The paint was flaking on the window frames, the wooden walls looked thirsty and dry, and there were tiles missing on the roof. It was some time since he'd seen Xander in the main street. He wondered if he was all right.

After Xander's house, he was at Reece Norman's plot. The ruins of the burned house were still there. They'd never been cleared, serving as a constant reminder of the tragedy that had occurred there. Reece and her children had taken refuge in the trailer on the land to the side of where the house had been, and—for whatever reason—she'd never moved on.

The plot looked like wasteland now. Some effort had been made as part of the fire investigation to clear the debris into charred piles, but they'd never been moved. The roof had completely collapsed and the walls were all but leveled, yet the front door frame had stayed in place, oddly defiant against the ravages of the flames.

Poor Reece, what a life she'd had.

The trailer was heavily rusted, having seen much better days. Another police car had replaced the one that was there the previous night. The other officers might have finished their shifts, but there would be no clocking off for Reece Norman, not until Poppy was found.

There was no yard, as such, but old, rusting toys littered the area immediately around the trailer. A small red kite, weighed down by half a burned brick, had been left by the steps up to the main door. Cory had never really looked at the plot before, other than to notice the ugliness of the burned ruins. As he ran by, he noticed how far the land went back before Reece's plot ended and the woodland began.

As he jogged past the trailer, he made sure to look straight ahead, hoping that he wouldn't be spotted if Reece was looking out one of the windows. He'd be back later, accompanied by Bianca, this time on official newspaper business.

He was into woodland now, the overarching branches creating an umbrella from the sunshine. There was a scent of dampness from the leaves and pine needles which hadn't yet dried off after the rain. The road to Shallow Falls was undulating; he didn't particularly notice in a car, but on foot he could feel the stinging in his calf muscles, and it was harder to breathe. The birdsong and stillness of the morning air invigorated him. However terrible the events of the day before, nature had done what it always does by getting up early the next morning and carrying on as normal.

As Cory neared Devil's Corner, he heard the first car engine of the day. Soon that road would be busy with commuters, but it was usually clear before seven o' clock. He looked behind him, trying to track which direction the vehicle was coming in, but he couldn't work it out. He switched to the other side of the road, thinking it was better to face the car from the direction it was approaching.

He passed some bedraggled plastic flowers, all that was remaining of a makeshift shrine to the last person who'd died on that treacherous corner. There were warning signs in both directions, but the small stretch of road leading to the falls had been called Devil's Corner for as long as anybody could remember. Town legend said it had claimed more lives over the years than anything else in Shallow Falls. It was a corner that Cory treated with the utmost respect, as a sailor does the sea when heading out on a fishing trip.

As he began to run around the outside edge of the curved road, he heard the heavy revving of a car behind him and cursed that he'd opted for the wrong side of the road. The car was upon him in moments, like a wolf leaping out from the darkness. The sturdy black SUV approached the corner too fast, forcing the driver to go wide and directly into Cory's path.

The driver sounded the horn and Cory leapt out of the way, just in time to avoid being clipped by the vehicle's enormous bumpers. He fell to the ground hard, adrenaline pumping like a high-powered hose. The car screeched to a halt a few yards ahead.

Cory began to push himself off the ground, aware of pine needles sticking to his palms and small grazes on his knees.

'What the hell do you think you're doing, running like that out here?'

It was Chief Tarrant, and he was livid. He wasn't the only one.

'Thanks for the apology,' Cory said, immediately thinking better of it. 'Do you always drive round Devil's Corner at that speed?'

'If you're running in the woods, you should at least be wearing some reflective clothing,' the chief yelled at him. 'I could have mowed you down just then—you might have ended up in a wheelchair, brain damaged, or even killed.'

There was something about the way Chief Tarrant reeled off the list of possible outcomes that made Cory feel like it was more of a threat than an itinerary of health and safety hazards. He decided to back down and let the chief win this one.

'You're right. Sorry, Chief—I should be wearing more suitable clothing. I only just switched my route at the last minute; I hadn't intended coming out this way.'

Tarrant's eyes narrowed and he studied Cory's face. Figuring he was being weighed up, Cory kept his expression straight.

'What are you doing out here, anyway? You must know we're looking for that little girl.'

'Any sign of her yet?' Cory asked. He wasn't going to let a near miss prevent him from doing a little fishing.

'No sign,' Tarrant replied, moving back to police chief mode and casting aside his angry dad persona. 'Just heading back now to get ready for this morning's briefing. If you've any sense, you'll head back yourself—it might be safer that way.'

Cory considered for a moment mentioning his broken window to Tarrant, but thought better of it. This didn't feel like the time for it. Instead, he waited for the chief to get back in his car and started to jog the same way he was heading, back into town.

As soon as Tarrant was far enough away, Cory turned around and headed back to the falls. He didn't particularly care about Tarrant's advice, and there was someone he wanted to talk to on duty out there. They'd already exchanged texts that morning, and he'd get more useful information out of her than he ever would the police chief.

NINE

Bianca was looking out her living room window when Cory pulled up. Within seconds, she was at the front door, calling to somebody else in the house then bounding towards the vehicle, her enthusiasm seemingly undampened by the events of the day before.

'I thought you might like to keep the engine running, bearing in mind the problems you've been having,' she said with a smile.

'Good call,' he replied. 'It wouldn't start again this morning. I absolutely must get over to the junkyard and get hold of a spare part, or I'm going to end up stranded one of these days.'

'So, what's changed overnight?' Bianca asked, getting straight down to business. Cory liked that she wasn't so much into chit-chat. Her mind always seemed to be on the job.

'Poppy's still missing. I went for a jog up to Shallow Falls early this morning to speak to a friend of mine who was out there on duty: Louise—Officer Louise Powell. They've been searching the falls since daylight, but there's no sign of her. Tarrant is briefing his team at nine o'clock. Hopefully, he'll call a press conference today and bring it all together... that's if he doesn't kill me first.'

'What?' Bianca asked.

'Nothing, ignore me,' Cory answered. 'Are you up for a visit to Reece Norman? It's going to be difficult, but we need to do it. You know her already, you said?'

'Only in passing,' Bianca replied. 'We're not best friends or anything like that.'

They wouldn't need to be. A familiar face for Reece might be just what was needed for Cory to get inside the trailer and start asking questions. It was time to dig a little deeper into the news story; bricks were not in the habit of hurling themselves at windows.

Cory drove slowly through the town, considering what he was going to say to Reece when they knocked at her door. She'd have a police officer present at all times, updating her with developments in the search—that could be tricky.

They reached the edge of town and arrived at Reece's trailer. Cory pulled the car off the road, looking for signs of life. It looked just as it had when he'd jogged past for the second time that morning, returning from his off-the-record chat with Louise. She'd been pleased to see him and thankfully unconcerned about the sweat dripping from his forehead or the patches of sweat around his pits and soaking his back. He'd certainly looked better, but that didn't seem to bother Louise.

'Okay, gently does it,' Cory said. 'Follow my lead and let's see if she'll speak to us.'

They walked up to the trailer, where they could hear subdued voices coming from inside. A child was singing. Cory put his foot on the flimsy metal step beneath the front door and tapped gently, not wanting to alarm anybody inside. The mumbles of conversation stopped and movement could be heard. Cory hoped Reece would answer.

The door opened. 'Can I help you?'

Unfortunately, it was the police officer, a kind-looking woman who he hadn't seen before. She looked relieved to have escaped the intensity inside the trailer; the air from outside seemed to lift her instantly.

'I'm Cory Miles from the Tribune. I wondered... could I have a word with Reece?'

One of Reece's children came to the door to see what was going on.

'I'm sorry, Mr. Miles—I don't think it's appropriate at this time.'

'Mom! It's that nice lady from the store.'

Cory heard a shuffling from inside the trailer, and the entire structure vibrated as somebody came to the door. It was Reece. She looked like she hadn't slept all night, her eyes red from tears or tiredness—probably both. She wore stretched gray jogging pants and a faded t-shirt which at one time had displayed a logo.

'Hi, Reece, I'm so sorry to hear about Poppy,' Bianca began. 'Is there anything I can do to help? Would the girls like to come out and play with me for a while?'

Cory watched the look of relief on Reece's face.

'That would be lovely. I'm sorry, we only know you as the lady from the store.'

'Bianca,' she replied.

The two girls were now eagerly waiting at the trailer door, like energetic dogs anxious to be let off the leash.

'Stay close, please,' Reece said, 'Stay where I can hear you, Bianca.'

The police officer looked like she'd swallowed a bee, but

she followed Reece's lead. They all looked like they were walking out of a sauna after being locked in overnight, taking in grateful gasps of air. Megan and Toni ran down the steps onto the sparse grass and Bianca took them off to play.

'What did you say your name was?' Reece asked.

'Cory. Cory Miles from The Shallow Falls Tribune. We'd like to help get the word out about Poppy. If there's anything we can do...'

'Be careful of the press,' the officer cautioned, but Reece cut her off.

'The police haven't found my baby yet, Officer Philpot. I'm sure the local paper can't do much worse.'

The officer was immediately chastened. Reece beckoned Cory to come in.

'If you don't mind, I'll get some air for a few moments,' Officer Philpot said. 'I'll keep an eye on the kids, too.'

She took Reece's silence as acquiescence.

'Reece is under enormous stress,' Cory whispered to the officer. 'She doesn't mean it.'

He guessed Officer Philpot was used to being chewed out by anxious parents, but he didn't want her to think he was gloating at her discomfort.

As soon as Cory sat down, Reece began to sob. He gave her a moment before asking any questions. The trailer was a mess, with cheap kids' toys strewn all over the floor. Coffee cups had been left on all the surfaces and the smell of cheap instant permeated the living room. Three discarded noodle containers had been left, half-eaten, on the kitchen counter. He'd have expected nothing less, with one of Reece's children missing.

'I'm going out of my mind,' she said without warning. 'There's nobody to look after the kids. I want to be out there looking for Poppy, but all I'm allowed to do is sit here with the officers, just waiting for news. I'm going mad in here.'

'Do you have any family nearby?'

'No, none. You've seen the house, haven't you? That's where my family went. I'm on my own.'

Cory considered for a moment probing the issue of the girls' fathers. He'd heard the mutterings from the local townsfolk the night before, and it would be useful to know. But he decided not to push his luck too early; instead he paused, waiting for her to pick up the conversation. Years of reporting work had taught him that silences are generally filled if you waited long enough. He noticed a bottle of prescription antidepressants placed on a shelf out of reach of the kids. Were they new, or had she been on them before Poppy disappeared?

'She's almost completely deaf, you know,' Reece picked up. 'Poor little thing, she lives in a world of her own most of the time. She must be wondering what's happening.'

Reece's eyes began to well up once again. Cory wondered if it was possible to run out of tears where a child's safety was concerned.

'I spoke to Chief Tarrant early this morning...'

'Don't you mention that man to me.'

Reece's tone turned instantly to scorn and her eyes blazed with fury.

Cory stayed quiet while she filled in the gaps. Just outside the window, he could hear Bianca playing a catch game with the kids. She'd already proved herself to be worth more than her weight in gold.

'That bastard called Child Protective Services on me. I love my kids—don't ever let anybody tell you otherwise. Just because I was late to pick them up from school...'

Cory needed to play things cautiously and avoid the possibility of spooking Reece.

'What happened?' he asked. Had Chief Tarrant had concerns before?

'All three girls went missing. Only for twenty minutes. I was delayed at my job, so they started walking home on their own. He thinks I'm some sort of unfit mother. Well, you try bringing up three girls on your own in a trailer like this, with no sight or sound or support from their fathers.'

At the sound of Reece raising her voice, Officer Philpot tapped on the door to check in on them.

'Everything all right in here?'

Reece nodded and indicated that she should leave them.

'It's part of his job,' Cory ventured. 'I'm sure he didn't mean anything by it. They have to get the CPS involved if they're concerned about the children.'

She paused for a moment and walked over to look at the girls playing outside.

'Look at them,' she said, 'They haven't got a clue what's going on. They think Poppy will just turn up like she's been away on some playdate. But they don't know the truth, do they, Mr. Miles? I've seen it on the television enough times. If they don't find a missing person within twenty-four hours, the chances are that when they do find them, they'll be dead.'

TEN

Cory and Bianca drove back to the newspaper office in silence. Cory needed some time to process what had just played out in Reece's trailer, and he was pretty sure his companion was thinking it all over, too. One thing had surprised him about Reece Norman, in spite of everything the townsfolk had been muttering about her. He liked her and thought she was doing a good job in very difficult circumstances. From what other people had said, he'd expected some kind of monster. Reece Norman was anything but that.

Bianca was studying the photographs of Poppy, turning them over and over in her hands, not venturing a word.

'What did you make of Reece?' Cory asked, deciding at last that it was time to share their notes.

'The girls are lovely,' Bianca replied, laying the photographs flat on her lap. Unusually, Reece had managed to lay her hands on printed images, which she'd removed from frames for them. Cory was more used to digital images being emailed. He'd noticed that they were all school photos. Reece's cell phone was a basic pay-as-you-go model; she probably didn't take many photos on that.

'I think Reece hasn't told them the full truth about Poppy. They've been told she's gone away on a special visit and that she'll be back soon. Kids know the truth, though. The first thing Megan said when we went outside to play was *Has that man come to tell Mom that Poppy's dead?'*

Cory swallowed hard.

'I think she's under tremendous pressure,' he began. 'I don't know how she's holding it together. She told me that if she can't get to work this week, she'll lose her job at the gas station. She's already behind on her electric and can't afford to refill the propane tank when it runs out. I can't imagine what it's like for her.'

They drove in silence for a minute while they mulled over that information.

'So, she's officially a missing person now?' Bianca said, after the silence had started to feel uncomfortable.

'Yes. It's a whole different ball game now. A lost child is a slightly more relaxed affair; now that she's officially missing, the investigation gets stepped up.'

'Do you think we should make some posters with these photos?' Bianca asked. 'Will the police do it?'

'Tarrant has already got that school picture out on social media—as has the paper—and I want to get these scanned and in our system right away. It may take a day or two to get the posters out, depending on how fast people get their acts together. It can't hurt if you want to stick up a few posters in town—it might jog some memories.'

Bianca paused, as if considering her next words carefully.

'Do you think she's dead?' she asked.

Cory thought about it. Of course, he'd been considering

that possibility since the moment the report about Poppy had first come in.

'There's only ever been one recorded murder in this town and that occurred before I got here. The biggest risk to your life in Shallow Falls is Devil's Corner. That's claimed more lives than anything else in this community; it's unbelievable that the road hasn't been rerouted through the woods. So no, I don't think she's been murdered. I think there's an explanation. She may have wandered off somewhere; perhaps she's lost or scared.'

'But will she be found dead?' Bianca asked. The issue was clearly troubling her and she was looking to Cory for guidance.

'This is the tough side of a reporter's job,' he began. 'It's definitely not for everybody. But if you push me, I'd have to say that there is a chance now that a dead body will be found. I don't believe yet that it'll be murder—I still think the most likely cause is that she wandered off, got lost and maybe fell, or, even worse, drowned. But that's just speculation; I'd never raise that in a newspaper article. We have to deal with the facts.'

'Did you know that two of the girls' dads are still on the scene?'

Cory took his eyes off the road for a moment, then quickly turned back.

'Did Megan and Toni tell you?'

'Yes,' she replied. 'Apparently there's always lots of shouting when they're around. The kids go outside and play, apparently. Neither of them is very interested in the girls; they just seem to come to see Reece. One is in the military and the other lives locally somewhere.'

'You know, you've got a talent for this work, Bianca.'

Cory smiled. 'You're always falling over interesting tidbits. Did they say anything about father number three?'

He pulled the car into the newspaper office's parking lot. As he switched off the engine, it ran on a little. He needed to get that fixed, especially with such an important story going on. Now was not a good time for his means of transportation to let him down.

Bianca was smiling, clearly delighted at the compliment he'd just sent her way.

'No mention at all of the third guy. He'd be Megan's father, I'm guessing, as she's the eldest. It must be a tough life for those girls.'

They climbed out of the car and made their way over to the office block. Walking through the corridors, they could see many of the offices were now vacant, the ghosts of magazine teams and advertising departments wandering the empty rooms in echoes of more vibrant times for the Tribune. All those other publications were long gone; all that remained was an almost skeleton staff and a single weekly paper. The magazines had been pulled first, then the daily edition. Cory knew that the weekly must follow, but he couldn't bring himself to look for another job just yet. It would take him away from his son and Shallow Falls; he'd have to head out to a larger city to stand any chance of finding a decent reporting job. He wasn't ready to give up on his marriage just yet.

'Hey, Cory, Bianca, how's it going?' Mitchell asked as they passed his office. It looked incongruous against the backdrop of the empty rooms throughout the rest of the building, but Mitchell's family had owned this building for just under a century. It was bought and paid for, and had become the only remaining asset in the company, aside from the old printing press.

'All good,' Cory replied, 'I'm just going to update the news copy on the website and feed in some new photographs of the missing child. Anything else to report here?'

'Since she hasn't turned up, we're going big on it for Friday's paper. There's a big splash of photographs—we've got the school, the search, and the police operation. It's going to be a bumper issue. Keep your ear to the ground. What we're lacking right now is a suspect, cause, or motive. And don't give everything away on the website. We need to make sure there's still a reason to buy Friday's paper.'

'Will do,' Cory replied, and continued the short walk to the newsroom.

'Good morning,' Oliver Vasey said as they walked up to Cory's desk. 'This story is looking good. Tell me you have more pictures of the child.'

Bianca placed them on his desk.

'Nice work. I'll have to see if I can remember how to use the scanner. Have you got more words for me, Cory? Mitchell just upped the coverage, so I'm desperate for anything you've got. He's even considered dumping Vasey's People this week to make more space.'

'I've got plenty of words for you—I'll get them filed now. Let's get those images on the website. Send the electronic versions over to Bianca, too, will you? She's going to make some posters.'

Cory made sure Bianca was logged on, then got his head down and began to file his updates on the story. Although the newsroom was an active and noisy environment, he'd long ago learned how to screen it out and maintain his concentration. He typed steadily, his fingers striking the keyboard at a furious speed. As he recorded his experiences chatting to Reece and talked about the searches over at

Shallow Falls, he was vaguely aware of phones ringing, conversations taking place across desks, and some new level of excitement.

'Cory.'

It was Bianca's voice, almost shouting at him, impatient to get his attention.

He'd been in the zone, crafting his words, creating compelling news copy to bring readers up-to-date with the story.

'Oliver's been trying to get your attention for the past minute.'

'Sorry,' he said. 'You know how it is when you're in the middle of a riveting story, right?'

'You need to file your story and get over to the police station,' Vasey said. 'They've pulled someone in for questioning about the kid.'

'Already?' Cory replied, 'That's fast work. Have we got a name?'

'Yeah, it's Xander Griffen, a young chap, lives over on Reece Norman's side of town. Bit of a weirdo, by all accounts.'

'Xander? He's almost her next-door neighbor. Does it look like it'll stand up?'

Vasey shrugged.

'Who knows? Tarrant will be under massive pressure, so he must have a reason for pulling him in.'

'But Xander Griffen? That seems a bit too easy,' Cory said, thinking aloud. 'He's an easy target, too. Especially after what happened to him last time.'

ELEVEN

Shallow Falls Library was fighting a losing battle against the ongoing ravages of the internet. Once a proud addition to the town's resources, it was now struggling from severely depleted numbers of users and the consequent lack of local government support that soon followed.

The early twentieth century building, which once stood confident and proud at the end of the main street, now looked a little worse for wear and in need of a good coat of paint. Like a gladiator struck down in the arena, it had fought a brave fight, but now, bloodied and dispirited, it had only to wait for the inevitable thumbs-down from the emperor to finally put itself out of its misery. It was there that Cory and Bianca were heading after their short walk to the police station.

'One moment,' Bianca urged.

She took the second-to-last poster out of a cardboard wallet and taped it to a lamppost.

'I'll save this last one for the library. At least we've done our bit to help Reece out.'

Cory stopped and read the poster one more time. A

photo of Poppy with her hair in a ponytail beamed out at him. Reece had said that the latest photo, which they'd been using, wasn't how Poppy looked most of the time. The school had made her remove the ponytail for the photo, insisting it was more appropriate for a formal photograph.

'But that's not how Poppy looks,' Reece had said. 'I hate that school photo. I wouldn't pay for it—they cost enough as it is. They made her do something different with her hair, but she never wears it that way. She thinks uncovering her ears will help her to hear better and I'm certainly not going to be the one to stop her. She looks uncomfortable in that picture; I don't want that in my house.'

Bianca had respected her wishes and changed it for another. Even though Poppy had grown up a little since the image was taken, Reece still felt it would help people to spot her better.

'That photograph catches Poppy's beautiful soul.' she'd said. 'That's how I want them to see my daughter.'

Have you seen Poppy Norman? the poster read. *Missing since 3pm on Tuesday May 3rd. Please contact The Shallow Falls Tribune or Shallow Falls Police if you can help.*

Cory wondered what lengths he'd go to to save his own son. It had been three days since he'd last seen him and less than a day since they'd spoken, albeit briefly, on the phone. The simple answer was that he'd do anything to save the life of his child. And, having met Reece Norman, he'd go just about as far to save the life of her child, too. If he could do anything to help her escape from the pain she was in, he'd do it. He never wanted to see someone in that state again; Poppy's disappearance was torture for her.

'How long until we'll hear about Xander?' Bianca asked.

She had a habit of asking precise questions directly. That was a great trait in a reporter.

'Who knows? It depends what they have on him. Poor guy—it's not the first time this has happened. Do you remember? It was after his parents died, some woman accused him of following her. I just felt desperately sad for him at the time—he clearly has learning difficulties of some kind. They'd be better off finding him some care, instead of hauling him back to the police station.'

'He's definitely a loner,' Bianca said. 'He'd come into the store and was painfully shy. I'd try and get him to speak, but I never heard him say more than a *thank you*. It's terrible how his parents died, too. I guess they cared for him when they were alive. I don't know who picks up the responsibility now they're gone. Does anybody?'

Cory shrugged. Truth was, he didn't really know. Xander was an adult, living in that big house all on his own. He must have money, because he certainly didn't have a job.

'You know they died on Devil's Corner?' he said.

'No, I didn't know that. I only knew it was an accident. I've never heard it called that until you said it, but I know my parents always take it slow—it's one hell of a corner. I just figure it's sensible to slow down a bit. What happened, did they skid off it?'

'Yes, something like that. It was icy, too—it's even more treacherous in winter. The car went hurtling down the embankment right into the river at the end of the falls. Crunched into a great big rock at the bottom. They had airbags, but the force of the blow was so great, it broke their necks. It was a horrible way to go.'

Cory saw Bianca's expression.

'I'm sorry, was that too much information? I forget that you're an intern. You're so good at this reporting business, I've begun treating you like a reporter already.'

'No, it's fine,' Bianca reassured him. 'It's just that I know the rock you mean at the river. We used to walk out there and mess around in the water when I was younger. I never realized so many people had died there.'

'Like I said, the town council should be campaigning to deal with that stretch of road. Right, we're here, let's see if Mrs. Franklin can help us.'

They walked through the grand entrance to the library, their footsteps echoing on the tiled floor. Cory opened the heavy oak door that led into the downstairs section, where they were greeted by a sign reading *Fiction & Children's*.

'I learned to read here,' Bianca said. 'Mom used to bring me twice a week, regular as clockwork. I must have read every book in the kids' section at least twice. Mrs. Franklin has worked here as long as I can remember.'

'Do you still use it?' Cory asked. 'I've only ever been on newspaper business. I don't get to read much these days.'

He surveyed the flaking paint on the high, ornate ceiling and observed how quiet it was. Just a couple of seniors were there, one reading last week's Tribune and the other engrossed in a book in the romance section.

'I read on my phone these days,' she answered. 'I guess we get what we deserve if this place finally falls apart.'

'There's Mrs. Franklin—let's see if she can help with my hunch.'

Imogen Franklin had worked all her life in the town's library. Some townsfolk believed they'd built it around her and that she never left the building. Several generations of children had grown up knowing her only as *the library lady*. They would look at her fearfully at first, scared of the single thick hair that was growing out of the mole on her cheek. She never plucked it—not in all those years. But when she asked them if they wanted to stamp their own books, they'd forget about her appearance, captivated by her magic and passion for books. Perhaps Imogen Franklin was there to teach young children their first important lesson in life—that you can't judge a book by its cover.

Cory and Bianca walked up the ornate period staircase which led up to the nonfiction section. Cory had spotted her reshelving books up there, pulling along her distinctive wooden cart. It was a wonder she never tired of putting books back on the shelves.

'Hello, Bianca, it's been a long time since I've seen you,' she said, immediately recognizing a former patron the moment she saw her. 'I gave you your first board book when you were a baby, and now look at you, a grown woman.'

'Hello, Mrs. Franklin.'

'Please call me Imogen. And what brings you here, with Cory Miles of all people?'

'It's the usual newspaper business, I'm afraid. I've got a planning question. You hold historical records here, don't you?'

'Probably,' she replied. 'What is it you're after? Are you working for the newspaper now, Bianca?'

Bianca nodded and smiled.

'Just think, it all began in this very building with that first book. A love of words, that's what it is. You're welcome here any time, you know, Bianca. Just because you're all grown up, it doesn't mean we won't have books that you'll like.'

Bianca's face reddened a little and Cory knew how she felt. He'd never once brought his son to the library. Hearing Imogen Franklin speak made him feel like he'd betrayed her in some way.

'I'm interested in the plot of land that Reece Norman's trailer is on.'

'Oh, that poor lady. What must she be going through

right now? And those lovely girls of hers—they're regulars in here, you know. I hear Reece telling them not to be like her and to learn to read properly. I'm sorry, I said too much... but it breaks my heart when adults can't read. They can get started at any time, you know. It's never too late.'

Cory hadn't realized that. Was Reece illiterate? It had never even occurred to him.

'Can you also pull out any information you have on that entire row of houses that border on the woods, including the Griffen residence?'

'It's going to take me a little time to lay my hands on them—old planning documentation is stored in the stacks on the third floor. One of my volunteers called in sick today, so I'm the only paid member of staff in the building. Can it wait a little while until I have a moment to look for you?'

'Yes, it's no problem.' Cory replied. 'Here's my business card—would you give me a call at that number when you find it?'

'Yes, I'll let you know right away.' Imogen replied. 'I know we have what you're after; you're not the first person who's asked for that particular documentation. In fact, there have been a few people who've wanted to look at the title information on Reece Norman's house in recent months.'

TWELVE

Cory needed a strong coffee, so he suggested to Bianca that they walk up the main street to Lacey's Diner. The place was completely different during the day compared to the evenings. Now it was packed with seniors and shoppers, catching a breath from retail and enjoying the best that the town's most popular eatery had to offer.

'We'll need to take stools at the counter,' Cory said. 'There's no chance of getting a booth in here at this time of day.'

Bianca located a second seat while Cory placed the orders. He was getting antsy about Xander Griffen, but he knew the procedure: there would be no more information from Chief Tarrant unless a charge or arrest was made, and that could be some time coming. Sitting in the diner and listening to people's conversations was the best bet for now. In the same way the initial search for Poppy had turned up the local gossip about Reece, so it would about Xander—except Cory knew a bit about Xander already.

'The coffees are on their way,' he said, as Bianca sat on a stool. 'It's buzzing in here today.'

'I'm not sure why anybody buys the paper,' she replied. 'They're all talking about Xander.'

'Pick up anything interesting?'

'Poor guy has been sentenced already, by the sound of it. Just walking to the far end of the bar and back, it was like gossip bingo. I heard *no smoke without fire, he's a strange one,* and *he's never been the same since his parents died.* Basically, he's been written off as the town nutjob. He never struck me that way when he came in the store. As far as I could, tell he was just painfully shy.'

'This is precisely why we need the local paper,' Cory began, 'because the people of Shallow Falls can't be trusted to get the facts right. Imagine if all we had was gossip. We'd be hanging people on the basis of a vote on Facebook if we did that.'

The coffees arrived: Bianca had an Americano, and Cory a double espresso. If she ever got a full-time job as a reporter, she'd graduate to espresso—she'd need it to sustain the long and erratic hours.

Cory's phone buzzed and he pulled it out of his back pocket to take a look.

'It's from Reece Norman,' he said. 'Must be important— she said she only had two dollars' credit left when we spoke earlier.'

Reece had left a voicemail rather than a text message. If she was unable to read and write, as Imogen Franklin had intimated, that made sense. Cory figured he must have missed the message when he silenced his phone at the library.

It's Reece Norman. Please call back when you can. I got a letter. I don't want to tell Chief Tarrant.

Cory called back immediately. There was no answer, so he left a message of his own.

Hi, Reece, it's Cory Miles here. We'll be right there. It's just after midday when I'm leaving this message. See you shortly.

As he ended the message, his phone buzzed again. Another missed voicemail. His phone was usually never that busy.

Hello, Mr. Miles, it's Lauren Clinton, the principal at Mountain View Elementary here. It's nothing to worry about, but Zach has had an accident and we're unable to get hold of your wife. Please call us as soon as you can.

'I've got to go,' Cory said, putting his phone in his pocket. 'I need to go to Westview to see my son. He's had an accident of some sort. You might want to go back to the office.'

'I'll tag along, if I'm not in the way.' Bianca replied. 'I won't have anything to do in the office without you there. If that's okay?'

'Yeah, sure,' Cory said, leaving a ten-dollar bill on the counter. As they walked back to the office to pick up his car, he took out his phone again and let the school know he was on his way. He held his breath as he inserted the key. It wouldn't start. He tried again. Nothing.

Cory could feel the tension rising through his body. He didn't want to curse with Bianca in the vehicle with him, but he was getting close to it. He tried it a third time and it fired into life. He started to breathe again.

A little too fast, he reversed out of the parking space and was out on the road in no time at all. As he passed Reece's trailer and entered the shade of the woodland road, he remembered he'd told her they were on their way. She of all people would understand that he'd been called away on a child-related emergency.

Cory hadn't realized how fast he was driving until

Bianca spoke up just before the stretch of road that lead to Devil's Corner.

'I don't want to be a backseat driver, but aren't you going a bit fast, bearing in mind where we are?'

Cory's immediate reaction was to chew her out, but he stopped short. She was right, he was going far too fast for Devil's Corner, especially in the light of what he'd been saying to her earlier that day.

'Yeah, I'm sorry, I didn't realize how wound up I was.'

He braked gently and the car slowed to a more appropriate speed.

'I used to do this drive to work every day; I've taken that corner from both directions hundreds of times. There's nothing intrinsically dangerous about it if you take it at the right speed. I, of all people, should know that.'

'So, you haven't always lived in Shallow Falls?'

There she was, asking her tight, laser-sharp questions again.

'No, I used to commute here when... um... when my wife and I were together. She's a hot-shot lawyer in Westview; it's her money that bought the house. When she kicked me out, I had to find somewhere fast. It made sense to stay in Shallow Falls because I can save on gas. The housing is cheaper, too. I miss Zach, though...'

Westview was ten miles away from Shallow Falls, an easy commute, though people were more inclined to say that in summer than during the winter months.

Bianca didn't probe anymore and Cory was pleased for it. The less she knew of his struggling marriage, the better.

Within twenty minutes, they'd arrived at Mountain View Elementary. Cory pulled into the small parking lot and spotted a vehicle in the visitors' parking.

'Nadia's here already,' he said.

He could sense Bianca looking at him from the side.

'Nadia's my wife,' he explained.

Cory parked the car, not bothering to lock it up, and Bianca followed him. They signed in at the reception area and rushed over to the principal's office. Cory tapped at the door and entered.

Nadia was sitting in front of the principal's desk with Zach on her lap. He had a small bandage on his forehead and Nadia was stroking his hand to comfort him.

'Zach,' Cory said. 'Are you okay? What happened?'

'What happened is that I had to come out of court to get here, because you couldn't get your ass over here fast enough,' Nadia seethed.

Principal Clinton informed Cory that Zach had bumped his head on a desk as he'd gotten up from the floor after playing with building blocks. It had made a small gash in his forehead, and they were being cautious in case of a concussion.

'Hey, Zachy,' Cory said, kneeling down to kiss his son on the head and inspect the covered wound.

'Hi, Dad,' Zach replied, moving forward to put his arms around Cory. Bianca hovered at the door, unsure what to do with herself.

'And who's this tagging along with you? Don't say you've found another woman already?'

Nadia was on the offensive, taking Cory by surprise. He got that she was anxious, but it seemed out of place in the principal's office. He tried to stay calm.

'This is Bianca Williams—she's doing an internship at the newspaper. I'm sorry, we were out on a job when you called.'

'Well, you might have got here a bit quicker,' Nadia continued. 'You know how important this case is and it was a complete embarrassment to have to ask the judge for a temporary postponement...'

'I'm sorry, I got here as soon as I could.'

'You're always sorry about something.'

Zach was cuddling into his mom, scared by the conversation they were having.

Principal Clinton intervened.

'Well, everything seems to be straightened out here. I suggest you get Zach checked out by your physician—I'm sure he'll be fine after a rest.'

Cory and Nadia thanked her and left the office, making their way along the echoing corridor towards the reception area. Cory was regretting bringing Bianca along; she looked unsure what to do. He couldn't blame her, bearing in mind what she'd just witnessed.

Fortunately, Zach saved the day, walking up to her and taking her hand.

'Hi, I'm Zach. Who are you?'

Cory observed that they had something in common— the ability to ask the correct blunt question at precisely the right time.

As Zach showed Bianca his painting on a wall display, Cory ventured some advice to Nadia. He immediately regretted it.

'You know, we ought to try and keep any tension between us away from Zach—and Principal Clinton, come to think of it.'

'Don't tell me how to behave in front of my own child.'

Nadia only ever got that way when she was stressed. He wanted to remind her Zach was *our child*, but thought better of it.

'I need to be focused at work more than ever, Cory. Do you realize how stupid this makes me look?'

'I got here as soon as I could.'

'But it wasn't soon enough, was it, Cory?'

'Sorry...'

'I'm trying to get Zach ready for school in the mornings and I've got no help at all. And we stretched ourselves on the mortgage—you know that—and I'm struggling to do it on my own.'

'Look, I'm sending over money regularly, but I have to have a place to stay.'

'But that's not the point, is it, Cory? If you hadn't been so married to that damn job of yours, we might not be in the situation we're in...'

'But you asked me to leave the house. I wanted to go to counseling....'

'Mr. and Mrs. Miles.'

The principal's voice boomed down the corridor. They stopped dead.

'If you must discuss your marital difficulties in front of your child, then I suppose I can't stop you. But I would politely request that you take any arguments away from my school. Your shouting is disturbing the children in their classrooms and I won't have it. Leave now please, and only come back when you are capable of behaving like civilized human beings.'

THIRTEEN

'I'm so sorry you had to see that,' Cory said to Bianca as they climbed back into his car. 'It wasn't our finest moment.'

Nadia was revving her car, clearly annoyed at the joint humiliation they'd just experienced in the school corridor at the hands of Principal Clinton. There would be no gold stars for the Miles family that week.

'Make sure you're here to pick Zach up after school tomorrow,' Nadia called across from her car, making no effort to conceal her anger. 'You promised, remember? Try to get here on time if you can.'

Cory tried to start up the engine, but it was having none of it. Nadia pulled out behind him and he gave Zach a friendly wave before her car disappeared down the road. Cory couldn't face the further embarrassment of a car that wouldn't play ball, so he waited until Nadia was off the scene. He tried again. Nothing.

'Goddammit,' he slammed his fist on the steering wheel. Bianca jumped at his side.

'I'm sorry,' he said. 'This feels like the final straw. Getting a ringside seat on my marital problems is not what you signed up for with your internship. It's really unprofessional of me. I'll say it again: I apologize.'

'It's fine, honestly,' Bianca reassured him. 'My mom and dad have fights all the time. I just figure it goes with married life. Zach's a lovely kid, though; you must miss him terribly.'

She'd done it again, got directly to the heart of the issue without beating around the bush. That's exactly why he and Nadia were arguing so much. They both wanted the best for Zach, but they were both feeling the strain of being separated and he felt like a big failure, letting his son down.

Principal Clinton was right: they'd have to do better. Zach didn't deserve to be exposed to all that tension. They'd need to work hard to keep him away from it. Cory resolved to speak to Nadia at the earliest opportunity, to see if they could cool things down a bit. Couples counseling would help, he was certain of that.

Cory's phone buzzed and he checked its screen.

'We said we'd go to Reece's; I forgot to let her know we'd been delayed. We'd better get over there. I'll speak to Nadia later and apologize to Principal Clinton, too. What a day.'

Cory asked Bianca to open the hood release again. He climbed out, tapped the troublesome engine part, and got Bianca to start the engine. It fired up and he felt a massive sense of relief. That was another thing to add to his list—to head over to Kelsey Baker's junkyard and see if he could get a used part to fix the car.

Cory was anxious to get to Reece's trailer, having learned through experience that contacts in news stories are best treated with respect. If he messed about and made her think he wasn't taking her seriously, she'd clam up on him.

The drive back to Shallow Falls was uneventful. Cory noticed that the police tape had now been removed from the road along the falls. Presumably they'd moved on to other things. Perhaps the questioning of Xander had sent them off in a new direction.

As he parked the car outside Reece's trailer, Cory could see that the accompanying police officer had changed once again, giving him a new gatekeeper to get past. He was helped by the fact that Toni and Megan rushed to the door when they saw Bianca was with him.

'Can we play with Bianca, Mom?' he heard them asking. There was a frosty reply from inside the trailer; a female officer by the name of Ambrose was guarding the door, the children at her side.

'I'm sorry we took so long,' Cory called through the door. 'I got called away on a family emergency and I had to drop everything and go.'

There was more mumbling from inside the trailer, then movement. Reece opened the door, staying behind Officer Ambrose for cover.

Cory made an appeal to her more forgiving nature.

'I'm sorry, Reece, it really was an emergency. The call came in just after you contacted me.'

Reece looked at the girls, who were straining at the leash to go outside and play. They looked sick and tired of being holed up like that. Reece was pale and exhausted.

'Off you go, girls—stay close to the trailer.'

They were like greyhounds out of the gate.

'Officer Ambrose, I'd appreciate it if I could have a few minutes on my own to talk to Mr. Miles, please.'

Ambrose studied Reece's face as if making sure that was coming from her, then nodded reluctantly and stepped outside.

'If you don't mind, I'm going to take ten minutes to pop back to the police station,' she said. 'There's something I need to attend to. Will you be here all that time, Mr. Miles? Are you happy for me to do that, Reece?'

Both nodded and Ambrose walked over to her car.

Cory guessed she was heading back to the station for a quick coffee and some banter with her colleagues. It must be an intense shift staying with the mother of a missing child; he wouldn't wish that situation on anyone.

She turned toward him. 'I've had a lifetime of being let down by dumbass men, Mr. Miles. Please don't become the next idiot on my list.'

Cory closed the trailer door behind him, feeling as self-conscious as when he and Nadia had been scolded by Principal Clinton.

Toni and Megan sounded like chirping birds just released from a cage, their childish joy a delight to hear.

'What did you want to discuss with me?' Cory asked, taking a seat at Reece's cue.

She walked over to the kitchen counter and pulled out an envelope from under a pile of magazines, handing it to Cory.

'It came with today's mail. It doesn't look like the usual bills and things. Wait until you see what's inside. I didn't want to show Officer Ambrose because...'

'What?' Cory asked, sensing her hesitation.

She paused a moment longer.

'Because I don't trust Chief Tarrant.'

'Any reason?'

'I just don't like the man. That's all. Don't ask me why. Besides, I told you what he did with the social services, reporting me for picking up the girls late at school. A man like that can't be trusted.'

Cory took the single piece of letter-size paper out of the envelope, which had an address sticker on the front. It looked like it had been printed at home rather than the mass-produced labeling that might come with a bank statement or something similar. The note inside was typed out in capital letters.

Take care Reece. I hope you see Poppy again.

Cory read it aloud, remembering what Imogen had let slip about Reece's illiteracy.

'I recognized my name and Poppy's,' Reece said, 'But I didn't quite catch the meaning. I didn't need to, I could see how it was written.'

'Do you think it's threatening?' Cory asked. 'It could just be from a well-wisher.'

'There isn't any signature on it, is there? I can tell that much. It's meant to threaten me, all right.'

Cory felt ambivalent about the letter. It might just be some anonymous person in town wishing her well. They might struggle with literacy themselves, hence the brevity.

'Is there anything going on which you haven't mentioned to the police? Are you holding back any information that they ought to know about? I'm wondering if you ought to have shown this to Officer Ambrose.'

'I don't want Chief Tarrant knowing about it. I want my Poppy back more than anything in the world, but the police don't need to see this.'

Cory decided to change the subject. The sound of Bianca and the girls playing moved to the back of the trailer, where he could hear a ball bouncing off the rear wall.

'What do you know about Xander Griffen?' he asked. 'You're sort of neighbors. Do you know him well?'

'He always seems like a shy boy to me. Never says much at all.'

'Do you think he's responsible?'

'I don't think he'd say boo to a goose. I know the folks

around here think he's strange. They also think I'm some sort of tramp because three of my men upped and left me with the girls. Well, Poppy's father may yet show his face again, but it's not looking good.'

'Who owns all this land on the edge of town, Reece? Your trailer has been here for years now and the ruins of the old house have never been bulldozed away. Is this your land?'

'You've figured out I can't read properly, yes? Well, the world can be a mighty confusing place if you can't make sense of words, Mr. Miles. Ma and Pa were talking to that Mr. Jones about the land when the house burned down--'

'It killed both your parents, right?'

'Yes, and my baby sister. Why else would I be living in this trailer with my three kids?'

'Was that Spencer Jones, by the way?'

'Yes, Mr. Spencer Jones. Spends most of the time drunk in Lacey's, as far as I can tell. Don't know what he was speaking to Ma and Pa about—it all went quiet after they died.'

'So how do you get along, Reece? Without being able to read?'

'The girls help me now. It gets easier as they get older. I've got something called dyslexia, according to my little sister, but she's not around anymore and I wouldn't know what to do about it. But I manage.'

'Didn't Xander's parents die, too? Around the same time?'

'Yes—well, within two months of each other. It's hardly a coincidence. Mine died in a tragic house fire due to an electrical fault. His came off the road at Devil's Corner. All I'd say is, don't buy a house next to me and Xander—it doesn't look like it's very lucky.'

The conversation was interrupted by the sound of gunfire outside. It sounded close; not right next to the trailer, but over where the woodland began. There was a scream from outside, signalling that Toni and Megan were startled by the shot, which echoed around. Cory and Reece jumped up and ran to the trailer door, throwing it open, desperate to make sure nobody had been hurt. Bianca emerged from the back of the trailer, her arms around the two girls. Toni was crying, and Bianca looked rattled.

'What happened? Did you see who it was?' Cory asked, urgently.

Bianca shook her head.

Megan was pointing to the two cars which were parked outside the trailer—Cory's and Reece's. Two bloody crows' corpses had been left on each hood, their flesh blown away by a shotgun.

FOURTEEN

It took longer to deal with the police over the matter of the crows than Cory would have liked. At Reece's request, he kept quiet about the letter, but he felt conflicted; what if the letter held the key to Poppy's disappearance? He consoled himself that there were no clues on the envelope or the letter itself. Any fingerprint evidence would be long gone, considering their circuitous journey through the mail system and the endless pawing by Reece.

Cory couldn't accuse Tarrant's team of skimping over anything: they were thorough and professional. The crows had been dead for some time, possibly the day before. Neither Bianca nor the children had seen or heard anything. The sound of the gunshot had come from the adjoining woodland, but the officers said the two things might not be related—the gun could belong to a poacher or even a farmer. Cory was skeptical about that, and he could tell that Reece was, too.

Officer Ambrose was in the doghouse for leaving her post. She'd have gotten away with it if it wasn't for the crows. Word came down the food chain that Reece was to be under supervision at all times, in case news came in.

Cory was pleased to see Officer Louise Powell had been called to the scene. They'd struck up quite a friendship in the time he'd been reporting on the paper and they got on well, finding each other easy company.

'Hey, Cory, good to see you again! I can tell you're sinking your journalistic teeth deep into this news story.'

As she smiled, her face lit up and her eyes sparkled. He liked her positivity; he needed a bit more of that in his life.

'How's the case going? I guess two dead crows don't help?'

'Probably some wacko with a grudge against Reece. They all come out of the woodwork at times like these. Poor woman, she's been two days without Poppy now. I can't imagine what it's like to be in that position.'

'Any news on Xander Griffen that won't land you in trouble with the chief if you share it with me?'

Louise looked around. Officer Ambrose was close by. She moved up to Cory.

'What are you doing this evening? Can you join me for a drink?'

Cory was taken aback for a moment.

'It's strictly professional,' she added. 'I can't speak freely here, but there are a couple of things I can share with you. Are you up for it?'

Other than calling Nadia to apologize and to chat with Zach before bedtime, Cory's schedule appeared to be clear that evening. It was clear most evenings.

'Yeah, sure. Not Lacey's, though, if you don't mind. Spencer Jones has made it his evening haunt, and I don't want to have to chase him away all night. How about that new wine bar that opened recently?'

'Chez Nous?' Louise offered.

'That's the place—how about we meet there at, say, eight o' clock?'

'It's a date.' Louise smiled, then corrected herself. 'It's a professional meeting to discuss pressing business matters.'

She gave Cory an impish smile and he returned it. He felt the excitement of collusion and a frisson of something that he couldn't put his finger on. He liked Louise, and that was that. He had a son to think about and a marriage that was down but not yet out.

'Are we good to go here, officer?' Cory called over to the senior officer on site. He got the nod and caught Bianca's attention. She was still playing with Toni and Megan, and the color had now returned to her cheeks.

As Bianca finished off whatever game she was playing, Cory moved over to Reece, who was sitting on the lower step of the trailer. He kept his voice low as he spoke to her.

'You sure you're going to keep that letter quiet? It might be better to let on.'

She nodded.

'Yes, let's keep it to ourselves for now. If I thought for one minute it would help me find Poppy, I'd let the police know.'

She began to sob, and Cory felt a desperate need to offer some comfort to her. But what could he say? She'll turn up safe? It'll all blow over? The simple truth was—and they both knew it—the longer that Poppy was missing, the greater the chance she'd be identifying a body, not picking up her little girl from the police station.

'I'm sorry, Reece, really I am. I promise you, we're doing all we can at the newspaper to get the word out far and wide that Poppy's missing. If you think of anything else, you have my number.'

Bianca was waiting for him at a diplomatic distance now. She'd left the girls and was ready to leave.

'Let's hope this car starts,' Cory said to her. 'I don't want a big performance about it when we have such a crowd watching.'

It didn't start right away, but it did start the second time, without Cory having to lift the hood and do his trick of tapping the starter motor.

'The internet says it's something to do with the brushes inside the motor. They're worn or something. Sometimes they make contact, sometimes they don't. A gentle tap usually fixes it. Eventually, it'll just stop working altogether.'

He looked at the clock on the dashboard.

'I'm not getting over to Kelsey Baker's yard today—I'm going to have to file updates for the newspaper. Shall we grab a bite to eat on the way back to the office? I'm starving —I assume you are, too?'

It was late afternoon by the time they got back to their desks, pre-packed sandwiches and sodas in their hands. Oliver Vasey brought Cory up to date with the layout of that Friday's special supplement, which had been mocked up on his computer screen.

'Mitchell might extend the coverage tomorrow,' Vasey began. 'It depends if the kid turns up—so keep these photos and the profile info flowing. Anything to report from today?'

'I've got more profile and background information to add, a couple of comments from police officers and so on. But nothing substantial.'

'What about the crows?' Bianca asked, then stopped dead, picking up on the glare that Cory had just given her.

'Crows?' Vasey asked.

'Oh, it's nothing.' Bianca recovered the situation. 'Just a

bit of a scare we had while we were out in the car. Nothing to do with a disappearing child.'

Oliver nodded and returned to tapping away at his PC.

Once installed back at their desks, Bianca came seeking answers from Cory.

'Why didn't you mention the crows?' she asked.

'A couple of reasons,' Cory replied. 'First is that it's probably the work of some weirdo. They tend to come out around cases like this. They can confuse the issue and set the police along the wrong path. Secondly, the senior officer at Reece's trailer asked me not to, for that very reason...'

'Do you always let the police decide what you say?'

Cory looked at her. She was clearly struggling with a basic journalistic principle: that of oiling the wheels.

He owed her some patience after his earlier bad-tempered displays that day.

'Think of it as information management. Sometimes the police don't want us to share certain pieces of information. We're here to help the police, not hinder them. If I thought releasing that information about the crows would help find Poppy, I'd do it in an instant. But I agree with the police. It's unsettling and it's not a good development, but it probably is the work of a weirdo. So, for now, it's best kept quiet.'

The remainder of the afternoon was spent filing news copy, importing new photographs and making check calls. Xander was still being questioned, but no charges had been made. Imogen Franklin hadn't gotten back to him. It was a little annoying, but she had told them she was short-staffed. And he'd sneaked off into one of the abandoned conference rooms to make a call, smoothing things over with Nadia and checking in on Zach.

'Is it okay if I drop you near my apartment?' he said to

Bianca as they were leaving the office. 'Are you okay to walk from there? It's a little closer to your house.'

'Yes, no problem,' she replied. 'I appreciate you giving me so many rides. I'll be fine. In fact, if you drop me off on the main street, I'll pick up some bits and pieces to take home. It'll keep me in Mom's good books.'

Cory stopped the car as close as he could to where she needed to be, without leaving himself running late for Louise. As Bianca walked off, he made a final check call into the police station to see if Xander had been charged. There was still no news.

He ended the call and moved to start the car. Something along the street caught his eye. It was only because there was something not quite right about it that he was even giving it a second glance. He strained his eyes to get a better look. Some young guy looked like he was getting very heated up about something or other. His body language said it all: cocky, confrontational, and arrogant. He was shouting at some young woman.

It was Bianca. She looked upset, so he pulled his keys out of the ignition, ready to step in and lend his support. He stepped out of the car, but Bianca walked off and the man—youth—whatever he was, walked away in the opposite direction. Cory stood and watched for a few moments to make sure that Bianca was safe.

Once he was satisfied Bianca was in no immediate trouble, he got back in the car. He'd ask her about it the next day, to see if he could help with anything. It was probably none of his business; for all he knew, it could be boyfriend trouble. He'd tread carefully, making sure he wasn't interfering where he wasn't wanted.

By the time he was sitting in Chez Nous with a glass of red wine at his side, he was feeling good. He'd forgotten about the episode with Bianca, had time for a shower and even managed to make arrangements through the landlord for the glazier to come and fix the window. And he didn't have to drive that night; Chez Nous was within walking distance of home.

Louise Powell looked like a completely different person out of her uniform, wearing her hair down. It was a stunning length and made her look spectacular as she entered the wine bar. She was wearing a dress, too; Cory had seen her in her uniform pants so many times now that he'd almost forgotten wearing a dress was an option.

She walked up to him, smiling, and ordered herself a white wine.

'Busy day?' Cory asked.

'You can say that again. A chilled white wine is exactly what I'm after.'

The conversation was easy, moving quickly from that day's incident with the crows to matters that weren't work-related: Zach's progress at school, Louise's new house, Cory's car problems, and Louise's mom's health. As they chatted and laughed, Cory noticed Louise moving a little closer. The bar was busy—it was probably so that she could hear him better over the sound of the chatter.

'What is it you wanted to discuss with me?' Cory asked. 'You mentioned something earlier at Reece's trailer?'

Louise tensed a little, now Cory was moving the conversation into slightly less personal territory.

'Yes, you're right, we've been gossiping away all evening like a couple of... well, yes, I did have something to tell you. It might be something, it might be nothing. It's Chief Tarrant. He's busting balls to get an arrest on Xander Griffin. He's determined that the interviewing officers find something and make it stick.'

'What have they got to go on? Anything?'

'That's just it. I know Officer Mansfield, and he thinks Xander is clean. The chief seems to want to hang the whole thing on him being a bit weird. But let's face it, if we were all arrested because we do odd things now and again, we'd all be in jail.'

Cory laughed. She joined in and as she moved forward, she placed her hand on his knee, as much to steady herself as anything.

Cory stopped for a moment as something hung in the air between them, something he couldn't put his finger on. They were looking at each other, neither saying a thing, caught in a silent moment in time.

Louise leaned forward, as if she were moving in to give him a kiss. For a moment, Cory considered reciprocating, but instead got up from his stool abruptly.

'I'm sorry, Louise, really sorry. I still need to sort things out with Nadia. We've got to do right by Zach. I have to go...'

Cory walked out of the bar, leaving Louise to figure out for herself what had just happened.

FIFTEEN

Wednesday—Day 3

CORY WOKE to the sound of his phone ringing. His mouth felt as dry as if he'd gargled with sand before going to bed the night before. He swallowed a couple of times to get his saliva glands working before picking up the call, trying to check the number but unable to focus on the digits.

'Cory Miles speaking...'

His voice was so weak that he couldn't quite make it to the end of the sentence.

'Hello, Mr. Miles, it's Imogen Franklin from the library.'

Jeez, what time is it?

Cory moved his phone closer, then further away from his eyes, trying desperately to find a focal point. It was after eight o'clock. He'd missed his run and would have to rush at the speed of a miser with a coupon code to get in to work on time. And there was Bianca to pick up, too.

'Hi, Imogen, have you got that information we were talking about?'

'Yes, some of it's here at Shallow Falls, but I'm going to have to request some of it from the county branch. They have more storage space than we do. Is that okay? It's not a rush job is it?'

'No, no, it's all good, Imogen, thank you.'

He could feel his voice working properly now; his eyes were beginning to adjust to the light and his brain had kicked in, too. It was the plywood panel that was covering the smashed window that had done it: the morning sunshine which normally shone in at that time of day couldn't break through. He'd been like a parakeet with a blanket thrown over its cage. It was a good thing Imogen had called.

'You start early at the library,' Cory said.

'Well, I'm pleased I caught you. I've seen you jogging around the town at this time of day. Did you have a good run this morning?'

Cory mumbled a reply and thanked Imogen for making the call. He switched off the phone and decided to go around to view the documents she had so far before picking up Bianca from her home.

He surprised himself how fast he could get showered, dressed, and fed with a slice of toast. The car even obliged him by starting the first time. Cory felt it was going to be a good day.

The library was quiet when he walked through the heavy doors. It was still before nine o'clock and the public hadn't bothered to turn up yet. Imogen was busying herself at the reception desk, getting ready for the day ahead.

'Good morning, Imogen. Thanks for digging out that information—I know you're busy.'

'Well, since my husband died, I'm just pleased to have this library to come to. We don't even open until half past nine today, but I honestly don't know what I'd do with myself if I wasn't here. Perhaps watch television all day. After a life reading books, that's not something I'm prepared to consider.'

'Good for you,' Cory smiled. Then the memory of how he'd walked away from Louise the night before came back to him. He cringed. What was he, some hormone-fueled youngster incapable of expressing himself? She had just caught him off guard. It was another apology he'd need to make, something he seemed to be doing a lot of recently.

'Here are the documents,' Imogen said, sliding them across the counter. 'I'm sorry I couldn't get everything you were after, but I promise I'll let you know as soon as the rest arrives. Have they found young Poppy yet? Are they any further forward?'

'Still no breakthrough,' Cory replied, shuffling through the papers that he'd been handed. 'This is fascinating. That piece of land has been in Reece Norman's family for generations. Does she have any idea, do you think?'

'I doubt it, Cory. Do you think she'd be living in that trailer if she did? It must be worth a pretty penny, I'd think.'

Imogen had placed some newspaper clippings in the file, too. They included the reports from the Tribune about the fire that destroyed Reece's house.

'My God, it was quite some place in its day. Look at this: was that really where those charred remains are now?'

'Yes. It used to be quite some property. All built of wood, of course. It went up in flames in no time; there wasn't a chance of saving it.'

'Any insurance involved? It must have been insured?'

'Well, that I do remember. The house had been on that plot for many decades. It was owned outright and was never insured. I assume that's why Reece has to live in that trailer.'

'The land must be worth something, though? If she sold it off as building plots...'

'Well, that's where you'll have to speak to somebody who knows more about those matters than me. Someone who knows about a register of deeds or something like that will be able to steer you in the right direction.'

'This is great. Thanks, Imogen. Okay if I make some copies?'

'Those *are* copies, Cory. I knew you'd want to take them with you.'

Cory tucked the paperwork into the folder that Imogen had provided and thanked her again for her trouble. He'd need to head over to pick up Bianca; she'd be expecting him.

Cory inserted the key and attempted to start the car. There was nothing. He tried again. Then a third time. He leaned over to flick up the hood and tapped the starter motor, then returned to start the car again. Five minutes later he gave up. There was no way that engine was firing up until he fixed the starter. Baker's junkyard was getting a visit that day, whether he liked it or not. He hoped Kelsey had the part he needed.

Cory phoned in to the office to let them know that he'd be showing his face late. Then he updated Bianca on his movements.

'Hey, Bianca, it's Cory. Sorry, but I'm going to be late. I have to walk over to the junkyard. The car has given up on me—it's stuck outside the library. I'll let you know how I make out, but you may need to get a lift or walk in today.'

Bianca was fine with that and said she'd start walking over.

He paused a moment, wondering if he should ask about the incident he'd witnessed the previous night. He went for it, even though he knew he should probably keep his mouth shut.

'Was everything okay when I left you last night, Bianca? You weren't in any trouble or anything? It's just I saw you with some young guy...'

'You saw that?' she asked.

'Yes. Tell me to keep my nose out of your business if you want to. But he didn't look like he was being very friendly.'

'You're right, Cory, it isn't really any of your business.'

Cory was taken aback—he hadn't heard Bianca speak as curtly as that before. He'd overstepped the mark, he knew it, but he had to ask. He'd been concerned about her safety.

'I'm sorry, I shouldn't have said anything. It's your own business; I shouldn't be prying.'

'And I'd appreciate it if you kept your mouth shut about it to my mom, too,' she snapped.

He'd upset her and clearly touched a nerve. She was an intern, not a friend; he'd need to remember that.

'I will. I apologize, I was just concerned for your welfare.'

He was wasting his time. Bianca had ended the call.

SIXTEEN

Cory was still worrying about how he'd offended Bianca when he walked through the gate of Baker's junkyard. He was also trying to fix in his mind that whatever happened that day, he had to be over at Westview to pick up Zach from his school that afternoon. After the run-in with Nadia and Principal Clinton, that was one appointment he could not afford to miss.

The junkyard looked like a fortress from a zombie movie, surrounded by a mix of corrugated iron panels and deadly, curled barbed wire fortifications. Scrap cars were piled up five high for as far as the eye could see. It was a wonder the planning department hadn't insisted on landscaping. Kelsey's yard was a blot on the landscape, its main saving grace being that it was based in an industrial unit well away from the tourism hot spots which brought visitor dollars into the community.

The other saving grace was that Kelsey's family had been located in the town since just before Henry Ford produced the Model T. If you dug down deep enough, and managed to tow away the piles of junked, rusted vehicles which littered the place, you would probably discover car-zero, the first-ever car to be scrapped there, and that car would likely be a Model T.

Kelsey was one of those business people who'd never bothered bringing his establishment up to twenty-first century standards and any attempt at branding or advertising had passed him by like a bee moving on from a pollen-depleted flower.

Above the entrance, daubed in red paint complete with globules from the drips, a sign announced *Baker's Scrap Vehicles*. That was it. No catchy phrase like *No.1 in Shallow Falls for bargain car parts* or *Watch your head, our car parts prices are low*. No beautifully produced signage using the trendiest fonts or latest design techniques. If it couldn't be scribbled on the bag of a pack of cigarettes or painted onto a metal panel with the last drops from a spray can, it had no place in Kelsey's yard.

Kelsey's office was located in a rusting shipping container just inside the entrance to the yard. There was a portable toilet just behind it; plumbing would have been too great an expense and the height of luxury. Kelsey sat at a simple desk, its surface smothered in oil drips, in a beaten up wooden chair which quite possibly arrived on the same day as the first scrap vehicle. Behind him were stripped car parts which sold well: starter motors, salvaged fan belts, bulbs, and side mirrors. There were two rusting filing cabinets to his side, and all around the front of the container, invoices and paid bills awaiting processing were hung up, held by bulging bulldog clips.

There was one concession to modernity: a telephone. Baker's had survived quite nicely for over a century without many of the niceties which most businesses enjoyed, but a phone had been considered an essential business tool for many years. Kelsey had even gone so far as modernizing the business by introducing a Nokia cell phone in 1999. That same phone sat at his side on the desk, smeared with oil streaks but working and holding its charge just as well as it did on the day he first took it out of its box, shortly before the end of the last millennium.

By the time he walked up to Kelsey's desk, Cory was in an agitated state of mind. He wanted to smooth things over with Bianca personally, not over the phone. But he had to fix his car first. Being able to get about town—particularly with such a big and important news story going on—was absolutely crucial. He'd also gotten an uneasy feeling as he was walking out to the Summerfields Industrial Estate, like he was being watched. He'd dismissed it as paranoia, scolding himself for being rattled by a brick through the window and a dead crow on his car. A similar thing had happened once before, over the newspaper's position on plans to close an old folks' home. Sometimes reporting the news made you unpopular, he knew that. Still, he couldn't shake the sense of unease.

'Good morning, Kelsey, how's things?'

He had a furrow in his brow. Very little ever seemed to rattle Kelsey Baker, so that seemed unusual.

'Nice to see you, Cory. I'll bet you're up to your ears, what with the news about that poor little girl?'

'You can say that again. Have you had the police around here?'

'Yes, they checked the yard thoroughly. I even managed to sell a couple of parts to two of the officers. What is it they say: every cloud has a silver lining and all that?'

'Well, I'm hoping you can help me out, too. I have a 2001 Ford Escape. The starter motor has gone. Do you have any in the yard?'

Computerization was another twentieth century luxury that had bypassed Baker's Scrap Vehicles. What Kelsey couldn't recall from memory wasn't worth knowing.

'We've got four of them in—your best bet is one that came in two weeks ago. It's an old model now, and most of them are worse for wear, but that one's in good condition. You'll find it just behind the crane. It's blue—you can't miss it.'

'Everything all right, Kelsey? You look troubled—that's unlike you.'

'Ernie Winters didn't come in today—he's my crane guy. I tried to get over there to move a couple of the cars myself before we opened, but I've been going like a house afire this morning. It's unusual for Ernie—he's a go-getter, would turn up if he was at death's door. It's just left me in a tight spot.'

'Sorry to hear that, Kelsey. Look, I'll get out of your way. May I take a couple of wrenches with me to strip out the starter?'

Kelsey indicated it was fine to help himself, so he picked them up and headed off into the yard.

Cory estimated the site was at least a couple of acres. It was a graveyard for the automobile industry, a Who's Who of favorite vehicles through the decades. Cars at the bottom of the stacks had generally been stripped clean. They were lucky if they had wheels, seats, or windshields left, let alone engines and headlights. The newer vehicles were generally positioned at the sides or higher up.

He wondered how health and safety figured in Kelsey's business. It seemed remarkable that some government agency or other hadn't made it illegal yet for ordinary members of the public to go scavenging car parts in environments which were jam-packed with sharp, hazardous objects and dangerous machinery. It was a good job it was still allowed, though, as it was the quickest, cheapest way for Cory to get the part he needed. There would be no such indignities for Nadia, as the high earner in the relationship. Her car went to the garage and only had dealer-approved parts.

Cory saw the blue vehicle behind the large crane and noticed the cab door was wide open, probably how Kelsey had left it when he'd had to open up to customers for the day. The Ford Escape was two vehicles up in a stack of three. He'd hoped it would be a little easier to get to.

He formulated a plan of attack. He'd need to climb into the car to release the hood. The passenger door had been stripped already, so he'd have to lean over to pull the lever on the driver's side. The driver's door on the other side was still intact, so he figured it would be easier to take the course of least resistance.

Cory pulled himself up, putting his right foot in the broken window frame of the car below, then grasped the frame of the Ford. He was pleased that Kelsey wouldn't have CCTV—if he did, Cory would likely end up on *America's Funniest Home Videos*. He heaved himself up over the passenger seat and reached over toward the hood release lever. Behind him he heard an engine starting with a deep diesel rumble. Some other customer must've gotten lucky and found an old engine that was working.

He couldn't quite reach the lever, so he reached across to get as close as possible. As his fingers gripped the lever and the hood eased open as far as the above car would allow, something began to shake the car. He jumped up and immediately dropped straight back down onto the seat as the roof of the vehicle came crashing down just above him. Glass from the windshield shattered and flew all over, covering his body with tiny shards.

'Damn it, Kelsey,' he cursed as the shaking stopped momentarily and he carefully tried to clear a safe path through the shards to pull himself back out of the car. As he started to shuffle out of the passenger's side, he pulled his dangling legs back in fast, aware of something coming straight at him from the long chain attached to the crane. Someone was swinging a car at him. Either they didn't know he was there, or they were trying to kill him.

The entire pile of cars shook violently as vehicle struck vehicle and Cory pulled his feet out of the way with only moments to spare. He could sense the crane moving again, no doubt preparing to smash the Ford Escape once more. He had to scramble over to the far side. If he could escape from the rear, he'd be able to take cover from the assault, make his way back to the entrance, and alert the police. But with the roof now crushed, he barely had any space to maneuver. One more strike from above, and he'd be crushed in there.

Cory found a floor mat on the passenger side, shook the glass from it, and placed it on the driver's seat as protection from the shattered glass. He pulled himself across the seat and began to push at the driver's door. There was a violent crash from above and the roof of the Ford crunched down just above his head. It gave him one small hope as the driver's door sprung open, forced out of its position by the bent frame. He could still hear the crane moving. One more impact and he'd be crushed. Even worse, he'd be pinned inside the car, bloodied and with broken bones, left to die slowly.

Cory thought of Zach. He had to get out for Zach; he had no intention of leaving his son fatherless.

A dark shadow formed overhead, the crane ready to drop its heavy load for a third time. Cory had only seconds left, but he was so constricted in the narrow space that he could barely move. Then, as the shadow grew darker and the inevitable crash moved closer, he heard a voice from just beyond the door.

'Cory, grab my hands.'

It was Bianca. Her face appeared just below the driver's seat. Cory pushed his arms forward and, with a strength one so young should not really possess, Bianca pulled him out of the Ford just as the final impact finally crunched what was left of the roof. He tumbled down to the ground, followed by more broken glass, landing at Bianca's side.

SEVENTEEN

Cory and Bianca waited for at least five minutes before daring to move. They huddled together, creating what cover they could to protect themselves from more falling debris if it came. Everything was silent except for the crane's engine, which was still running. At least it had stopped moving.

It was Bianca who broke the silence.

'Kelsey Baker has been knocked unconscious—he's out cold on the floor in his office.'

'Did you get a look at who was in the crane, Bianca? Did you see who did this?'

'No, I crept around the cars when I realized what was going on. I just wanted to get you out.'

'Thank you, Bianca. Thank you so much—I'd have been crushed if it wasn't for you. Why are you even here?'

'I felt terrible about cutting you off like that, it was really rude. You just... you caught me off guard. It's not something I want to talk about. What happened at school is still very raw for me. And I'm embarrassed, too. I'm sorry about the way I behaved on the phone. I wanted to meet you here and tell you as soon as possible. In person.'

'Well, I'm pleased you did. And honestly, it's no problem. I shouldn't have been prying. We should check it's safe now—we need to get help for Kelsey if he's out cold.'

As Cory stood up, tiny fragments of glass tumbled to the ground. Pulling his sleeve down over his hand to protect his skin, he carefully brushed off the remaining shards. He could barely believe that he'd escaped unharmed. All he could feel were a couple of cuts on his legs and one of his arms, nothing life-threatening.

Having checked that the crane was without a driver, Cory climbed up into the cab and made a best guess at what was required to shut down its engine. He pulled out the key and locked up the cab, then he and Bianca ran over to the office.

Kelsey was slumped on the floor, a single wound at the back of his head where he'd been struck by a heavy object. His attacker wasn't spoiled for choice of weapons—there were plenty of solid metal objects littered all over the yard. Kelsey's mouth had been taped up, as had his legs and hands.

Bianca knelt down and felt for a pulse.

'He's alive,' she said. 'We learned how to do this at school. Can you bring me that first aid kit—the one hanging up on the wall over there? We should make him comfortable while we wait for an ambulance to arrive.'

Cory did as requested, then looked for the Nokia phone that was on the desk earlier. It had been smashed. The cord leading to the landline phone had been torn out of its socket and cut. Whoever had been operating that crane did not want to be disturbed while they were trying to finish Cory. He was bizarrely relieved that he'd fallen out with Bianca earlier on. If they'd parted on good terms, she'd never have felt compelled to seek him out to apologize.

He felt a sudden rise of anxiety, a panic attack; he hadn't had one since he was a teenager, but he recognized the symptoms. The cocktail of fear, danger, and the unknown exploded through his veins and he had to take a seat at Bianca's side for a few moments while he tried to regulate his breathing to conquer the demon.

Bianca tended to Kelsey with a confident hand, removing the ties from his feet and hands, gently peeling the tape from around his mouth, and cleaning, then loosely bandaging, the wound on his head. Finally, she rested his head on one of the floor mats that Kelsey had salvaged, then took her cell phone out of her pocket.

By the time the call to 911 had been placed, Cory had settled himself and was ready for the inevitable police frenzy that was about to follow. Sure enough, within minutes, the sirens could be heard across the town. The police car arrived first, swiftly followed by the ambulance.

Things were going from bad to worse. Of all the police officers who could have stepped out of that car, of course one of them was Louise Powell. She saw Cory right away and—just for a moment—paused. Her face colored slightly as she walked up to them. Her colleague checked Kelsey and made certain everything had been done to make him comfortable while the ambulance arrived.

'Hi, Cory, are you okay? You look like you've been in a fight or something.'

She'd decided to tough it out and he was grateful for that. He was in no shape for an emotional confrontation at that moment.

The arrival of the emergency medical personnel created a useful distraction and Kelsey was quickly moved to a stretcher, then into the vehicle waiting to take him to the town's small hospital.

'Will he be okay?' Cory asked.

'This young lady did an excellent job of patching him up,' said one of the ambulance crew. 'There may be some concussion, perhaps even a fractured skull, but he'll be right as rain soon enough. I'm as sure as I can be that there's no lasting damage.'

Cory thanked the ambulance worker for her update and watched as she closed the rear doors and the vehicle drove off down the street, away from the junkyard.

'We'll need to get a statement from you both,' Louise said, kicking into full professional mode. 'There's no need to go to the station if you're happy to do it here. We'll need to check for fingerprints, to see if we can find any clues about who it was.'

Bianca and the second officer took the police vehicle for their chat and Cory sat in Kelsey's old wooden chair. Louise sat on the table, having placed one of the floor mats over it to prevent her uniform from getting oily. When Bianca was safely out of earshot in the police car, Louise started to speak quietly.

'I'm so sorry about what happened last night.'

'It's fine. Really, it's no problem.'

'No, I need to apologize. I know you have your son to consider.'

'We'd both had too much to drink, we didn't know what we were doing...'

'But I did know what I was doing, Cory. It was nothing to do with the drink.'

There was silence. They both looked to the ground.

'I knew what I was doing, too, Louise. I owe you an apology, as well. I just can't start a relationship right now. I have to sort things out with Nadia.'

Louise looked towards the police vehicle to make sure

they weren't being watched. She touched Cory's hand, then took it away.

'I know,' she said. 'I won't push you. Take care of your family first.'

A second, then a third, police car arrived. Before long, officers were all over the place, dusting for prints and taking photographs, making sure they understood exactly what had happened. Louise took a statement from Cory, and Bianca finished giving hers shortly after.

'I don't suppose I can still get that starter motor, can I?' Cory asked. 'I'll make sure I settle up with Kelsey once he's back at work, but I really do need it.'

Louise made certain that her colleagues had done every-thing they needed with the Ford Escape and then gave Cory the nod.

'I suspect Kelsey will be happy to offer you free parts for life, after the way Bianca helped him. Off you go, but make it quick, please. And you'd better settle up with Kelsey, or the chief will eat me for breakfast.'

Without the pressure of a mystery assailant trying to kill him, it was surprisingly easy for Cory to release the starter motor from its bracket. The damage was to the roof of the car; the engine compartment remained fully intact. Cory grimaced as he saw how near he'd been to getting crushed.

As he wrapped the extracted starter motor in old news-paper found on the floor in Kelsey's office, he heard his phone ringing in his back pocket. It was Oliver Vasey at the newspaper.

'Hey, Cory, Oliver here. You okay? We heard there's been an incident at the junkyard at Summerfields—nothing nasty, I take it?'

'It's a long story, but we're fine. I'm heading back to the office shortly.'

'Pleased to hear it. We've had a tip-off from that poster Bianca hung all over town. A good one, too, bearing in mind Xander Griffen's been in custody for twenty-four hours.'

'What is it?' Cory asked, immediately intrigued. 'Anything that moves the story on?'

'You might say that,' Oliver replied. 'It's an anonymous tip-off. The caller said that Xander Griffen's cell will be found thrown away in the bushes just along from his house. And the caller insists that if the police get their hands on that, it'll confirm his whereabouts on the day Poppy disappeared.'

EIGHTEEN

Cory was grateful for the lift that Louise gave him and Bianca back to his car. The sooner it was fixed, the better.

'You should get those cuts cleaned up and checked out, Cory,' Louise called after him as the patrol car drove away.

Cory gave her a wave to acknowledge the advice, but it would have to wait until the car was fixed. He'd wasted enough of the day already and he wanted to chance another visit to Reece Norman, too. There was something on his mind about the land on which the trailer was located. He had to remember that he was picking Zach up at five o'clock, too.

'What will happen about Xander's phone?' Bianca asked as she peered into the engine compartment, watching closely as Cory pulled the wires away from the broken starter motor, then released it from its fixing and moved the new one into place.

'We have to report information like that directly to the police; we can't take the law into our own hands,' Cory explained. 'Our intelligence could help to free an innocent man, and we'd be obstructing justice if we dealt with it as a newspaper. Besides, I think that anonymous call came just in the nick of time for everybody—they have to decide what they're going to do with Xander within three days. The pressure usually starts after twenty-four hours. Chief Tarrant looks sillier the longer he holds him without a charge after that, especially if they do have to release him after seventy-two hours.'

'It seems complicated to me,' Bianca said.

'I think you'd be grateful for those seventy-two hours if you'd been wrongly arrested,' he replied, tightening the final bolt on the newly installed motor. 'Right, let's see if that's done the job. Fingers crossed.'

Cory reattached the electrical wires and got into the car on the driver's side. For a moment, he had a scary sense of deja-vu. Only two hours previously he'd been trapped in a car just like his own, fearing for his life. And now he was sitting in the driver's seat like nothing had happened. He forced the thought to the back of his mind. The car started the first time, and Bianca let out a victory cheer.

'Oh, yeah, we're back in business,' Cory declared. He put the old starter motor, along with the tools that he'd borrowed, back into the trunk of the car, ready to return to Kelsey when he was released from the hospital. While the car was idling, Cory made a couple of calls: firstly to the newspaper office to let them know his whereabouts, and secondly to the police station to ask after Xander Griffen.

'Released without charge,' Cory said to Bianca as he ended the call. 'Xander's been released. He had photographs on his phone that showed he wasn't even in town when Poppy disappeared. The cell towers confirm it. He has a full alibi. I wonder what made the chief so keen to pull him in?'

'Don't you think there's a lot of weird stuff going on?'

Bianca asked out of the blue. 'I don't just mean Poppy. You had your window broken, there was that thing with the crows, and now the junkyard.'

'I agree, and it's why I'm trying to get to the bottom of this land ownership situation. It doesn't help that Imogen hasn't gotten all those documents for me yet. My journalistic senses are working overtime and I can't help but think there's more to this than meets the eye. So yes, Bianca, we're on the same page with that feeling. But until the police turn up a fingerprint, a decent witness statement, or a suspect, we're all taking shots in the dark.'

'That cut on your face looks sore—do you think we should drop in to the ER before we see Reece? We can check up on Kelsey, too, while we're there.'

'Good idea,' said Cory as he pulled out of the library parking lot.

Within the hour, they were back at Reece's trailer. Cory had had three pieces of glass removed from his legs and a small sliver taken out of his cheek. The wounds had been disinfected and bandaged, and after a couple of routine checks on his heart and blood pressure, and a condition check on Kelsey, they were on their way. Kelsey was fine— one night in the hospital for observation, and he'd be back at work in no time.

'Let's not tell Nadia about what happened,' Cory said as he set the emergency brake. 'I think it's one complication too much at the moment. Hopefully, this cut on my cheek will have calmed down a bit by the next time I see her.'

Bianca agreed not to mention it and they walked over to Reece's trailer. Officer Ambrose was back on shift and answered the door. She knew better by now than to challenge Cory and Bianca; she let them in right away.

Reece seemed to have lost weight since they last saw

her, and her face was drawn and pale. Poppy's disappearance was obviously responsible for her puffy, bloodshot eyes and the way her hands were shaking. Cory could have cried for her. He hoped more than anything that the police would be able to signal some sort of breakthrough soon.

'You've heard that they released Xander?' she asked, not even bothering to greet them.

Bianca sat at the table with Megan and Toni, joining them in their coloring. It struck Cory that there had been no gifts of flowers or food for Reece; how lonely it must be for her.

'At least it wasn't your neighbor,' Cory tried to reassure her.

'I honestly don't care who it is at this stage,' Reece replied. 'I just want to know where my little girl is. Not knowing is killing me. Even Officer Ambrose has begun preparing me for the worst. They're not talking about what happens when she comes home. They're asking me to think about who will identify her when a body's found.'

Reece began to sob gently, and Cory wished desperately that there was something he could do.

'Reece, I know it's a horrible time for you, but I want to ask you something. It might just be something about nothing, but I have to ask. It might help us to find out what's going on with Poppy.'

'If you think it'll help find my little girl, do what you have to. Anything to get Poppy back—I don't care what it is.'

'Did you know that you own all of this land around the trailer?' Cory asked gingerly. 'And do you know if the old house was insured?'

'I don't know anything about that,' Reece answered. 'My Ma and Pa used to deal with all that, and Spencer Jones used to advise them. I couldn't read the paperwork, it made no sense to me. When Ma and Pa died, Jerry took care of things.'

'Jerry?' Cory asked.

'He's Toni's father,' she replied, 'And a complete waste of space, too.'

She spoke those words quietly, making sure that Toni was engrossed in her play.

'So Jerry was around during the aftermath of the fire? Have the police checked out the girls' fathers? Presumably they're potential suspects. Are there any custody issues?'

Officer Ambrose chimed in.

'One of the fathers has been questioned in connection with the case.'

She looked at Reece for approval. 'Do you mind if I tell him?'

Reece shook her head.

'Megan's father is dead, a drug overdose. Toni's father, Jerry Hunter, lives in the next town. He's estranged from Reece and his daughter. He's been questioned already and has a firm alibi.'

'What about Poppy's father?' Cory asked.

'AWOL,' Reece answered.

'How do you mean?'

'Absent without leave. He's a private in the Army. He's been missing for two months. I haven't seen him for over seven months. As far as I'm concerned, he's best out of our lives.'

'Does anybody know where he is?' Cory persisted.

'Not a clue,' Reece laughed. 'But I'd expect nothing less from Harry. The moment the going gets tough, he always bolts for the hills. He's been in and out of Poppy's life since she was born. He's best out of the way; things get difficult whenever he's around.'

'I assume the police want to question him?'

Cory addressed his question directly to Officer Ambrose.

'Of course we do—we've got an interstate search out for him. But if the man doesn't want to be found, he doesn't want to be found. And if the Army can't lay their hands on him, I don't hold out that much hope for the police. Like Reece said, it sounds as though he bolted, probably responsibility isn't his thing.'

Cory changed the subject.

'So, Jerry dealt with all the paperwork after the main house burned down. What did he tell you about that?'

'Just that there was no insurance and that the landowner said I could live on this piece of land until I was told to move on.'

'But that's not right, Reece; you own all this land,' Cory continued to push. 'Or your family does, at least. And that's you now, isn't it?'

'You know, Reece, I'll be happy to come around and help you with your reading, if you like,' Bianca offered. 'After they find Poppy, that is.'

Reece looked over at Bianca with a warmth that suggested it was the first kindness anybody had shown her in a long time. It made Cory feel immediately guilty. He'd been all about the news story, forgetting that there was a real family suffering because of it.

'I'd like that, Bianca, when they find Poppy. Thank you.'

'I have to be in Westview at five o'clock to pick up my son from an afterschool activity. Would you have any objections to me paying Jerry Hunter a visit while I'm there?'

NINETEEN

'Why do they call it Shallow Falls?' Bianca asked. 'I've lived here most of my life, but I haven't got a clue.'

'When I started work at the Tribune, they gave me a written guide about the locality. There are all sorts of interesting bits and pieces in there about the community. I've been telling Mitchell that we should publish it and sell it to the locals and tourists. One thing I remember about it, though, is where the name Shallow Falls came from. It started as a warning in the late nineteenth century when people first started to settle here.'

Cory looked over as the water cascading down from the rocks, its white froth skipping like pure white lambs, a beautiful array of rainbow colors breaking through as the sun kissed the water.

'You see how the water crashes down and you'd expect it to be really deep? Follow my finger towards that ledge over there, just below where the parking lot ends, by that wooden post. People used to try and jump off that ledge into the water. But they'd break their arms, legs, or necks because it's really shallow—in spite of how it appears. So, it started as a warning sign and became the name of the town. If you look really carefully, you'll see a couple of hazard signs attached to the rocks just behind the ledge there.'

Bianca squinted. The sun's rays catching the water made it difficult for them to look directly towards the falls, but she nodded; Cory took it that she'd managed to get a proper glimpse.

'It was a good idea of yours, coming out here for a late lunch,' Cory said after swallowing a bite of his sandwich. 'It's been quite a day so far. It's not every day someone tries to crush you in a junkyard.'

'Did the police have any ideas about what's going on? I mean, that's not normal, is it? A brick through a window, somebody trying to kill you... and Poppy missing, too. I'm no detective, but there's something going on.'

'I think you just hit the nail on the head, Bianca.'

Cory looked at her, admiring the insight that she was displaying at such a young age. She seemed to have that knack of making connections, a good sign for someone interested in becoming a reporter.

'How interested are you in a newspaper career?' he asked. Most of their interns at the newspaper were just passing through, more interested in getting on TV or becoming a news anchor. They didn't want to do the ground work that was necessary to become a great journalist. Bianca was different—she seemed to get it.

'I'm very interested. I'd like to major in journalism in college. This problem I had with school might cause a bit of an issue for me, though...'

Cory decided to chance his luck and push for a bit more information.

'So, what happened there? Spencer Jones was pretty rude to you in the diner. I know you well enough by now to realize that you wouldn't do anything terrible. Were you set up by somebody?'

'What do you think?' Bianca replied abruptly.

This was clearly still a very sensitive issue for her, but Cory wanted to know. The altercation on the street the previous night was still bothering him. It had looked threatening and aggressive.

They both took a bite of their sandwiches, allowing the sound of cascading water to distract them from the uncomfortable silence. Bianca looked out onto the river as it flowed calmly into the woodland.

'I wish I could be like that water,' she began, 'so calm and still after all that crashing and drama. It's not quite so easy in real life, though.'

Above them, out on the road just beyond the parking lot for the falls, Cory heard the screech of brakes as yet another car took Devil's Corner too fast and had to make a sudden speed adjustment.

He sighed. 'You know, the newspaper should start a campaign to get that stretch of road made safer somehow. The number of near misses there must be practically every day...'

'It was Chief Tarrant's son.'

It came out of the blue, like Bianca wasn't even listening to him.

'What was?'

'Dean Tarrant and his friends—that's who caused the problem at school.'

'How?' Cory asked, intrigued.

'It was horrible. I get why you said Reece doesn't want to speak to Chief Tarrant. If he's anything like his son, he's a nasty piece of work.'

'I didn't even know Tarrant had a son. I mean, I guess I

do, but I wouldn't be able to pick him out of a crowd if you asked me to.'

Cory thought about it. Dean Tarrant was just another face in a stream of teenagers to him. He simply hadn't registered him.

'Come to think of it, he's not the kid who won the football scholarship, is he? He was called Dean something—was that Dean Tarrant?'

Bianca snorted.

'Yes, that's the one,' she said. 'He's an entitled little shit. Excuse my language, but he is. Securing Dean's scholarship was more important to the school than getting to the truth. They threw me under the bus because it was less damaging for everybody. Everybody except me, of course.'

'What did he do?' Cory asked. He felt a rising surge of indignation flowing through his veins. It wouldn't be the first time a sports jock had gotten away with something in order to ensure his career continued on its stellar trajectory.

'Let's just say he tried to force himself on me at a house party. And his friends were cheering him on. I managed to get out of the room and run home. My parents came with me to report it to the police. There was even video evidence, I saw someone filming it in the bedroom.'

'Did he hurt you, Bianca?'

A single tear ran down her cheek.

'No, I pushed him off. But it was frightening and humiliating. He would have hurt me if I hadn't escaped. They were like a pack of wolves. They were my classmates, Cory. They shouldn't ever behave like that, should they?'

'No, there is never any excuse for acting like that, Bianca.'

'We reported it to the police and the whole thing was covered up. There was no sign of the video—it mysteriously disappeared, even though the police were supposed to have investigated. With no reliable witnesses on my side, the dialogue soon began to change. It was suggested to my parents that I'd led him on and taken it too far—that maybe it was a false claim. Dean's friends backed up his version of the story, saying I encouraged him. I hadn't, Cory.'

'I know,' Cory reassured her. 'I believe you.'

They sat in silence for a few moments. Cory needed some time to think.

Bianca broke the silence.

'How do you make a complaint about the chief's son?'

He didn't answer, sensing she wanted to talk.

'I never stood a chance. It turned out that Dad had let his insurance expire on his car soon after—it was a genuine omission—but somehow, Chief Tarrant was able to work it out before Dad realized. He got a caution from the police, and they let him off. They basically warned him that if news of him not being insured got to the newspaper, it could ruin his business and his reputation. At the same time, the school came up with a settlement package. I was asked to withdraw all claims about Dean Tarrant and take a hit with the yearbook and prom. They said I was making false claims which could have ruined his promising career. I was made out to be the villain. In return, they'd let me leave school quietly, with a reference intact, so long as I stopped making a fuss. They wanted to paint me out of the picture for the trouble I was supposed to have caused. I don't know if Dean even got a rap on the knuckles.'

Cory was thankful for the background noise of the water and birdsong filling the silence, as Bianca's story simmered between them.

'Dean's still threatening you, isn't he?' Cory said.

'Yes,' came Bianca's answer. It was a single word, tinged with pain and sadness.

'Do you think you're in any danger?'

'He keeps taunting me whenever he sees me. I try to ignore him, but sometimes I get angry and frustrated. That's what you saw the other night. I was telling him to leave me alone. He keeps goading me with it. *I had a great time in the bedroom that night, Bianca, how about a rerun sometime?* I don't know how to make him stop.'

'Look, I'm pleased you told me, Bianca. I know it's hard. But when you're out working with me, you're safe, okay? If you need anything, just let me know. I'll act as a witness—bullies like Dean Tarrant don't scare me. And I don't care who his dad is.'

'Thanks, Cory,' she said. 'It feels good to discuss it with somebody. I don't talk about it with Mom and Dad anymore. Dad thought he might lose the business if word got out. He's already struggling with all these internet realtors; he can do without a local scandal.'

'I understand the pressure to keep it quiet, Bianca,' Cory replied, shocked by her story. 'But if there's one thing working as a journalist has taught me, it's that the truth always surfaces, one way or another.'

TWENTY

As Cory and Bianca approached Westview, the trees started to thin at the side of the road and they began to drive past industrial developments at the far end of town. Cory's phone buzzed a couple of times.

'We're out of the cell phone dead zone,' he announced. 'Could you scan the numbers and see what came in while I've been driving?'

He took one hand off the wheel, passing his phone over to her and activating the screen with his thumb print in order to give her access.

'Two voicemails,' she said. 'Both Shallow Falls exchanges.'

'Can you play them? There's nothing private in there.'

Bianca tapped to access the voicemails.

'Voicemail PIN?' she asked.

'Don't laugh,' he smiled, 'but I don't have one. There's never anything private on there anyway.'

The first message began to play.

Hey, Cory, it's Oliver. A couple of messages to pass on from the office. I've emailed this to you, too, so hopefully you'll pick up one of these. Still no word on Poppy Norman. The police have put official posters up now and Chief Tarrant was all over TV and radio this morning getting the word out. Kelsey Baker is fine, he's been discharged from the hospital, but he didn't see anything...

'At least Kelsey's fine,' Bianca said.

'Thanks to you,' Cory replied.

...whoever it was struck him from behind. As for Ernie Winters, his crane driver, he'd received a call purporting to be from one of Kelsey's family, saying the junkyard was closed for the day and not to come in. Take care out there, Cory—this thing is beginning to stink.

'There's something going on in this town, I'm telling you,' Bianca said, accessing the second voicemail.

'I think you're right. I keep trying to explain it away as coincidence, but it sounds to me like somebody's trying to cover something up.'

He was interrupted by another familiar voice coming through the speaker of his phone.

Hello, Mr. Miles, it's Imogen from the library. I just wanted to let you know that the planning documentation has arrived and it's ready to be picked up whenever you can pop in. I'll be in the library until nine o'clock today. Just give the front door a bit of a shove—we're closed to the public at that time, but I'll still be around. I think you're going to be very interested in what's in the paperwork. See you later, bye.

'If my hunch is right, we'll have a better idea about what's going on once I've spoken to Imogen,' Cory said.

'But how is it connected to Poppy going missing?' Bianca asked, handing the phone back to Cory.

'I'm not sure that it is. I just think that I may have found a way that we can help Reece out a bit. I don't think it's related to Poppy, though—I don't see how it can be.'

'Do you want me to make myself scarce while you're at your son's event? I don't want to cause any trouble.'

Cory thought about her suggestion. Things had been a bit tense last time he saw Nadia.

'Nadia can't be there today, but I'll have to drop Zach off at the house afterwards. Maybe you could hang back in the car while I do that. Let's see how the land lies today—hopefully things will have cooled down a bit. And you're okay to see Reece's ex before we head back for Shallow Falls? Your mom and dad know you'll be back late?'

'All good,' Bianca confirmed.

Cory parked the car on the road outside Zach's school. He was relieved that the replacement starter motor appeared to have done the job, even if its procurement had not been without a considerable amount of drama.

'How does the cut on my face look? It doesn't look like I've been in a fight, does it?'

Bianca took a close look at Cory's cheek.

'It's still a bit raw, to be honest with you, but it's not too bad. Just tell your wife that you got the scrape in the junk-yard. It's the truth.'

Cory laughed. He'd leave out the bit about nearly getting crushed to death if he had to explain it to Nadia. If she thought for one moment that his lifestyle might put Zach at risk, she'd give him a hard time. She'd be justified in doing it, too.

Zach's game passed uneventfully, with the exception of a brief encounter with Principal Clinton.

'Nice to see you here supporting Zach,' she'd said as she passed by. 'His head looks fine after the accident yesterday, which is more than I can say for your cheek.'

She had registered Bianca, too. It suddenly occurred to him that she might think she was a new girlfriend. His face reddened at the thought. Surely she'd see the age difference and assume it was a professional or family connection?

'My cheek was an accident. And Bianca is an intern at the paper,' he'd clumsily blurted out, as if explaining himself.

'No need to explain anything to me, Mr. Miles, what you do in your own time is your own business.'

'But she really is an intern.'

'So long as we don't have a repeat of the incident on the school premises yesterday, there's no need for me to get involved in your private life, unless somebody new will be coming to pick Zach up from school. We need to know that for child welfare purposes.'

There was a cheer and Zach came running towards Cory with a big grin on his face.

'What happened?' he asked Bianca.

'Zach just scored.'

Principal Clinton had moved on, leaving Cory feeling like he was still ten years old and just got into trouble for something he didn't do.

The game passed without further incident, but Cory was annoyed that he'd missed Zach's goal. It didn't seem to bother his son, who'd taken to Bianca immediately. He was happy to share all the details of his game and the day at school as they sat eating a burger in one of the local fast food restaurants. Then they headed back to Nadia's house, the house they used to share together.

As they pulled up outside the house, Nadia was speaking to a neighbor in her driveway, briefcase still in hand. It was Dan Sweeney, local pain in the neck. It looked to Cory like he'd caught her on her return home from work.

As Cory stopped the car beside them, he watched as Nadia bent down a little to get a good view of who was sitting in the rear seat with her son. For a moment, he saw her expression change as she recognised Bianca from yesterday.

He got out of the vehicle, then opened the door for Zach. His son reached over to give Bianca a hug before he got out, as if they'd been best friends for years.

'Nice to see you, Cory,' Dan said. 'Is that your new girl-friend in the back with young Zachary? She's a bit young for you, isn't she?'

Cory cringed.

'That's Bianca, she's an intern at the newspaper. We're working together,' he began a little too emphatically.

'So you keep telling me,' Nadia said. 'Zach seems very comfortable with her already.'

'She's just like that with kids,' Cory replied. 'They seem to gravitate towards her.'

'Kids don't seem to be the only ones,' Nadia muttered under her breath.

Cory didn't respond; it was best to change the subject.

'I scored a goal, Mom,' Zach declared as he ran over to hug her.

'Nice to see you're getting lots of sports in still,' Dan said. 'It's important to carry on doing boyish things even when you haven't got a dad in your life.'

Cory couldn't keep his mouth shut this time.

'He has got a dad around,' he cut in sharply. 'Where do you think I've just been?'

'Steady, Cory,' Nadia cautioned, 'I'm sure Dan didn't mean it that way.'

'I'm pretty sure that's exactly how Dan meant it,' Cory replied.

'I only meant that it's important for a child to know who

its parents are. It can be confusing when girlfriends get involved, kids get muddled.'

'For the last time, Bianca is an intern. She is not my girlfriend.'

Cory couldn't help shouting, even though it was the last thing he wanted to do with Zach around.

'If you must know, the only woman I've seen socially since we split up is Louise Powell, and that's for professional...'

He instantly knew he'd said too much. Nadia had suspected for some time that Louise carried a torch for her husband. Cory was oblivious to it, but it hadn't stopped her from commenting.

'You've said enough, Cory. Just say goodbye to Zach and leave now. And I'm sorry, Dan, I apologize for my husband's behavior.'

Cory opened his mouth to defend himself again but thought better of it. He apologized, said his goodbyes to Zach, and got back in the car. Bianca was already back in the front seat, having climbed through the gap while the others had been talking. Her cell phone buzzed as he sat in the driver's seat. He slammed the door.

'I'm sorry you had to see that again,' he began, looking over at her. She wasn't listening. Instead, she was reading a text that had just come in on her phone. Her face was white. Cory could read it clearly from where he was sitting.

Want to meet up sometime for a replay? You know you like it, even if you play hard to get.

There was no name, just a number. Cory didn't need a name to know who'd just contacted Bianca. It was Dean Tarrant.

TWENTY-ONE

'I've found where he lives on the map. Are you sure you're up to this?'

Cory looked away from his phone. Bianca had just had a shock and he didn't want to push her too hard. He had to keep reminding himself she was only eighteen. He already thought of her as a colleague.

'I'm fine, honestly. It's not the first text he's sent like that. He uses one of those cheap throwaway cell phones—he's not so stupid to do it on his own phone or use his name. If I report it, it'll only look like I'm causing problems again, and I can't prove it's him sending them.'

'Why does he have your number?' Cory asked.

'People I knew at school have my number, it was never a big secret. He's only just started sending these. But you're right—I need a new number.'

'Save those texts, don't delete them,' Cory advised. 'They may come in handy as evidence if he slips up. Right, let's go and see Jerry Hunter. He's Toni's father, right?'

They chatted in the car as Cory drove through Westview. Many of the streets were familiar, reminding him of his married life in the town. This was where he and Nadia had met, where they'd fallen in love, gotten married, and had Zach. It was also where everything had gone wrong.

He wasn't familiar with the area where Jerry lived, but it was more affluent than he'd expected. They pulled up at a large, detached house surrounded by a well-kept yard. Cory guessed it had four or five bedrooms. It was nice—he wouldn't have minded living there himself.

'This might get difficult, so let me take the lead. We call this door-stepping. It can go either way, but sometimes it gets a bit hostile. Just follow my lead and stay behind me. And be prepared to pack up and go at a moment's notice if it turns sour.'

They walked up the short driveway and Cory rang the bell. He followed it up moments later with a loud knock.

Voices came from inside: a man's, then a woman's, then the sound of someone thumping down the stairs. The door opened.

'If you're trying to sell something, then you can get lost.'

This had to be Jerry. Cory took an immediate dislike to him, for the leering expression on his face and his unkempt appearance. His beard was in need of a trim and he smelled of stale sweat. He looked past Cory, staring at Bianca with a predatory look in his eyes. He was only wearing boxer shorts and an undershirt, and he had nothing on his feet.

'I'm from the local paper...' Cory began.

'You want to talk to me about my stupid bitch of an ex-wife? You got ID?'

The man had barely spoken more than twenty words and already Cory's hackles were up. How could such an unpleasant man have fathered such a lovely kid? He knew the answer, of course. It was because of Reece; it looked like the father had very little to do with it.

Cory pulled his ID card from his back pocket and handed it to Jerry, who proceeded to study it with great care.

'What's this about? Poppy?' he asked.

'Yes, I'm just doing a bit of background on the story. Mind if we come in? This won't take long.'

Jerry looked Bianca up and down, smirked, and indicated that they should step through the door.

The living room was tastelessly decorated, with prints of sports cars hung unevenly around the walls, and the biggest television that Cory had ever seen in the corner. White leather couches were marked with what he assumed were beer stains. Jerry didn't offer them a seat; he put on a pair of pants that were draped over the back of one couch. Then he walked over to a desk in the far corner of the room and took something out of the drawer, putting it in his pocket.

A high-pitched voice came from upstairs.

'Who is it, Jerry?'

'Stay in bed—I'll be back up in a couple of minutes.'

He looked at Bianca.

'Unless you want to join us?' he leered.

Bianca flushed, and Cory stepped in.

'If we can just ask a couple of straightforward questions, we'll be out of your way.'

'Shoot,' Jerry said, putting his hand down his boxers to adjust himself. Cory was pleased Jerry wasn't the sort to shake hands.

'Nice house,' Cory said, looking around.

'What of it?' Jerry replied, immediately defensive.

'You've done well for yourself,' Cory continued.

'Yeah, I have,' came the smug reply.

'What do you make of Poppy's disappearance?' Cory asked.

'Take a seat,' Jerry said at last, waving them both towards the couch opposite the TV set. 'It's been a long time since it's had someone as good-looking as you sit on it,' he said to Bianca with a wink.

Cory came in quickly with a follow-up question, desperate to get Bianca out of the house as quickly as possible.

'Do you have any idea what might have happened?'

'It's that stupid bitch of an ex-wife who's to blame. The dumb woman would forget her brain if left on her own long enough. She probably left her somewhere and now she's trying to blame someone else.'

'Do you ever see your daughter? Toni, isn't it?'

Cory could feel Bianca's discomfort. She already knew men like this; he would never have brought her along if he'd known.

'Nah, I don't have time for stupid kids, if you know what I mean?'

He sneered again and nodded his head towards the bedroom upstairs.

'Do you pay child support?' Cory asked. He knew he was pushing his luck.

'Now look here,' Jerry said, immediately riled at the question. 'If that stupid bitch was dumb enough to get pregnant, that's on her. She was supposed to be on the pill or something; it was just a bit of fun as far as I was concerned. I didn't want no kids...'

'But you were together long enough to get married.'

'Yeah, and it was too long, as far as I was concerned. Two years too long.'

'Did you know Reece at the time the main house was there—before the fire?'

Cory could see from his face that he remembered that, all right.

'Yeah, we lived together in the house when we were a couple. Nice little house, too—crying shame it burned down. Spoiled a good thing.'

'How long were you around after the fire?' Cory asked. 'Did you ever live in the trailer?'

'Hey, if it wasn't for me, that stupid bitch would be homeless. It was me who ordered that trailer and got it placed there. I handled the electric and everything. She can't even read, the stupid bitch. I had to do everything for her.'

'How long did you stay around afterwards?'

'I was out of there the moment she told me she was pregnant. That's not what I signed up for. She already had that snot-nosed little brat Megan when we were together. Her previous husband had died. Probably of boredom.'

He laughed at his own comment and Cory sensed Bianca tensing on the couch. He gave her a glance, silently urging her not to venture a challenge to Jerry.

'So, do you even know Toni?'

'Nope! Never really seen her. Don't want to, either. I like my freedom, if you know what I mean?'

Once again, he smirked and looked up towards the bedroom.

Cory shuffled a little, and after a pause, asked his next question.

'What happened with the insurance money after the fire? If you were the one who could read, surely you handled everything after the accident?'

'What are you saying?' Jerry replied, immediately

defensive. His hand moved toward his pocket. 'You said you were here to talk about Poppy. I've seen the police—they asked me their questions, so they know I didn't do nothing. Who are you, IRS or something?'

'Not IRS, Mr. Hunter, just the local paper. But I'm following up a lead that Poppy's disappearance may be related to Reece's land in some way.'

Jerry drew a small gun on them. Bianca jumped in her seat. Cory knew he had to stay calm, even though a drop of sweat ran down his forehead as he tried to assess if Jerry was the kind of man to do something stupid.

'You need to shut your mouth and get back to your shitty little paper. I hear it's brilliant for litter boxes and lining birdcages.'

He waved the gun from side to side, his finger loosely hovering over the trigger. Cory began to stand up.

'Sit down,' Jerry shouted. 'Now tell me, why are you really here? What do you know? Why are you snooping around?'

All Jerry's smugness was gone now, and Cory was worried for Bianca's welfare. He knew he'd have to play this one carefully if they were both going to get out of here.

A woman appeared at the door, wearing only a silk nightgown. Her hair was ruffled, but she'd been quiet coming down the stairs; none of them had heard her.

'What's going on, Jerry? What's holding you up?'

The sound of her shrill voice caught Jerry by surprise and the gun went off. A single bullet hit the plaster just above Bianca's head and a cloud of dust exploded over her hair. She jumped up and Cory followed her, terrified that she'd been hit.

'You stupid bitch, look what you made me do,' he screamed at the woman.

'I told you to get rid of that damn gun,' she yelled back at him. 'Look what you've gone and done—we'll have to get the ceiling redone now.'

'We're going,' Cory said. 'That's enough, Jerry. We're walking out of here and you need to stop talking now. And put that damn gun away.'

Cory looked at Jerry directly in the eyes, so he knew he wasn't messing around. He ushered Bianca out of the house, helping her to shake off the plaster dust as he did so.

So that was Jerry Hunter. They'd finally met one of Reece's men. No wonder she was in such a mess.

TWENTY-TWO

Cory and Bianca said nothing as they ran over to the car and got in their seats. Cory started up the engine and drove off two hundred yards or so before stopping, desperate to get away from that house. His hands were shaking.

'Are you okay?' he asked at last, when he could be sure his voice would be steady enough to get the words out.

Her eyes were wide with shock.

'I can't believe that just happened,' she murmured, her voice wavering.

'The man's an idiot. He could have killed you with that shot.'

They sat in silence, broken only by the rumbling sound of the engine.

'Should we report him to the police?' Bianca asked.

Cory considered that one.

'It's not illegal to have a licensed gun in your own home. And although that man is a complete fool, I don't think for one minute he meant to fire that weapon. Did you see his face? He was as scared as we were.'

'But still, he got all angry when you started pushing him about the insurance on Reece's house. He must be covering something up. We should tell the police about that, shouldn't we?'

Cory paused a moment. This was the gray area between journalists and police officers and he wanted to make sure he said it in a way that Bianca would understand.

'If you want to report this to the police, I certainly won't stop you. In fact, I'll back you up fully and will happily be a witness. However, I think we're best sitting on this one, certainly until I've got a look at those documents that Imogen has for me at the library. I suspect there's another story mixed in with all this, and I don't think it involves Poppy's disappearance. But there's something going on and I don't like the smell of it.'

He paused, trying to think of the right words to persuade her.

'I think we can help Reece more if we bide our time a while longer. The police have already interviewed Jerry, and they're obviously happy that he has nothing to do with Poppy's case. So, if we can get over the fright of what just happened, I think we should wait a little longer and find out if this runs any deeper.'

The way Bianca looked at him, he could tell she was thinking it over.

'Do you think Jerry did anything? Other than being a crappy father and leaving Reece to pick up after the mess he made?'

'I think he may have deceived Reece,' Cory said. 'But if my hunch is correct, I think a number of people might have been doing the same. That's why I want to wait. I want to find out more. If I thought it was in any way connected with

Poppy, I would go to the police immediately. But at the moment, I can't see how it could be.'

Bianca exhaled a long, deep breath as if she was expelling all the tension of the past half hour.

'It's getting late,' Cory remarked. 'It'll be dark soon. I take it your parents know your whereabouts? Are you keeping them informed? The life of a reporter can be a bit irregular at times.'

Bianca confirmed that she was keeping them up to date via text messages. After checking that she was fine to continue, Cory began the drive back to Shallow Falls.

As they left the streetlights of Westview behind and moved into the enveloping darkness of the woodland that linked the two communities, Cory decided it was high time he gave Bianca a way out if she wanted it.

'It's been one helluva day, Bianca,' he began. 'If you're thinking better of your internship at the Tribune, I won't hold it against you. What's happened these past few days is not typical, I assure you. But if you want out, I'll write you a glowing reference and there'll be no hard feelings on my part, though I'll be sad to see you go. I've enjoyed having your company and—to be perfectly honest—I'm not sure I could have managed the last few days without you. You're a complete natural.'

He sensed Bianca smiling to his side, but his attention was fully on the road now.

'Are you kidding?' she said after a few moments. 'I can't remember the last time I had so much fun. I mean, I was terrified back there when Jerry had that gun out. And he was a horrible little man; I'd like to have given him a good kick in the you-know-whats. But I love what we're doing here—it really feels like we can make a difference. I want to help Reece and her kids. I'm desperate for them to find Poppy. But if we can make any kind of positive impact on this situation at all, then I'm in, with both feet.'

Cory smiled this time. It was exactly the kind of *Hell, yeah!* answer he was after.

'Well, I'm pleased to hear it. I honestly believe that if you stick with this, you've got great instincts. People are happy to talk to you; you'll make a great reporter. And I promise, getting crushed in old cars and having guns pulled on you is definitely not a typical part of the job.'

They both laughed, desperate for a release of the tension after the incident at Jerry's.

'We're nearing Shallow Falls now, so excuse me while I concentrate fully on the road for a bit,' Cory said. 'I always take a deep breath when I drive this stretch...'

'Stop the car,' Bianca shouted.

'What is it? I can't just stop—the road is too narrow.'

'Pull over as soon as you can.'

Cory looked for a stretch between the trees where it might just be safe to stop.

'What is it—are you going to be sick?'

'No, there's someone out there in the woods. I saw a fire through the trees.'

Cory applied the brakes and slowly pulled the car in between two trees. It wasn't the best parking in the world, but they were out the way and at least it was safe.

'Are you sure? You didn't just catch a reflection from the headlights?'

'I saw it. It was a campfire.'

'It could be campers, or something like that,' Cory suggested.

'Shouldn't we investigate? If there's any strangers in this

area, the police need to know, especially with Poppy missing.'

Cory turned off the engine and left the sidelights on.

'Okay, let's take a look,' he said. 'Have you got a flashlight on your phone? It's going to be pitch black out there.'

They crossed the road and began to make their way through the woods. The ground was soft and yielding underfoot, but spiky twigs on low-hanging branches scratched their faces, making movement through the trees slow and occasionally painful.

'Where was it?' Cory asked. 'Are we heading in the right direction?'

'It was definitely over there,' she pointed, shining a beam from her phone.

'I don't see any flames,' Cory remarked, beginning to wonder if they were on a wild goose chase.

There was the crack of a twig up ahead.

'Shhhhh,' Bianca cautioned.

'If there's anybody camping out here, we'll frighten the life out of them. Shouldn't we announce ourselves?' Cory whispered.

Suddenly, to the side of them, there was a startled movement. A deer darted towards them, but on seeing the light from Bianca's phone, it bolted off in the opposite direction.

'Something startled it, and it wasn't us,' Bianca whispered. 'Look, over there, I can see the embers from a fire.'

Cory had experienced quite enough frights for one day and was eager to get out of the woodland and back to the car. But Bianca wasn't letting this drop. He owed her that, at least, bearing in mind the danger he'd placed her in at Jerry Hunter's house.

Bianca began to rush through the trees, ignoring the low branches and intent on reaching her destination.

'Look,' she shouted through the trees. 'There's a camp-fire here.'

She waited for him to catch up.

'Hold your hand over it. See, it must have been extinguished with water—some of the wood is still warm. Somebody was here—they must have heard us coming.'

'It might have been a vagrant, for all we know,' Cory suggested, beginning to feel a little exasperated.

'Yes, and it might be connected with Poppy's disappearance, too. We need to report this to the police—we can't sit on this information.'

She was right, and Cory told her so.

'I promise I'll let Louise know tomorrow morning, first thing. We'll keep it away from Chief Tarrant. I'll ask Louise to take a look out here off the record and we'll see what she thinks. Is that okay?'

Bianca nodded, and they headed back towards the car.

As they neared the edge of the road, Cory realized he couldn't see the car's sidelights.

'We didn't take a wrong turn, did we, Bianca? We ought to be seeing my car by now.'

'This is right, I'm sure,' she replied. 'Look, there it is, just across the road there.'

She shone the beam from her phone. There it was, exactly as they'd left it. But there was no sign of any sidelights.

'Damn,' Cory cursed. 'I've run down the battery. That new starter motor can't be charging it fully. Either that, or I didn't connect the wiring properly.'

He climbed into the driver's seat and tried to start the engine. It was dead.

Once again, he got Bianca to assist him while he messed around under the hood. Now he was smeared in oil, as well as covered in fresh scratches. Eventually he gave up trying to fix it.

'I'm so sorry, Bianca, the battery is gone. There's no hope of me getting a phone signal out here to call for a tow truck. We're going to have to walk back to town in the dark.'

TWENTY-THREE

'You know, if we're quick, we'll just catch Imogen before she leaves the library,' Cory said as they were greeted at last by the welcome appearance of streetlights. 'We've got ten minutes—do you think you can keep the pace up?'

'Yes, why not?' Bianca replied. 'I'll text Mom and let her know. I've got my signal back now.'

'Me, too,' Cory said, checking his phone. 'I'm going to call the garage and see if I can get the car towed back to my house this evening.'

They caught the library in the nick of time. The lights were still on, but the sign at the entrance informed them that it had been closed to the public since seven o'clock.

'Imogen must live in this place,' Cory said. 'I hope I have half her energy when I reach her age. She was working when I dropped in first thing today and she's still at it.'

Bianca took the lead, straining at the heavy wooden door. 'I guess with her husband dead, it gives her something to do. She's always lived for the library. This door's locked.'

'Imogen said to give it a shove. Let's push together, okay? One, two three...'

The door opened. The lights had been dimmed to indicate that the library was not open for business.

'Mrs. Franklin?' Bianca called out. 'It's Bianca and Mr. Miles...'

'Call me Cory, you're making me sound like a teacher,' Cory said with a smile.

'Mrs. Franklin—it's Bianca and Cory.'

There was no sound.

'Maybe she's upstairs?' Cory suggested. 'I hope she's not wearing headphones—we'll frighten the life out of her.'

'Let's check between the shelves first, then head upstairs,' Bianca suggested. 'You take the first half of the alphabet, I'll take the second half and let's meet up in Mystery and New Adult, that's somewhere near the middle.'

Methodically, they worked their way up and down the rows of books, all the time calling out for Imogen.

'I hope she's okay,' Cory said as they met up in the central rows of shelving. 'Let's head upstairs to nonfiction.'

They made their way up the grand staircase to nonfiction and called out again.

'Imogen! It's Cory Miles—are you here?'

Still no answer.

They used the same technique as they had on the ground floor to work through the shelving. Cory half expected to find her engrossed with a book somewhere, but there was no sign of her. The lights had been turned down as if she'd been getting ready to leave the building, but there was no sign of anyone.

Bianca rejoined Cory at the political books section.

'I know,' Cory said, with a flash of inspiration. 'Imogen left that message for me earlier. If she called me from her cell, I'll have her number. I'll call it now, and we'll hear it ringing.'

Cory found the voicemail notification and worked through the screens until he found her number.

'Lucky,' he said, looking up at Bianca, 'It's a cell phone. She must have called me on her lunch break.'

He called the number, and they listened.

'Can you hear anything?' Cory asked.

Just to the side of them a fluorescent lamp was flickering and buzzing.

'I might be imagining it, but I think I can,' Bianca replied. 'It's very quiet, though. Look, the light switches are over here —let's see if I can turn off that light so we can hear better.'

Bianca messed around with the switches, at one point plunging the entire level into darkness. Eventually she found the combination she was seeking.

Cory called the number again. It had switched to Imogen's voicemail.

'Yes, I definitely heard a ringing,' Cory said. 'It was upstairs, though. I don't think that area is open to the public. It's restricted access, I think.'

'Well, she's expecting us,' Bianca replied, 'and if she's had an accident, we ought to check up on her—just in case.'

Cory nodded and they headed back to the staircase, beginning the climb to the third floor.

'I've never been up here before,' Bianca remarked. 'It feels quite naughty.'

At the top of the staircase was a flimsy barrier on which a photocopied sign had been attached.

Staff only beyond this point.

'I guess you don't need a lot of security in Shallow Falls,' Cory said with a laugh. 'If you've managed to climb three flights of stairs, you deserve to be here.'

He called Imogen's number again. This time, it was

more audible, but the sound was still not as clear as it should have been.

The lights were on across the entire level. It appeared to be used for archives and documentation. There was a local history section and several microfiche machines, too.

'It's like an old treasure chest up here,' Bianca said.

'Imogen? It's Cory and Bianca. Are you up here?'

Still no reply.

'I'm beginning to worry,' Cory said, calling Imogen's phone once again. They followed the sound of the ringing phone around a corner and into a walled area in the center of the upper floor. A door with a manual keypad lock had been left propped open with a chair. The light was on inside. That's where the ringtone was coming from, but it was still muffled.

'Imogen?' Cory lowered his voice, now they were entering a more compact space. They were in the stacks, a long room packed with movable shelving. At the end of each heavy metal shelf was a tri-spoked, rotating handle which allowed the shelves to be moved up and down tracks for easier access and more efficient storage.

'Imogen?' Cory asked as they walked up and down the stacks, peering into the gaps between the shelves to see if she was in there.

Towards the end of the rows of shelves was a cluster of five which were all bunched together, tightly grouped and firmly clasped. Desperately concerned now, Cory called Imogen's phone again. The ringtone sounded from the middle of the cluster of compacted shelves.

'On my God,' Cory said, realizing what must have happened. 'Bianca, start to wind those shelves outward. I'll take the two at this end.'

'She might have just left her phone on a shelf by accident,' Bianca began, not sounding too convinced.

They wound the handles, first turning them the wrong way, then getting the hang of it. As the handles were turned, the heavy shelving moved along the tracks and the rows began to part. Bianca was on her last shelf and there was still no sign of Imogen or her phone.

Cory looked at her as she began to turn the handle.

'You might not want to look, Bianca. I'm not sure I want to, either.'

As the handle was turned and the final shelves began to separate, Cory saw it before Bianca did. Imogen Franklin's dead body had been caught within the shelving, the force of the impact crushing her to death. Her arms were up high, as though she'd attempted to pull herself over the tops of the shelving, but she'd failed to make it. Either the shelves were too high, or she'd been unable to summon the strength to pull herself up. Once the shelves were parted, her body slipped off the shelving and slumped to the floor.

Cory gasped.

'Don't look, Bianca,' he warned, but she ignored him and peered around the shelving anyway. She flinched when she saw the body.

Cory didn't hesitate. He called the police, then found a couple of chairs just outside the stacks for them to sit on while they waited for help to arrive. They took advantage of the water cooler on that floor, and when the ambulance crew and police team arrived, they were sitting sipping cool water from plastic cups, their faces gray and stunned.

Cory was pleased to see Louise there, knowing there would be a million questions to answer. It was going to be a long night, but at least there was a friendly face among the uniforms.

Amid the frenzy of activity around them, his phone rang. He took the call.

'It's my car,' he said to Bianca. 'It's been towed back to my house. I left the hood unlatched, so they've taken a look at it. It was the battery—one of the cables from that starter motor was a bit oxidized. It just needed a rub with a bit of sandpaper to improve the contact. We're back in action.'

He said the words, but he knew it didn't matter after what had just happened. The ambulance team had confirmed that Imogen was dead.

The forensics and investigations experts moved in, swarming like bees, each one knowing their job and sticking precisely to the hierarchy. Even Deputy Cabera was there, out of uniform, no doubt called out from his home for such a big news story.

'Looks like Poppy Norman will be sharing the front page in Friday's newspaper,' Cory said. 'I'm supposed to be reporting the news, not making it.'

'Hey, Cory.' Louise attempted a smile, in spite of the circumstances. 'I'm coming off shift shortly—do you want me to run you and Bianca back home once you're done here?'

'We're not suspects, are we?' Bianca asked.

'Not at all.'

Louise smiled at her and Cory noted the effort she was making to reassure Bianca.

'We'll have to take detailed statements from you and eliminate your fingerprints and DNA from the crime scene, but no, don't worry. This is either some tragic accident, or we're hunting for a murderer.'

Those words hung in the air as they all thought about what that might mean.

'Look, I don't mean to pre-empt the investigation,' Cory

began, 'but there's no way this was an accident. Imogen Franklin was intending to share some interesting local information with me tonight. My bet is that you won't find those documents in this building any more. If they've gone missing, I'm telling you for certain—somebody needed Imogen Franklin dead. And if they wanted her dead, then I'm onto something big -something that runs deep into the heart of this town.'

TWENTY-FOUR

Thursday—Day 4

THE NEXT MORNING, Louise brought Cory a coffee into his bedroom. It took him a few seconds to search his mind for what had happened the previous night.

She had offered to run them home, dropping off Bianca and then returning with Cory to his apartment. As they were chatting in the car on the road outside, Cory noticed that the board over his bedroom window was gone; the landlord had gotten the glass replaced after the damage to the property earlier that week.

Not wanting to stop the conversation with Louise, he invited her in for a coffee. She'd finished her shift, after all. They'd carried on talking until the small hours and he'd poured them a whiskey each. He certainly needed one after the day he'd just had. Then what had happened? His memory was fuzzy.

'Don't worry, I slept on the couch,' Louise said, as if

reading his mind. 'You don't have to apologize for anything—you were a perfect gentleman.'

'For a moment there... What time did I fall asleep?'

Cory was relieved. He liked Louise—a lot—but there was his son to consider. And he loved Nadia, too, after all the years they'd spent together. He had no intention of throwing it all away.

'I told you to go to bed, after I was talking to you and you started snoring in the middle of an anecdote. You barely made it without falling asleep. I hope you don't mind, but I couldn't risk driving with those three whiskeys we drank. So I made myself comfortable on the couch.'

'At least nothing happened...' Cory began.

'Well, that's not entirely true.'

Louise was perched at the edge of the bed now, a grim look on her face.

'Oh no, what happened?' Cory asked.

'Well, did you know we both have the same make of cell phone?'

'No,' Cory replied, preparing to grimace at what was coming next.

'Well, Nadia called first thing to let you know that Zach's head is okay. She sounded like she was going to apologize for something, but she got all worked up when I answered your phone. She asked why I was at your place.'

Louise had a pained expression on her face, as if trying to warn Cory about what she was going to tell him.

'I'd make a terrible criminal—I can't lie to save my life. I'm sorry—I told her I'd stayed the night.'

'You didn't, did you?' Cory sighed in deep despair.

'Sorry—Nadia put the phone down before I could explain.'

'I'll call her now.'

'I'd advise against that,' Louise cautioned. 'She was pretty pissed. I'd give her some time to cool down if I were you.'

'This week is getting worse. I can't believe what happened to Imogen last night. It's like a bad dream.'

'It's pretty shocking stuff for Shallow Falls. Who the hell would want to murder Imogen Franklin? I agree with you; it seems ridiculous.'

'Well, I missed my morning run again. I'd better get showered and pick up Bianca. I want to have a word with her parents. I know she's not a minor any more, but still, with what's been going on, I ought to have a chat with them and let them know their daughter is safe.'

'You'll both need to get swabbed for DNA and finger-printed at the station, too, don't forget. Speaking as Officer Powell, the sooner that's done the better—it'll help speed up the investigation. And save me from having to make an official house call.'

'You'll check out that woodland at Shallow Falls, won't you? Please don't mention it to Tarrant just yet, but I'd be grateful if you could. If it's just some harmless drifter or campers, fine. But I'd never forgive myself if it was connected with Poppy in any way.'

'Yes, I promise—I'll make sure I do it today. And don't forget to call Nadia later. If you need me to, I'll speak to her and reassure her that nothing's going on between us. I've a feeling that might just make things worse, though.'

'I think you're right about that,' Cory replied. 'Surely this week has to start getting better soon? I'm going to have Mitchell Kane on my back today, too. He won't be happy about having to rewrite the entire front page of the newspaper.'

Cory showered, grabbed a light breakfast, and saw

Louise out. He looked up and down the street to make sure nobody was about; wagging tongues in Shallow Falls were all he needed while he was fighting for his marriage.

He was relieved that the car appeared to be fixed—for the second time—but he winced when he read the handwritten bill sitting on the driver's seat. He'd had to pay a higher rate for the nighttime call-out and tow; it was more than he could comfortably afford that month.

As he drew up outside Bianca's house, he could tell immediately that something was up before he even knocked on the door. From his previous visits, he knew Bianca's mom and dad were out of the house early in the mornings, but it was after nine o'clock and both cars were still in the drive. There was no sign of Bianca looking out the window, either, awaiting his arrival.

Cory checked his phone to see if she'd sent him any kind of warning. There was nothing there.

He walked up the driveway and knocked. The instant movement towards the door suggested he was expected. Bianca's dad answered.

'Ah, Mr. Miles, come in, please.'

There was no outstretched hand to shake, no smile, and he'd opted for the formal 'Mr.'.

Mr. Williams led Cory into the kitchen in silence. Bianca and her mom were sitting at the circular table. Mrs. Williams was stonefaced. If Cory didn't know better, he'd call this an intervention.

'Have a seat, Mr. Miles.'

His tone was curt and abrupt. Bianca made an apologetic face as Cory sat down.

Mrs. Williams began to speak.

'What on earth have you been up to with our daughter,

Mr. Miles? Does your newspaper not have a duty to care for your interns?'

Mr. Williams laid in, too, before Cory could respond.

'Bianca comes home late at night with scratches all over her arms and face, and then we find out she's smack in the middle of a police investigation due to the murder of our local librarian. Does that not give you any cause for concern, Mr. Miles? Bianca has had a difficult year at school; we're already worried enough about her future. And now this.'

It sounded like Bianca hadn't mentioned the gun. Or the narrow escape in the junkyard. Cory was grateful for small mercies.

'I don't know where to begin--'

'I'll bet you don't,' Mrs. Williams retorted.

'Mom,' Bianca intervened.

'I can't explain what's going on in this town at the moment; I've yet to figure out how to connect the dots. Imogen Franklin's death is tragic, but we just happened to be the first on the scene. If it wasn't for Bianca's help, that poor woman might have been there all night.'

He felt their hackles retracting a little. If he was going to get away with this, he'd need to be conciliatory.

'As for the scratches, it was due to Bianca's excellent observational skills that we may have found a lead to help with finding Poppy Norman. If it wasn't for your daughter, I'd have driven straight past it.'

Bianca smiled a little.

'I have to compliment you on raising a very impressive young reporter,' he began, deciding to pick up on Bianca's hint and spread it on thick. 'She's an absolute credit to you and a complete natural at this job.'

He watched as Bianca's parents looked at each other, then visibly relaxed in their chairs. They'd clearly been working themselves up for a confrontation but had discovered instead that their daughter was the hero of the hour. He'd keep quiet about the other stuff; there was no way a couple of compliments would get him off the hook if they knew their daughter had narrowly missed being hit by a bullet the day before.

'Can I get you a cup of coffee, Mr. Miles?' Bianca's mom asked, her tone now completely softened.

'Cory, please,' he smiled.

'Well, good to meet you, Cory,' Mr. Williams said, his arm now outstretched. They shook hands.

'I'm delighted to hear that Bianca is doing so well after her troubles at school. If she can turn the corner and put all that behind her, we'll be very happy.'

'Don't worry, Mr. and Mrs. Williams.'

'Please, Cory—it's Paul and Denise.'

'Don't worry, Paul and Denise, I'm certain that Bianca is going to go far in this line of work.'

Cory's coffee arrived, thankfully straight and black.

'So what is it you do?' Cory asked, trying to deflect them from tricky territory into calmer waters.

'Hasn't Bianca told you yet?' he asked.

She had mentioned it, but Cory didn't let on. He wanted this conversation firmly back on safe ground.

'I'm a realtor,' he said, proudly. 'I built up my own business, but you won't see my name on the boards. I call the business Absolute Realty.'

'Oh, yes, I've seen your signs about town. How's business? Are people moving much these days?'

'The housing market ebbs and flows, but it's the big developments where the future of Shallow Falls lies.'

'Oh, yes?' Cory asked. 'Anything I should know?'

'Only that there's an awful lot of money about to be invested in Shallow Falls. And some people are about to get very rich. Particularly those people who own the right plots of land, that is.'

TWENTY-FIVE

'I think we just about got away with that.' Cory smiled at Bianca as they walked toward the car.

'I thought they were going to put an end to the internship last night—they were furious about what happened. The scratches from the woods didn't help. It was a stroke of genius talking me up like that. They seem to think my career is over before it's started, after what happened at school. It makes life difficult, but I'm sure we can work around it.'

They were soon seated and belted up in the car, ready to move off.

'What do you think your dad meant about the investment that's coming into Shallow Falls? He got all cagey with me after he dropped that piece of information. Anybody would think I was a reporter on the local newspaper, the way he clammed up when I started asking questions.'

They laughed and Cory started the car, taking a moment to be thankful that the starter motor problems now seemed to be fixed. He left the car idling while he finished the conversation. There was something he wanted to suggest to Bianca, and he wasn't certain how she'd take it.

'What your dad told me—about the investment money that's heading our way—nothing's been raised in formal council meetings yet, as far as I'm aware. You wouldn't dig a little, would you? See if you can get your dad to share a little more information. It'd be off the record—I'd have to validate it via a third-party source.'

'Good luck with that,' Bianca replied. 'Ever since the events at school, it's been difficult to talk to Dad. He's gotten very secretive about what he's up to. I mean, the regular house sales are fine. But he seems to be handling something big at the moment. He doesn't even talk to Mom about it.'

'If you hear him drop any more snippets of information, let me know, will you?'

'Yes, but he won't get into any trouble, will he? I think I've tarnished the Williams family name quite enough for the time being.'

'I have no reason to think your dad is up to anything. It's perfectly normal to be discreet about deals that are being negotiated in the background. I'm just seeing a lot of different things in play at the moment, and I've a feeling some of them might link up.'

Cory moved the car slowly away from the sidewalk. He noticed Bianca's parents watching them from the windows and wondered what they were saying. It was an unusual alliance, a young intern and a middle-aged man, but something about it worked.

'Where are we heading, the office?' Bianca asked.

'Later,' Cory answered. 'We'd best check in at the police station and make sure they have everything they want from us. I need to file some news copy about Imogen. Oliver Vasey texted me on the drive over here to tell me they've already published the basics on the website, so the pressure is off for an hour or two. And I want to pay a visit to Xander Griffen. Are you up for that?'

'After our recent escapades, what could possibly go wrong?' Bianca replied. 'Besides, poor Xander doesn't have anyone to talk to, as far as I know. He must be terrified. He'll probably be grateful for a bit of moral support.'

'I want to ask him about that cell phone. Cell phones don't just appear in bushes, somebody must have thrown it there. Somebody who wanted to point the finger at him as a suspect.'

'I can't believe it's Thursday already and there's still no sign of Poppy. It feels like we're doing more than the police.'

Bianca had made a good point.

'There are more police officers about town, working through all the leads they have. Jerry Hunter's been questioned already, for instance. But they must be getting suspicious now, what with the incident at the junkyard and Imogen Franklin's death. Something is going on in Shallow Falls, and it stinks.'

Cory was frustrated to learn that Chief Tarrant was out in the field when they stopped off at the police station to make sure the investigating team had everything they needed from them. There were no witnesses, no leads, and no security camera footage. The police had drawn a complete blank on Imogen's death. And, as Cory suspected, there was no sign of the documentation she'd had sent over for him.

Before leaving the police station, Cory put a call into Oliver Vasey, asking him to chase whatever Imogen had sent over from the county branch of the library. He needed to see that documentation.

Next stop was Xander's house. They'd passed it several

times during the past few days, but it was high time they checked in on him. Cory would have liked to get it out of the way sooner, but the previous day had been challenging, to say the least.

He parked the car a few houses away from Xander's property, on the opposite side to where Reece's trailer was. He didn't want Reece to know that they'd been in the neighborhood without dropping in to see how she was. He could only imagine how she was feeling, on the fourth day since Poppy had disappeared without a trace.

'Go gently with Xander, won't you?' Bianca asked. 'He's shy and will get spooked easily. He knows me from the store. Maybe I can take the lead?'

'Sure, that makes sense,' Cory replied. 'I'll play good cop, you play great cop. I won't push him—he sounds like he's quite vulnerable.'

Cory surveyed the house. If ever a property needed several cans of paint, a re-roofing and a landscape gardener, this was it. The house looked careworn, tired, and in desperate need of a refresh, though as a turn of the century property it had probably survived much more than a bit of neglect. Although it bordered Reece Norman's property, it was quite a distance away from her trailer. Those old properties were not short of land.

Bianca tapped at the door. The old brass knocker was tarnished and had corroded so much that it was stiff and resistant.

There was movement in the house, then silence.

She tapped again, a little harder this time.

Cory thought he heard sobbing, but assumed he must be mistaken.

'There's somebody in there,' Cory said. 'Shall we walk around, see if we can get his attention?'

'Maybe he doesn't want to speak to us?' Bianca suggested.

'Let's see if we can encourage him,' Cory replied. 'We don't have to be pushy, but the most reluctant talkers usually have the most to say when it comes to a news story.'

They walked around the side of the house, moving close up to the living room window and peering in. Cory saw Xander ducking down behind the couch, hiding from them. The room itself was a wreck, filled with discarded pizza boxes, plastic instant noodle containers and abandoned soda cans with their pull-tabs sticking up. Unwashed cutlery and laundry sat on any available surface. It was quite clear from a simple glimpse through the window that this was a young man who was struggling to cope.

'Xander, it's Cory Miles from the local newspaper. I'm here with Bianca Williams from the store. We just wanted to make sure that you're okay. Will you let us in?'

'Leave me alone,' he shouted. He sounded terrified, as if he was being hunted and he'd had enough.

'We're here to help,' Bianca said gently. 'We just want to see that everything is okay. Please—can we come in?'

They watched through the window as Xander tentatively peered above the back of the couch, like a meerkat checking if the coast was clear.

'You promise those men didn't send you?'

Cory looked at Bianca and raised his eyebrows.

'We promise,' Bianca said. 'We're only here to see if we can help.'

They walked back to the front door and waited. Xander blinked as he opened up, as if he hadn't seen direct sunlight for several hours. He checked that Bianca and Cory were alone before inviting them in.

The house smelled of moldy food remains and dampness. Once upon a time it must have been splendid inside, with its high ceilings, period furniture, ornate centerpieces, and brass light fixtures. As Cory took it all in, he thought it would make an excellent location for one of those hoarder shows on TV.

They cleared the pizza boxes off one of the couches and sat down. Xander looked as nervous and suspicious as a caged animal.

'How are you coping, Xander?' Bianca asked, more gently than Cory had ever heard her speak.

'I didn't do it,' he replied, defensive, like he'd already said it a hundred times. 'I wouldn't touch those children. I like Reece—she's always been nice to me.'

'We don't think you did it,' Cory said, copying Bianca's nonconfrontational tone. 'What happened with your phone?'

'I only use it to order takeout—I don't have any friends to call on it. I don't know how to take photos on it or anything like that. I told Chief Tarrant where it was and when I was in the police station, they said they couldn't find it. They said I was lying and that I'd hidden evid... ev... they said I was hiding secrets on it. They said I took Poppy.'

He began to sob.

'I didn't hurt Poppy. I wouldn't hurt children. Reece's children are nice to me, why would I hurt them?'

Cory took a moment to compose himself. They had to get Xander some help from social services. He couldn't carry on living like this.

'Why were you scared about *those men*?' Bianca asked. 'Who are they? What do they want?'

Xander's entire form seemed to contract when she asked the question, like a snail rapidly retreating into its shell.

Cory studied an old photograph on the wall. It looked

like Xander's parents had been quite old when they died. He was pictured as a child—maybe five or six years of age— yet their hair was fully gray even then. He looked like any other child of that age: happy, carefree, and loved.

'They want to take this house...' Xander began, talking quietly.

Cory and Bianca said nothing, encouraging him with the expressions on their faces.

'They said if I don't do as I'm told, I'll end up sleeping on the streets or in the woods. They say I'll be cold and hungry and that animals will come and eat me. That Mr. Jones says if I don't accept the compuls... comp... the order, I'll be thrown out.'

'Compulsory purchase order? Is that what he said?' Cory asked.

Xander began to sob again.

'Yes, he said if I don't do what he says, I'll have no money and I'll starve on the streets.'

TWENTY-SIX

'What the hell is Spencer Jones doing frightening the life out of Xander?' Bianca said indignantly as she sipped on her double espresso. She'd taken Cory's suggestion: he'd told her that it would keep her awake through the day, after the punishing events of the night before.

It was a beautiful day, so they'd taken their drinks out onto the deck of Lacey's Diner which was drenched by the sunshine. Many other customers had had the same idea, and the buzz of conversation filled the air. The topic most talked about was the death of Imogen Franklin. It seemed that everybody had an opinion on the matter.

Cory took out his laptop and began to type.

'What are you working on?' Bianca asked. 'Anything I can do to help?'

'I'm just adding some detail to the Imogen Franklin story. The police always give the bare bones of it, but I can add in a little more detail. As we're witnesses, I can't reveal everything that we saw—it might jeopardize the investigation. But we can definitely do better than name, age, approximate time of death and a bland comment from the police chief.'

'I'm really bothered about Xander. He was terrified. I'm pleased we managed to get the house cleaned up a bit before we went. He needs a care giver or a support worker, or something like that. And who the hell protects somebody like Xander when a shark like Spencer Jones is sticking his nose in and causing trouble?'

Cory stopped typing and looked up at her. He'd not heard her speaking like that before. She was very passionate about the topic.

'I promise you, we'll do our best to get him some help as soon as we can. But right now, I need you to try and push your dad a bit about those contracts that are supposed to be coming into the town. I think we've stumbled upon a completely different story to Poppy Norman's disappearance here, and we need to keep at it like a dog with a bone.'

He continued to type out his news story, aware that Bianca was sitting looking about the place while he did so. Cory was just about to click the *publish* button, when she jumped in her seat, reached out, and tapped his arm.

'Chief Tarrant's here,' she whispered. 'He looks really pissed, too.'

It was no surprise. Lacey's sold the best coffee in town, and the cops were in and out of the diner all day.

'He's gone inside to order; I'll see if I can get a word with him,' Cory said, sending his story and closing the laptop.

'He's coming out again,' Bianca whispered, 'He's going to drink it outside.'

Cory kept his head down until Tarrant was almost level with their small circular metal table.

'Chief Tarrant,' he said, in a hijacking move.

Tarrant was standing directly next to them, so there was no way he could pretend not to have heard or noticed.

'Hello, Cory,' he said, resigned to having been ambushed. He was clearly annoyed, but being out in public, he looked like he was straining to play nice.

'Any news on Poppy Norman?'

There was a sudden lull in the conversation as it became evident that the surrounding coffee drinkers had caught wind of what was going on. Out of politeness, they continued to chat, but Cory knew their ears were firmly tuned to what was being said.

Tarrant lowered his voice.

'You'll have seen the latest press release, Cory, since you had one of your reporters at this morning's press briefing. We're following up every lead we have, but we've drawn a complete blank.'

He moved in, speaking confidentially.

'You know how this plays out: we keep searching until we have a suspect or a body. At the moment, we have neither.'

'What about Imogen Franklin?' Bianca asked. Cory looked at her, impressed that she didn't seem intimidated by Tarrant.

'What of her?' he replied. 'We still haven't ruled out that her death might have been a tragic accident. We're working through the list of volunteers who were in the library yesterday. It's quite possible that one of them is responsible for crushing Imogen in there. But just like Poppy Norman, we have no leads to suggest that she was murdered. She was well-loved in this town.'

Cory decided to press his luck.

'You know that she was looking for some planning documents for me?'

'What of it?' Tarrant replied. Cory could see he'd caught him unawares.

'Well, you must have read our witness statements. The planning documents were not found. It looks like somebody may have wanted to stop us from seeing them.'

The chief swallowed hard.

'That seems a little far-fetched,' he replied, speaking louder now.

'Does it, though?' Cory continued to push. 'Are you aware that Xander Griffen's cell phone appears to have mysteriously disappeared sometime after you were in his house. Do you have any thoughts on that?'

Cory knew he was playing with fire. If it had been just him and the chief at the police station, he'd have been shown the door by now. But Tarrant had been caught out in public and he had an audience to please—a coffee drinking audience.

'That boy is... he has learning difficulties,' Tarrant seethed as quietly as he could manage. 'We have a duty to leave no stone unturned when it comes to the investigation over the disappearance of Poppy Norman.'

'It's high time you found that poor girl.'

A woman from the adjacent table chimed in, looking scornfully at Chief Tarrant. There was a general mumble of approval from the surrounding customers.

'Shame on you, not finding her yet,' somebody else shouted. 'And here you are drinking coffee while that little girl is out there terrified somewhere—and what are the police doing to find her?'

Tarrant became aware that he was now playing to an audience, and a hostile one at that.

'You know I can't comment about an ongoing case, ladies and gentlemen, but I do assure we are doing everything in our power to find Poppy Norman and return her to her mother safe and sound.'

'But what about Imogen Franklin? You're supposed to keep this town safe. Some chance of that.'

Cory sensed it was beginning to get ugly, with the crowd beginning to bay for blood. Maybe he'd been reckless taking a swipe at the chief in a public place like that. He'd meant their conversation to be private, but the woman on the opposite table had piped up, and now it was getting uncomfortable.

'I can only assure you that the Shallow Falls Police are doing their very best to bring both of these sad and terrible incidents to a satisfactory conclusion as soon as possible, and that your safety in this town is our first priority at all times.'

Tarrant sounded like he was at a town hall meeting rather than on the outside deck of the local diner. It seemed to do the job. The hubbub continued and the hostilities ceased.

'Thank you very much for that, Mr. Miles. I shall be having a word with Mitchell Kane about your behaviour.'

That riled Cory immediately.

'You're an officer of the public, Chief Tarrant. You're obliged to answer the concerns of the public.'

'And you'd do well to remember your position in this town, Mr. Miles. You need to do your job and stick to reporting the facts. Leave the police to do the investigating. Amateurs like the local press just stir up trouble where it's not needed.'

'You're not threatening me, are you, Chief? As far as I'm aware the press still enjoys its freedom in this country.'

'No threats, Mr. Miles—just a friendly warning between two professional colleagues, that's all.'

Cory saw how uncomfortable Bianca looked and he suddenly felt outraged that Tarrant was trying to use the same bully-boy tactics that his son had been using.

'You need to watch that threatening tone, Chief, it might rub off on someone close to you—like your son.'

'Cory,' Bianca snapped at him, her face bright red.

'What's that supposed to mean?' Tarrant asked.

'Only that it's like father, like son, when it comes to throwing your weight around. Do you know that Dean has been hassling young Bianca here? Are you aware of what your son is doing while your back is turned?'

'Enough, Cory, I don't want you fighting my battles for me.'

Tarrant's face turned red, and his expression was twisted, as if he was about to have a heart attack.

'I'm going to walk away now, Mr. Miles, but your newspaper will be hearing from me. It's completely inappropriate for you to be talking to me in this manner. If you have a complaint to make, please do so to my face.'

'Cory, I want you to stop.'

Bianca was looking very agitated now, as if she was about to bolt. But Cory couldn't resist sneaking in the final word.

'But that's just it, isn't it, Chief Tarrant? You run this town; everything passes through you. What if it involved you, though? Can we be sure it'll be dealt with properly?'

'I'm leaving now, Mr. Miles.'

Tarrant placed his now-cold coffee onto the metal table and walked off slowly toward the parking lot. Bianca glared at Cory, her face bright red, and stood up.

'I don't need you to speak up for me. I can look after myself.'

She spoke quietly and assertively, but the emotion in

her voice showed she was hanging on for dear life to prevent the tears from falling.

Bianca walked off, leaving Cory sitting alone. He'd gotten so carried away he'd forgotten that they were sitting on the deck surrounded by the other customers. And now, all of them were completely silent, just looking at him.

TWENTY-SEVEN

Not for the first time in recent weeks, Cory realized he'd screwed things up. He was particularly annoyed with himself about Bianca. He kept forgetting her age. He should have shut his mouth the moment he saw her discomfort, but something inside him wanted to keep on pushing; he wanted to get some justice for her.

His coffee was cold now. At least the other customers had started chatting again, bringing the painful silence to an end. Cory took out his cell phone and called the office.

'Hey, it's Cory. Can you put me through to Mitchell, please?'

'Mitchell Kane's phone.'

'Hey, Mitchell, it's Cory.'

'Nice piece on Imogen Franklin, Cory. I can't believe you discovered the body. If that doesn't boost sales, nothing will.'

Cory told him about the altercation with Tarrant; it was best to get in first.

'Did you swear at him, punch him, or say anything that wasn't true?' Mitchell asked.

'No.'

'Did you steal from him, sell him drugs, or rob his grandma?'

'No.'

'Then Chief Tarrant can get as huffy as he wants. As far as I'm concerned, you're just doing your job. He's a public servant; stuff him! If he calls the office, I'll give him short shrift. You're doing great work, Cory—you'll hear no moaning from me.'

At least he was off the hook at work. He'd need to speak to Louise and make sure the information continued to flow. That's so long as she was still speaking to him.

With the Tarrant issue attended to, Cory knew that he would have to suck it up and apologize to Bianca. He knew he'd pushed it too far; he'd have to take any punishments that were coming his way. He decided to leave the car in Lacey's lot and walk up the road after her.

He didn't have to go far.

Bianca had found a bench directly opposite Lacey's and was sitting there watching the world go by.

'You okay?' Cory asked, walking up to her. She hadn't been crying—that was a good point from which to start clawing things back.

'I'm sorry I rushed off,' she began.

That was better than he'd hoped for. He waited for her to continue.

'I'm pretty furious with you still, but thank you—thanks for sticking up for me.'

'I know I went too far, Bianca.'

'I just wish my Dad and Mom had shown half your balls.'

Cory was speechless. He hadn't expected accolades.

'I was just overcome with anger on your behalf,' he said, quietly.

'I know you were—thank you. When it all happened, my Mom and Dad got scared, panicked, embarrassed, and humiliated, but they never got angry on my behalf. They just rolled over and did whatever Tarrant or my principal asked them to do. I don't think I ever felt so let down in my entire life.'

'Wow,' Cory said. 'That's a strong thing to say about your parents. I'm sure they were just trying to do their best by you.'

'Well, a bit of faith would have been nice,' Bianca replied. 'I still wonder if they ever suspected that Dean Tarrant's side of the story might have been true. You'd only just met me and you didn't question it—you knew I wouldn't have done those things.'

He sat down beside her and they stayed there in silence, watching the customers at Lacey's come and go, eyes following the cars as they drove past. Cory would never claim to be an expert in emotional intelligence, but even he could see that Bianca needed a short time to cool off and get her head straight. While they were sitting there, there was a buzz from his phone. He checked it and read the text that had just arrived.

'Take a walk up to the main street? Louise wants to have a quick word with me before she clocks on for her shift.'

Bianca nodded and they stood up. It was only a couple of hundred yards to the center, barely worth moving the car.

'What does she want?' Bianca asked. 'Anything new about Poppy? Or Imogen?'

'It's personal, I think,' Cory replied.

They walked in silence up to the small, square seating area in the heart of the main street. It was surrounded with benches and beautifully planted with seasonal flowers by the town's council, a favorite place to eat sandwiches and takeouts for those townsfolk who wanted a break from their desks during the working day. Louise Powell had secured a bench and her face lit up when she saw Cory and Bianca approaching.

'I won't be a third wheel, I'll let you speak alone,' Bianca began.

'It's not like that. Louise—Louise—and me, we're professional colleagues.'

'You might think that,' Bianca said with a smile, 'but she thinks otherwise. If you haven't noticed it yet, you must be blind.'

Cory didn't know what to say.

Bianca started to walk across the road.

'I'll hang out at a discreet distance. I'll be over here when you need me.'

Cory felt his face reddening. Damn, he'd forgotten to call Nadia to explain why Louise had picked up the phone earlier.

'Hi, Louise, ready to clock in for another day?'

'Yes, I went back home and got a bit more sleep after I left your place this morning. Where's Bianca gone off to? And did you call Nadia yet?'

'Bianca thinks there's something romantic going on. And no, I haven't called Nadia yet.'

She changed the subject.

'I hear on the grapevine that Chief Tarrant is pissed. He stormed into the office ten minutes ago, yelling at everybody in his path. That's why I'm sitting out here. There's no way I'm starting my shift early—I'm going in at the last possible moment to give him time to cool off. What did you do, run over his toes with your car?'

Cory laughed.

'Not quite. He might have been a little less angry with me if I had done that. Let's just say I pushed him a bit hard for information about the cases. I'm not his best friend at the moment.'

'I took a drive out to Shallow Falls after I'd had my morning nap. I went as an interested citizen rather than in an official capacity. I hope you don't mind?'

'No, I just wanted a second opinion,' Cory replied. 'Did you see anything out there?'

'I think you're right. I found two campfires out there. They looked fresh to me and they'd been covered up properly. They weren't easy to find.'

'You think there's someone out there?' Cory asked.

'It could just be campers or a drifter. But bearing in mind what happened to Imogen Franklin last night, and with Poppy still missing, I think we need to check out who it is. Once Chief Tarrant calms down, I'll suggest it to him. Or I might go straight to Deputy Cabera if the chief's still like a bear with a sore head when I go in there.'

'I appreciate it, Louise,' Cory said. 'I'd never forgive myself if we'd spotted something which might help to find Poppy and didn't follow it up. Did you have anything to do with Xander Griffen's arrest?'

She looked over towards the bank, distracted by something, then returned her attention to Cory.

'I saw him being processed, but I didn't go to the house. I don't think I've ever seen a man so scared; most of the idiots we get in the station look cocky and arrogant. I wouldn't have put Xander down as a criminal mastermind. Why do you ask?'

'I think he needs help from social services. Can the

police get that in motion? Surely you can refer him? He certainly needs it, if you ask me.'

Cory could see that she was distracted, but whatever it was she was looking at was behind him. He didn't wish to appear rude and turn around to look.

'I heard that from my colleagues,' she said. 'His place looks and smells like a pigsty, apparently. I'll have to ask around in the office—I haven't been serving long enough to have dealt with a case like his yet. But sure, I'll check for you.'

She frowned and stared over his shoulder. 'What the hell is going on over there? That's Bianca, isn't it?'

Cory had suddenly become aware of raised voices across the street. He shuffled around so that he could take a proper look at what was going on.

Bianca was across the road, outside the bank. Standing right in front of her, his hands clenched into fists and his face fired by fury, was Dean Tarrant. He was shouting into her face, and she was trying to give back as good as she was getting, but she was fighting a losing battle.

Cory shot up off the bench.

'That little shit,' he cursed.

He stormed across the square and began to cross the road, focusing on Dean and Bianca, intent on getting there before too much damage was caused. Instead, he walked directly out into the path of a car that was approaching in the opposite direction. The last thing he recalled before the impact was the sound of Bianca calling Dean Tarrant a lying bastard.

TWENTY-EIGHT

Cory felt the impact of the fender against his legs before he was pitched across the hood. The next thing he knew, he was on the ground, looking up at a sea of faces.

The first person he saw was Ida Maddison. Where was he? A thudding sensation filled his head.

'Cory, are you all right? Stay still a moment—we've sent for an ambulance.'

Above the hubbub of concerned and gossiping voices, Cory picked out Louise. She was frantic with worry; he could make that out above everything else.

A horn sounded along the main street and somebody shouted impatiently at the driver.

'Can't you see there's been an accident here, you idiot? Pipe down while we help the man.'

In spite of the inevitable chaos that the incident had caused, Cory knew he was okay and that it was a lot of fuss about nothing. Shallow Falls cars were restricted to twenty miles per hour in that zone, so it had come as more of a shock to Cory than anything else. The moment he'd felt the fender, he realized what a stupid thing he'd done and all but threw himself onto the hood to avoid any serious damage to his legs. Like a stuntman from Starsky and Hutch, he'd rolled across the hood and onto the road at the side of the vehicle.

Granted, he'd whacked his head on the side of the car as he fell to the ground, but metal was a better option than asphalt, and he managed to break his fall before receiving a nasty blow to the head. All in all, it rated higher on the embarrassment scale than the pain threshold.

'How are you, Cory? Have you broken anything?'

Louise was kneeling at his side, with the look that she might give a fallen soldier.

'I think I've shattered my dignity,' Cory began, forcing out a smile.

He wriggled his toes and moved his fingers, the amateur's quick test to confirm sentience and mobility. He had both.

'Doctor Parsons is here now,' somebody shouted.

A gray-haired man pushed through the crowd, an old leather doctor's bag in his hand.

Cory wanted the ground to open up and swallow him. Doctor Parsons ran through the obligatory checks and confirmed very quickly what Cory had known all along: his body and mind were still very much intact. It was just his pride that might need to be rushed to the ER for urgent cardio attention.

'You should stop by the hospital and get checked for a concussion, but I'd say you're good to go,' the doctor announced.

'How about you get your ass out of the road,' the horn-blowing motorist yelled, having seen that it was now socially acceptable to express impatience once again.

Louise offered Cory a hand and he took it, getting back to his feet cautiously.

'Yeah, and about time, too,' the angry driver shouted as he pulled past the car that had struck Cory and carried on with his journey.

'Bianca...' Cory said, remembering why he'd been in such a rush in the first place.

'Steady,' Louise warned. 'Don't go rushing off before you've taken a few moments.'

'I'm fine,' Cory insisted. 'Bianca needs my help.'

'Hadn't we better exchange insurance details or something?' the driver of the car asked. Cory noticed how drawn her face looked; he imagined he'd given her quite a fright.

'Hey, I'm so sorry about running out in front of your car,' he began. 'It was entirely my fault, I accept full responsibility.'

The driver looked relieved.

'Is there any damage to the car?' Cory asked, checking over the vehicle. He looked up the main street, but could no longer see Bianca.

'Nothing that I can see,' the driver said, looking to Louise for official confirmation.

'I'm happy to let this drop, Louise—if that's all above board?' Cory asked.

'Are you happy with that?' she asked the driver.

The driver of the car nodded.

Louise took out her notepad.

'I'll take your details before you continue your journey, but I think we're all good here.'

'I'm going to check on Bianca while you're doing that,' Cory said, 'I want to make sure she's okay.'

Louise seemed reluctant, but Cory went anyway. At first his legs were weak and unsteady, probably from the shock, but he could tell there'd been no permanent damage done. He thought of the times he and Nadia had warned Zach about running into the road, and there he was doing it himself; he just hadn't thought before rushing off to help.

Bianca had only moved a hundred yards or so in the opposite direction. He heard her raised voice first of all, then he saw her. She was still dealing with Tarrant's son, the arrogant little punk. It riled Cory just seeing him with that entitled, sneering look and aggressive body language.

'Are you okay here, Bianca? Is this man bothering you?'

'Hey, grandpa, this is none of your business. This is between me and the girl, okay?'

Cory felt his fist clench, but he just as quickly loosened it again. This was Chief Tarrant's son; he had to be very careful how he dealt with him.

Bianca was clearly distressed, her eyes red with tears and her face flushed, probably with frustration and anger, he thought.

'Bianca is my friend, and you're harassing her,' Cory replied, moving closer to try and separate Tarrant and Bianca. Dean blocked him, standing directly in his path. Cory hadn't realized what an intimidating presence he was. His arms were muscular and thick, his chest broad, his stomach toned and trim. He was in all respects the typical sports jock; a perfect physical specimen in stark contrast to Cory's more conventional vital statistics. But no bully was going to threaten him.

'Now listen here, kid,' he began. If Tarrant was going to refer to his age, he might just as well play the same game. 'There are laws about harassing young women. It's quite clear to me that Bianca wants nothing to do with you and you should respect that.'

'What are you, her sugar daddy?' Tarrant sneered in his face. 'Or some kind of pedo?'

Cory felt his fist forming again. As a man who'd never had to resort to violence in his life, this jerk brought out a rare fury in him.

'Okay, that's enough,' he replied.

'She's my girl, old man. We just want to be left alone to make out in peace without some old fogey like you in the way.'

'I'm not your girl, and I want nothing to do with you,' Bianca shouted at him.

Tarrant moved in and put his arm around Bianca's shoulders.

Cory had to intervene now—he couldn't ignore such blatant provocation.

'That's enough,' he said, moving in to push Dean Tarrant aside. But it was as if his hands had met a mass of concrete; the kid's body was solid and he didn't budge an inch.

'Come on, Bianca, give me a kiss, for old time's sake. You know how you love a bit of Dean—you can't resist.'

Cory moved in a second time, this time pulling Tarrant's arm away from Bianca as she struggled to escape from him. Tarrant's response was immediate and instinctive. His spare arm came at speed in Cory's direction, clasping his shirt tight and pulling him in so close that Cory could feel his breath on his face.

'Look here, little man...'

Dean Tarrant lifted Cory slightly off his feet. Cory was not a skinny man, in spite of the jogging. It took more than a morning run every now and then to offset the ravages of middle age. But Tarrant's arm barely seemed to register the weight he was lifting.

'I don't appreciate you interfering in my business, little man. If I say this pretty lady is my girlfriend, then she is, right? You're just an annoying little dick who writes for a paper that nobody reads any more, and you have no say in this situation at all. So how about you take a stroll and leave me and Bianca to get a little closer? She's a bit of a handful, you know—has she told you what we get up to when we're alone?'

Cory felt the rage burning through his body. He pushed his right arm against Dean Tarrant's chest as hard as he could. Tarrant immediately released him and fell to his knees.

'My god, did you see what he just did, he hit me, this man hit me!'

Tarrant was now playing it up to the small crowd that had gathered.

'Did you see what he did, Louise? That was assault! We've got witnesses, too, this pedo just assaulted me because I was trying to protect this young woman from him. Arrest him, Louise, he's hurt me... he punched me—you saw that, right?'

Dean Tarrant had spotted Louise approaching before Cory did. He'd timed it beautifully; Cory figured Louise must have seen his ineffectual attempt at getting his assailant to release his grip.

Tarrant gave a triumphant smile. 'Arrest this man immediately, Louise. Or else I'll report you to my father for ignoring an assault that took place right in front of your eyes.'

Dean Tarrant played the crowd for a few minutes longer, then stormed off, swearing he'd report Cory to his father for harassment and threatening behavior, and that Louise would lose her badge for not intervening. Bianca was in a high state of distress; Cory cared more about her than he did himself at that moment.

'That jerk,' he said to her. 'Are you okay, Bianca? Did he hurt you?'

She shook her head. Louise remained silent.

'What started that altercation?' Cory asked.

'I just happened to meet him on the street,' Bianca replied, calmer now Dean was out of sight. 'This is what it's like, Cory. Ever since we backed down over the school, he knows there's nothing I can do.'

'He's a bully, that's all he is,' Cory said, trying to reassure her. He was struggling with his own rage; Dean Tarrant had both infuriated and belittled him. 'What do you say, Louise?'

'It's difficult to know what to do about a little prick like that. His father could make life difficult for me if he wanted to, but I doubt he'll say anything. As you say, Cory, he's just your regular bully. But I'm not sure if I can raise this with the chief. You can imagine how that'll play out, can't you?'

'He's got me over a barrel,' Bianca said after a moment. 'If I create a fuss, it'll get back to the school and it could mess up my references.'

'I'll make sure you get a good report,' Cory said.

'Yes, but when it comes to college, school references will hold the biggest sway,' Bianca reminded him.

'You need to get yourself over to the hospital to check for a concussion,' Louise reminded him. 'You heard what the doctor said.'

'What happened?' Bianca asked. 'I saw something going on along the road, but I had a problem of my own to deal with. That wasn't you, was it?'

Cory opted to make light of it, to avoid burdening Bianca any further.

'It's nothing, Bianca, but Louise is right: if it's good enough for Zach, it's good enough for his father. Are you okay to run me over, Louise? I'd better get the all-clear before I drive.'

'Haven't you been run over enough for one day, Cory?'

Cory realized what he'd said and started laughing.

'Sure, Cory, my shift starts in twenty. I'll drop you off beforehand.'

'How about you, Bianca?' Cory asked. 'If you wanted to take some time off, I couldn't blame you. Not after the experience you've just had.'

'I want to complete an errand at Town Hall,' Bianca replied, perking up. 'I was heading over there when I ran into Dean Tarrant. I've got one of those journalistic hunches that you get, Cory.'

She smiled at him.

'Do tell,' he urged.

'Later.' She walked off, grinning. 'But if you're finished before I am, that's where I'll be. Hope everything is fine at the hospital.'

Cory and Louise followed her along the street so they could be sure that Dean Tarrant wasn't lurking around. Satisfied, they left her alone as she turned a corner.

'Best get a move on,' Cory urged. 'You don't want to be in the chief's bad books, especially if his jerk of a son is making threats.'

They arrived at the hospital and settled down to wait. Thankfully, he was called quickly.

'Second time in a week, Mr. Miles,' the nurse said, smiling at him. 'Working on a local newspaper's obviously more dangerous than I thought.'

Louise's phone buzzed. She excused herself and walked out into the corridor to answer it.

The nurse ran through the list.

'Nausea? Vomiting? Headache? Neck pain? Blurred vision?' she asked.

Only as a result of meeting Dean Tarrant, Cory thought.

'No, all fine. Nothing unusual to report.'

He glanced over to the corridor. Louise had a deadly serious expression on her face.

The nurse ran some routine checks on him, shining a small flashlight into his eyes, taking his blood pressure, and running a few simple sight and speech checks.

'Everything okay?' Cory asked as Louise came back in.

'You're all clear here,' the nurse informed Cory. 'Please try not to come again. I mean that in a nice way. If I see you here again this week, you'll be getting your own room.'

She gave Cory a warm smile and left.

'I've got to go,' Louise said. 'Are you all right to call a cab or walk back into the center?'

'Yeah, sure,' Cory answered. 'What's up, anything interesting?'

'I can't tell you the details, but all hell just broke loose at the station. They want me over at Shallow Falls ASAP.'

She came closer.

'Keep this to yourself, Cory. They've found a body.'

'Oh my God. Not Poppy?'

Cory thought about Reece Norman in her trailer, with her two girls.

'I can't say yet,' Louise replied. 'I don't know the details, but there's a body up at the falls. If you want to get your scoop, follow me up in ten minutes. Please don't make it look obvious that I told you; I'm worried enough already about what Dean Tarrant might say to the chief. You sure you're okay on your own?'

'Go, Louise,' Cory urged. 'You've got a job to do. Get over there as fast as you can.'

She paused for a moment, as if she was about to lean in and kiss him. Cory decided he'd accept it if that's what she intended; after all it was just a concerned kiss from a friend, not a betrayal of Nadia. But she evidently decided against it and left the room. Cory felt more disappointed than he ought to.

He pulled out his phone and texted Bianca.

Where are you? I'm clear now—can we meet back at the car? We've got a crime scene to attend.

Cory checked in at the office, too. They'd already heard about the police scramble and had sent over a photographer.

'Mitchell is mad as hell,' Oliver Vasey said, laughing. 'He can't make up his mind what to put on the front page. He's been walking around ranting that nothing ever happens in Shallow Falls, then we get a decade's worth of news in one week. Just pull in as much material as you can —I'm collating it all in the office. We're spoiled for choice this week; it'll all find a slot somewhere.'

Cory jogged from the hospital back to Lacey's, eager to get going and not miss out on the action at the falls. If they'd located Poppy, it would be huge news. He hoped she'd be alive, but he knew the chances of that were slim. All he could think of were the faces of Reece, Megan, and Toni. He wanted to cry at the thought of them being told Poppy was not coming home.

Bianca was waiting for him by the car, appearing completely recovered from her run-in with Dean Tarrant. They got into the vehicle, Cory feeling they were fast becoming like a couple of TV detectives, constantly screeching off to some incident or another.

'How did you get on with your visit to the Town Hall?' Cory asked. The car appeared to be behaving now. He shuddered, thinking how bad it would be if it had let him down on a serious job like the one they were about to attend.

'I had a crazy idea,' Bianca explained, obviously pleased with herself. 'I have an old school friend who works in the planning department, so I paid her a visit.'

'Oh, yes?' Cory replied, intrigued now.

'She let slip some information which I think you may find interesting,' Bianca continued. 'I think it relates to what you were investigating before Imogen Franklin died.'

They both fell silent. Imogen had only just died and there he was falling out with a punk like Dean Tarrant; it seemed so insignificant in context. With Poppy still missing and the death of someone as much-loved as Imogen Frank-lin, they had bigger fish to fry than the chief's idiot son.

'Did you know a grocery chain wants to build in this town?' Bianca asked.

'No,' Cory replied, 'it's not come up in planning meetings as far as I know.'

'Exactly,' Bianca said, as if she'd just made some scientific breakthrough. 'That's because it's not generally known. Apparently, they've been looking for some time. It's all hush-hush, nothing formal yet. But they're looking for a substantial site away from the usual industrial areas. I imagine my dad might know about it, too—remember what he said about big deals and secrets when he was speaking to you?'

They'd just driven past Reece Norman's trailer and were about to enter the tunnel-like entrance to the wooded area. He wondered if the police had told Reece a body had been found. Would she be sitting in that trailer in paralyzed fear, knowing what terrible news must surely follow?

'And none of this is official yet? That's why I wouldn't have seen it in the minutes of planning meetings, right?'

'Correct,' Bianca replied. 'My friend only knows about it because she listens in on all the conversations that the bigwigs have. They think she's just a stupid teenage kid, and they don't know she's friends with me.'

'I've gotta tell you, your instincts were spot on with this, Bianca—well done. Anything else you managed to pick up? This is great information.'

'We're at the falls now. Pull the car over before I tell you. I don't want you losing concentration while we're on this section of road.'

She had a point. Cory slowed down as he took the Shallow Falls corner and pulled across the road into the parking lot for tourists. It was now packed with police vehicles and secured with yellow crime scene tape. A TV satellite van was there already—it was a feeding frenzy.

Cory found a place to park, stopped the car, and applied the brake.

'So, what is it that might distract me so badly, driving round the bends at Shallow Falls?'

Bianca was looking at the activity at the falls; so many people were buzzing about that it looked like someone had kicked a hornet's nest.

'Guess who's been having meetings at the Town Hall? Who do you think is out there scouting for available land?'

Cory had a think, but nobody came to mind. They needed to be moving on; it was probably Poppy's body that had been found.

'It's only Spencer Jones, isn't it? The same Spencer Jones who's been bothering Xander Griffen about his land. The same creep who was bothering us in Lacey's the other night.'

THIRTY

'Spencer Jones is becoming a bit of a bad penny around Shallow Falls,' Cory said. 'This is excellent intelligence, Bianca, but you know what I'm going to say, don't you?'

'Yes, we have to verify it first. I'll see what I can find out from my dad. But there's a foul smell coming off our town, I'd say. I hope Dad isn't involved.'

Cory looked at Bianca, then over to the activity by the falls.

'Yes, we need to check this out. Careful who you speak to, though. If my near-miss at the junkyard is anything to go by, we're playing for high stakes here.'

She nodded. 'Do you think they're after Xander's and Reece's plots?'

'Yes... yes, I do,' Cory answered. 'If what you say about the grocery chain is true, I think the vultures are moving in. That's residential land, mind you. It would take a lot of effort to build a store there.'

'Yes, but if you leaned on the right people and had the right contacts, you could make it happen, couldn't you?'

Cory thought it over, considering how matters like this

progressed through legal and administrative processes. It was the less interesting side of working on the newspaper, but if you dug deep enough, you could discover some real nuggets of gold in planning committee minutes. He'd seen enough of how local councils operated to know that a word here, a great contact there, the occasional greased palm, and you could achieve virtually anything. Some councilors regarded planning regulations as a loose guide-line—the sort a couple of kids might have in a game of hopscotch.

Shallow Falls was a small enough community to be able to get away with stuff like that. And with land rights and property ownership going so many generations back, the rules could be easily bent into shape.

'We need to get out there,' Cory said, breaking away from his thoughts. 'I hope it isn't Poppy out here; it's going to be a very dark day for Shallow Falls if it is.'

'Hey, Cory, how's it going?'

Another of the Tribune's freelance photographers—known only to Cory as Micky—was on the scene already. He had the biggest lens Cory had ever seen on his Nikon DSLR. Micky was young, not that long out of college.

'You know it's serious when the telephotos come out,' he grinned. 'Who's this?' he asked, beaming at Bianca.

'Hi, I'm Bianca Williams,' she replied, holding out her hand confidently. 'I'm working as an intern with Cory. How about you?'

'Micky Nolan. Pleased to meet you.'

They shook hands and lingered just a second longer than they should have.

Cory was pleased to learn Micky's surname now; it had become embarrassing after such a time not to know it. Micky was one of those guys who turned up on news stories every now and again. He didn't know him well, but they always chatted.

'Do you two know each other?' he asked.

They drew their hands away.

'No, we haven't met before,' Micky replied. 'It's nice to see someone around my age on the job. Most of you are dyed-in-the-wool news hacks. When you're my age, it's good to see a fresh face every once in a while.'

Cory had seen Louise working beyond the police tape in the area overlooking the falls. He couldn't catch her attention; she had her mind fully on the job.

'What have you got to report?' Cory asked.

'Well, it's a body, we know that much.' Micky replied. 'They're staying tight-lipped about who it is. They got it all sealed off fast—the area's already under cover. There's no way I'm getting any pictures from this distance, even with a lens this size.'

'It may be Poppy,' Cory conjectured. 'If it's a child's body, the police will move super-fast to get it covered up from telephotos and drones. Mind you, with this level of tree cover, even a drone is no use out here.'

'Any idea who found the body?' Bianca asked.

'That's a dead end, too,' Micky explained. 'Most times it's a dog walker who finds the body. This time it was a couple of police officers, following up a lead about some campers being out here, or something like that.'

'They must be following up on our lead,' Bianca said. 'I assumed they'd just ignore it because they were too busy.'

'Louise must have succeeded in getting them to take it seriously. I wonder if the body might be a camper—or perhaps the hobo who lit that camp fire?'

Cory wasn't even convincing himself. He just couldn't face the prospect of it being Poppy.

There was a screech of tires behind them, and Chief Tarrant's car flew at great speed into the parking lot, squeezing into the last remaining space. As Tarrant got out of the car, a TV reporter ran up to him, followed by a camerawoman.

'Five minutes,' he shouted at them. 'You'll get your interview—give me five minutes for a briefing from my team.'

He rushed off. Cory thought he sounded like he was on a shorter fuse than usual, if that were even possible.

'Maybe Dean had a word with him after all,' Bianca said, her straight face turning to a smile.

'Yeah, we haven't had much luck with the Tarrant family so far today. Are there any other family members we haven't fallen out with yet?'

Micky had left them, ever alert to the next photo opportunity. He'd snapped Chief Tarrant getting out of his car, talking to the TV reporter, and now chatting to his officers inside the yellow tape. Cory wished he could catch Louise's attention, but he knew better than to compromise her at work.

Two officers were crossing the tape to walk over to their cars.

'The chief will speak to you in five,' one of them said to the TV reporter, pre-empting their request.

The TV station was based over at Westview and had a poor reputation in Shallow Falls because of their patchy coverage of local news stories. They were also struggling to regain their credibility after one of their reporters had sent out a tweet calling the town *Shallow Minds*. The rivalry between the two communities was historic, but it did the TV station no favors reminding everybody about it.

Cory decided to cash in some goodwill. He was

delighted to find out it was the two officers he'd bought coffee for in Lacey's earlier in the week.

'This is why we oil the wheels,' he murmured to Bianca. 'Follow me, and let's see how much they enjoyed that coffee.'

'Hey, officers, how's it going?' Cory asked.

'Hey, Cory, good to see you. It's not good news, I'm afraid. One body, recently deceased. The family have now been informed. We still need a formal identification before we release the name; that should come later today.'

'Is it Poppy Norman?' Cory asked.

'Come on, Cory, you know I can't tell you that. Under normal circumstances, I would. But we have to remain tight-lipped on this one, in case it compromises a different investigation.'

'That all sounds very cryptic, but a man has to try.' Cory grinned.

'The chief is going to brief the press in a couple of minutes. I suggest you make sure you're around for that.'

The officers made it clear there was no more information coming from their lips. They made their way back to their vehicle and drove out of the parking lot, turning back to Shallow Falls.

'What do you think?' Cory asked Bianca. 'Poppy or not?'

'They didn't give any clues,' she said. 'Would a couple of hardened cops show it on their faces if it was a child down there?'

Cory thought not; most seasoned police officers would have seen every horror that life could throw at them after a couple of years in the job.

He started walking over toward the falls area, where the

TV crew was. It provided an ideal backdrop for their interview with the chief.

There was a huddle of police officers and forensics staff just beyond the tape, above the shelf of rock that he and Bianca had been looking at the previous day. The water was still crashing down at the base of the falls. The place where they'd eaten their lunch was now cordoned off, the white tent positioned on the other side of the river from where they'd been sitting and chatting.

Had Poppy's body been there all the time? Had they been casually talking only yards from where Reece Norman's dead daughter lay? Cory shuddered at the thought.

Bianca was off chatting to Micky; the two of them had hit it off right away. It hadn't occurred to Cory that he and his colleagues must all seem like seniors to a woman as young as Bianca. Meeting someone just a couple of years older than her was probably a blessed relief, especially as Micky was a good kid. He was nothing like that Dean Tarrant jerk.

Right on cue, Chief Tarrant stepped over the police tape just as Cory was considering his son. The TV crew went straight to him, setting up the shot and moving him into position. Cory knew how it worked in the media pecking order: TV first, radio next—if they were even there —then, finally, the papers.

The TV reporter cut straight to the chase, asking Tarrant the question that was on everybody's lips.

'So, Chief Tarrant, have you found the body of Poppy Norman?'

THIRTY-ONE

Cory couldn't recall when he first realized Bianca was missing. There was such a huddle around the chief as he gave his briefing that it was difficult to keep track of who was where.

'I can confirm that there has been a fatality at Shallow Falls overnight. We are informing the family as I speak and there will need to be a formal identification process before we release the name of the deceased.'

'Can you confirm if it's the body of a child?' the TV reporter asked. Cory hadn't seen her before; he knew most of the local press, but it looked like the big guns had been dispatched.

'I can't confirm the age or gender of the deceased before we have completed the formal identification process. I hope you'll appreciate that with Poppy Norman missing at the moment, it's important that the press do not get ahead of themselves. You must await a formal confirmation of the tragedy that's occurred here. We also need to be mindful of the recent tragic death of a well-loved librarian in Shallow Falls—Imogen Franklin. I would urge you not to jump to conclusions. This is a complex police investigation which will be impeded if the press starts the process of idle speculation.'

Micky's camera could be heard clicking away as he captured the scene from every angle. Once upon a time, there would have been at least three newspapers in attendance. These days, it was just the Tribune. It was more cost-effective for the other newspaper outlets to pay Mitchell Kane to syndicate his news copy than to dispatch a reporter to the job. With two murders and a missing child, Cory had a feeling the nationals would be descending on them in no time.

'Do you have any leads in the case of Poppy Norman? Do you believe her disappearance is connected to the death of Imogen Franklin?'

The TV reporter was getting all the important questions in. That suited Cory fine because he figured the chief wouldn't have much time for the Tribune after their run-in at Lacey's. He took detailed notes in shorthand; things were moving so fast there was no way they'd be able to avoid a bumper edition of the paper.

'We do not believe at present that the two deaths are connected. I cannot comment on any links to the disappearance of Poppy Norman because I can't risk the press rushing to the wrong conclusions. Until we get a formal identification, you should continue to treat these sad events in isolation. However, I can confirm that at present we do not believe this death and the death of Imogen Franklin are linked. It is possible that Imogen Franklin's death was a tragic accident, but a full and thorough investigation by Shallow Falls police will confirm if that is the case or not.'

'How true is it that Shallow Falls police are dragging their feet with the investigation into Poppy Norman's disappearance? It's been four days and you still don't have any leads.'

Cory watched as Chief Tarrant's face turned beet red. He was riled again.

'That's it for now,' Tarrant declared. 'I'll call another press briefing as soon as we have any more information.'

With that, he stormed through the small crowd that had gathered around him like a bulldozer smashing through a brick wall. Tarrant walked over to his car, got in, and drove off. That was it, the short press briefing was over.

'What do you think?' Cory asked Micky. 'Is it Poppy?'

'Can't tell,' Micky replied. 'He's got a good poker face, Chief Tarrant—his facial expression bears no relation to the words coming out of his mouth. It's like a badly dubbed foreign film—the words don't quite match what you're looking at.'

Cory laughed.

'It's going to be a devil to write up for the newspaper,' he said. 'A story like this one, with so many twists and turns— it's likely to change the moment we go to print.'

'Well, I've got hundreds of pictures, and Mitchell is getting lots of syndication requests, so if one of my images makes it to the nationals, it'll be a great payday for me this month.'

Cory had noted on several occasions the incongruence of the press benefiting so much from human misery. Personal tragedies like Poppy and Imogen were a feasting time for the press. Circulation would be up, newspaper editors would see a glimmer of hope that the medium wasn't quite dead yet, and people like Micky could build their careers on one lucky snap.

'Hey, I hope you don't mind me asking,' Micky began

hesitantly. 'Is Bianca seeing anybody? Does she talk to you about stuff like that?'

Cory felt like her father; immediately protective and at the same unwilling to think of her as the subject of a romantic attraction. He stumbled and searched for the right words.

'Um, well... now that's a difficult question. We don't really have that kind of relationship; we mainly talk about the job. It's probably best if you chat to her yourself, Micky —I'm not sure it's appropriate for me to get involved, as her mentor. But if it's any help, I'm not aware of anybody.'

'Sorry—I didn't mean to put you on the spot. She's nice, and I'd like to ask her out for coffee sometime. I just didn't want to put my foot in it in case there's some football jock on the scene. Guys like me have to try a little harder; a football beats a camera any time.'

Micky walked off to finish taking photos.

If only Micky knew about Bianca's recent experiences at the hands of the high school jocks, he'd probably see that a guy with a camera was probably an infinitely safer option for her at the moment. It was none of his business and he had no intention of playing cupid in any way, bearing in mind his own recent marital difficulties.

Louise had spotted him and was dipping under the police tape to have a word.

'No Bianca?' she asked.

Cory looked around, first seeking out Micky to see if he'd gone to chat to her. He couldn't spot her on a cursory glance.

'She's here somewhere,' he replied. 'Is there anything more you can tell me?'

Louise shook her head.

'Much as I'd love to, I have to follow the chief on this

one. It'll be a disciplinary matter if we discuss any details. Tarrant is prickly as hell about it, terrified one of you guys is going to screw it up and get it wrong.'

'It's not Poppy down there, is it?'

Louise looked at him sternly.

'Come on, Cory, I could lose my job over this. The chief's been very clear. You'll have to wait for a briefing, like he said.'

One of her colleagues called her over, so she said her goodbyes and left him on his own. Even Micky was heading back to the office to file the photographs, and Cory would have to do the same, too. The beast that was the website needed to be thrown constant scraps of food.

He checked his cell phone for a signal. As he'd expected, the density of the surrounding foliage, the cover of the leaves and branches overhead, and the rural location of the falls meant he was in a dead zone. He needed to find Bianca and get on his way.

This was unusual for her. He scanned the falls area; there was no way she could have wandered off down there, because the police had it cordoned off securely. Nobody was getting anywhere near that body.

He looked across the road; had she gone off looking for more evidence of the vagrant that she thought she'd spotted? It seemed unlikely, but Cory didn't have any other ideas. And he needed to get that story filed.

Feeling irritable, he crossed over the road, taking great care that there wasn't some maniac about to fly around the corner at great speed in an SUV. Nobody seemed to have spotted him heading into the woodland on the opposite side of the falls, so he carried on, looking for some sort of indication that Bianca might have been there.

'Bianca,' he began to call, but not so loud that he'd attract police attention. 'Are you out here?'

It was easier to move through the trees in the daylight; this time Cory could see the low twigs before they scraped his face and hands. He weaved in and out, the ground soft and damp underfoot, the sound of birdsong rapidly replacing the voices of the police officers. He began to shout, now that he was away from the crime scene. Instinctively, he checked his phone again, hoping that he might be able to rustle up a weak signal and call her. Nothing.

'Bianca! It's Cory. Are you out here?'

He felt stupid calling out to her, but he knew this much already: there was no way Bianca would have left the area without telling him. Which meant she had to be in the woods somewhere.

Quickly his irritation turned to concern. What if she'd fallen or had an accident? What if she'd found her vagrant and been attacked? He knew he was overreacting, but the stillness of the woods and the complete lack of response from her was creating a rising tide of panic.

He took less care walking through the trees now, allowing the low twigs to push against him, like spindly hands trying to force him back.

'Bianca?'

Then he saw something up ahead, hanging from a tree. He sensed it was an article of clothing before he was close enough to confirm it. Hung up in the V between a narrow tree trunk and one of its branches was Poppy Norman's dress, the same one that she'd been wearing in one of the photos that Reece had provided. It was streaked with mud and looked wet; Cory's instinct was to reach out and touch it, but he knew the police would need it kept exactly as it had been left.

Something caught his attention several yards ahead. He struggled to make it out among the dense undergrowth. As his eyes focused on the object ahead, he realized what he was looking at. On the ground was a circle of stones where a campfire had been made and extinguished. And next to it, motionless on the leaf-covered ground, was Bianca.

THIRTY-TWO

'Bianca! Are you okay?'

Cory rushed toward her still body. To the side of her head was a stone, a splash of blood on its side. He put his hand on her arm, trying to get a response from her.

'Bianca? Can you move? Are you hurt?'

She began to stir. Cory hadn't realized that he'd almost stopped breathing with the tension.

'My head hurts like hell…' she began, struggling to find her voice.

'Can you move?' Cory asked, relieved that she was speaking to him now.

'Yes, nothing is broken. I fell. I can't believe I'm so stupid.'

'Take a moment,' Cory advised. 'Can you sit up?'

'Yes, help me up, will you? My head is spinning.'

Cory took her arm and she sat upright. She moved her legs and arms as if running an inventory check to make sure everything was where it needed to be.

'What happened?' he asked.

'I saw somebody,' she began. 'I'm certain it was a man.

But there were two of them. He might have had a dog; I couldn't tell. They were moving camp, and I picked up a sense of panic and urgency.'

'Why did you even come out here on your own?' Cory asked.

'Impatience. I'm sorry. But we told the police that we thought there was someone out here. And what have they done about it?'

'Louise came out here after I spoke to her. She raised the issue, as she promised, and some officers came out. Maybe Tarrant doesn't think it's important enough to check thoroughly. They have to take it seriously now that a body's-
-'

'The dress... oh, no, I found Poppy's dress!'
Bianca was suddenly distraught.
'I saw it, too. You didn't touch it, did you?'
'No, I learned my lesson after what Cabera told me when I handed over the stuffed toy. Oh, no... Cory, do you think that means it's her body down there? If her dress is so close, maybe she wandered down there and fell? What if somebody had snatched her and was keeping her out here? The poor child, she must have been so terrified.'

The same possibilities had crossed Cory's mind; he'd tried to banish any thoughts of the terrible things that might have happened to Poppy. Poor Reece. A discarded dress was a terrible thing to find, whether it was Poppy's body down at the falls or not.

'We have to stay calm,' Cory said gently. 'Chief Tarrant didn't say if it was Poppy's body or not. We have to tell the police about the dress right away, as soon as you're fit to move again. How did you fall?'

'I was trying to creep up on whoever it was in the trees and get a good look at them. But I disturbed a bird in that hedge over there and it startled the life out of me. I shrieked when it flew off and, in my panic, I tripped over the camp-fire. I guess from the feel of my head, I must have landed on one of those stones—they're pretty big.'

'We need to get you checked out at the hospital. I can't believe we're going back there for the third time this week. At least it's you this time and not me.'

Bianca did her best to laugh, but her hand moved to her head, feeling the small gash that the edge of the stone had left there.

'I bet they'll put a stitch in it,' she said. 'There'll be no hiding it from Mom and Dad. We'll have to face this one head-on. If we can get ahead of it, even better.'

'I'm beginning to think I'm a danger to you,' Cory said. 'Nothing like this run of events has ever happened to me before, I swear. It's normally such a safe job to do—it's not like this every day, I promise you.'

'I think I'm all right to get up now,' Bianca said. 'Can you help me up again? My legs feel wobbly.'

Cory did as she asked, ready to support her if she needed more help.

'I'm okay,' she said. 'Do you have a tissue to stop the blood trickling down my face?'

Cory felt in his back pocket and pulled out a clean tissue. Bianca seemed a little vague, as if she was dazed. He knew that concussion was a possibility from the nurse's questions to him after his own run-in with the car on the main street.

'Let's get you back to the car and let the police officers know where that dress is,' Cory said.

As they passed the dress, Cory hesitated about whether to take a photograph. He knew what Mitchell Kane would say: it's the photo of the century, a poignant reminder of the stakes in Poppy's disappearance.

Cory paused. What if it was Zach's clothing? His Spiderman t-shirt perhaps. How would he feel if his own son had gone missing and some opportunistic reporter had taken a photograph of his discarded clothes like that? He couldn't do it to Reece, even though he knew what a high price Mitchell Kane could put on an image like that.

He walked on by, doing his best to recall where the dress was located so that he could give clear directions to the police.

It was Louise who spotted them emerging from the woodland and she ran over to help when she saw that Bianca was having some difficulty walking.

'What on earth happened?' she asked. 'You've got more than half of Shallow Falls police force out here and still you manage to get into trouble! What happened to you, Bianca?'

'You need to get officers out there right away,' Cory urged. 'Poppy's dress is there—it's been left on a branch.'

For a moment it looked like she might give the game away, but she corrected herself quickly.

'But that can't be...' she began. 'Are you certain? Where was it, exactly?'

Cory gave her the details.

'Did you take a picture on your phone?' Louise asked.

'No, it didn't seem right,' Cory replied, feeling sheepish now. Some journalist he was. He'd never get a career-changing scoop if he let his integrity stand in the way.

The three of them crossed over the road and Louise caught the attention of Deputy Cabera who was now on the scene. Immediately he dispatched officers to check the area. Cory watched as three of them broke off and checked in with him to get directions.

Louise walked back over.

'Nice work, Cory; Cabera says he's going to get dogs out there once they have the dress. If there's someone out there, we need to track them down and find out if they have anything to do with all this.'

'*If* there's someone out there?' Bianca said, breaking her silence. 'There *is* somebody out there! I'm not imagining it, and it's high time you started taking it seriously.'

'Whoa—steady, Bianca, let's get you to the hospital and checked out.'

Cory was keen to prevent fallout over the deployment of police resources. They were checking out the dress, so it was being taken seriously.

'I'll catch up with you later,' Cory said to Louise as he moved toward his car.

Cory was anxious to get the story filed. He'd have Mitchell Kane on his back if he didn't. With no phone signal at the falls, the best option was to dictate the story to one of his colleagues on the phone when they got to the hospital.

They were back in the ER within ten minutes. Seeing how out of it Bianca was made him thankful that everything was just a short drive away in Shallow Falls. The town's hospital would be better described as a very large doctor's clinic. It was hardly state-of-the-art. However, one thing that it did boast was a short waiting time to be seen by a nurse. Cory was pleased to see it wasn't the same nurse who had patched him up twice that week. It was becoming embarrassing.

'I'm going to leave you while you get checked over,' Cory said to Bianca. 'I'll just be in the waiting area outside. I have to check in at the office. I'd best call your mom and dad, too.'

'Do you have to, Cory? They'll stop me working with you.'

'I have to, Bianca. I can't keep this quiet—they'll need to keep an eye on you after your fall.'

He moved outside the waiting room, relieved that she was now in a safe pair of hands. He called in to the office and dictated some copy to Oliver, who typed it directly into the online system as he spoke. Vasey checked it back for accuracy and then asked if it was okay to press the publish button.

'Go ahead,' Cory confirmed. 'Let's get this news story out there.'

Directly after hanging up with Vasey, Cory pulled up the contact numbers he'd gotten for Bianca. He'd keyed them into his cell phone the week before, ahead of Bianca's arrival. Emergency contacts were standard practice for the younger interns. It had been an administrative nuisance at the time, but now he was pleased he didn't have to go hunting for that information.

The phone connected immediately; he'd gotten her mom's work. He was put through to her extension.

'Hey, Mrs. Williams. It's Cory Miles. It's nothing to worry about, but Bianca has had a small accident.'

He would have reacted exactly the same if it was her informing him that Zach had just had a fall.

'That's the last straw, Mr. Miles. We didn't think we were placing our daughter in danger when we let her work with you, but it's become quite clear to me that you're incapable of keeping her safe. I'm coming over to the hospital now and taking her home. That's the end of Bianca's internship with the paper, Mr. Miles. It's over.'

Cory was about to plead his case with her, when he heard Bianca trying to get his attention from the treatment room. He could hear her voice from behind the curtain that had been drawn for privacy.

'Mrs. Williams, I'm so sorry, but I have to go. I promise we'll talk later.'

As he ended the call, he just caught her last words. 'Your editor will be hearing about this.'

Cory entered the curtained-off area of the treatment room after checking that it was okay for him to do so.

'I need a quick word,' Bianca said.

The nurse had gone off to fetch a dressing, so she was on her own now. She seemed considerably more alert.

'It'll take one minute,' Bianca said. 'Quick, before the nurse comes back. I don't want her to know that I passed this on to you. I'm supposed to keep it to myself, but this is dynamite.'

'Go on, tell me, then. Your mom wants you to stop working at the paper, by the way. She's going to land me in it with Mitchell Kane. Just so you're prepared.'

'Damn. Okay, I'll deal with that one when she gets here. Guess who the nurse is married to?' Bianca smiled. She had the color back in her cheeks now.

'Go on, tell me.'

'Only the medical examiner.'

She had a broad smile across her face. If it wasn't for the two small stitches in her forehead, you'd never know what had just happened. She looked a lot better with the blood cleaned off her face, too.

'You're joking,' Cory replied. 'It'll be a crime if your mom stops you working at the newspaper. You've got a knack for this work. What did she tell you?'

'She can't tell me whose body it is, but it's not Poppy's.'

'Seriously? Are you certain?'

'Yes,' Bianca confirmed. 'She said all she knows is that it's a male adult. It could be my drifter.'

'Could be,' Cory said, thinking it over. 'Did she give away any more clues? I'll have to verify it all before we run it in the paper, but it's good to have a heads-up.'

'Yes, this is the best bit about what she said. She wouldn't give me the man's name, but it's a local councilor. It looked like suicide; he was found hanging from a tree. But wait until you hear this. He was involved in town planning.'

THIRTY-THREE

Cory ran through the list of councilors in his head. There weren't that many and some of them were women. He sent a text to Oliver Vasey, asking him to stay alert for two names coming up. If one of the freelance photographers took a drive past their houses, it would probably become quickly obvious which of the two it was. A police car out in the street, and a number of cars pulled up in the driveway —it was easy to spot if you knew what you were looking for.

'The nurse is coming back. Make yourself scarce,' Bianca warned. 'I'll see if I can squeeze any more information out of her.'

Cory walked back to the seating area. He felt a massive sense of relief that the body was not Poppy's, but it made the discovery of her dress even more sinister. He forced those thoughts to the back of his mind; he couldn't bear to think about it. So long as they were all working to find Poppy and get her back with her family, that was all that mattered.

Cory had barely sat down again when Bianca's dad

came rushing up the corridor, a look of panic on his face as if someone had just given a five-minute nuclear warning.

'Where is she, Cory? What the hell have you done this time?'

'Whoa, calm down,' Cory said. 'She's fine, Paul; we've just been chatting. She's right through there, in the second cubicle—you can hear her talking to the nurse. Does that sound like someone with a bad injury?'

Paul Williams listened and visibly relaxed.

'I got a call from Denise,' he explained. 'I was viewing a property nearby, so I ran over. She's on her way in the car. The way she was talking, it sounded like an emergency.'

'Bianca just had a fall—she'd gone off into the woods on her own and was startled. I thought we'd better get her checked out just to be safe. She's had to get a couple of stitches in her forehead, but my little boy Zach did a similar thing earlier in the week. It was just an accident, honestly.'

'Okay, I know how much she's enjoying working with you. I think Denise might give you a hard time, though. I'll do my best to smooth things over, but don't hold your breath.'

There was a brief moment of collusion between the two men, an unspoken agreement that they'd tackle Denise as a team when she arrived and started demanding answers.

'So, what happened?' Paul asked. 'Why were you out in the woods?'

'Can I speak in confidence?' Cory asked, sensing an opportunity to pump Bianca's father for more information.

Paul Williams nodded. 'Of course. As a realtor, I hear all sorts of information as I'm traveling about town. I learned a long time ago that if you keep your ears open and your mouth shut, that information tends to flow a little more freely. I'm all ears.'

'This will be of interest to you,' Cory began, building up the story. 'There's been an alleged suicide at Shallow Falls, a councilor, apparently. This is all unconfirmed, so you must be discreet.'

'No problem—I understand how important this is to Bianca. I wouldn't jeopardize her position at the newspaper. Carry on, I'm intrigued. Do you have a name?'

'Not yet,' Cory answered, as his phone buzzed. He looked down at the screen and read the text from Oliver.

'Turns out I do have a name,' he continued, 'But this is unconfirmed. We've just put the pieces together, so this information is not from official sources. One of our free-lancers says it's Councilor David Ingram. Do you know him?'

Paul Williams' face looked as white as his daughter's had been half an hour ago.

'Oh my God...' he began, visibly choked up. 'Suicide? Are you certain?'

'No, none of this information has been confirmed at the moment. What do you know about David Ingram? From the newspaper's point of view, he was just your average councilor: a family man, with long-term service to the town. Nothing unusual about any of that.'

'Where is she? Where's Bianca?'

Denise Williams had arrived and was blowing along the corridor like a tornado in a temper.

Paul stood up in an attempt to intercept her, but she was in no mood to be placated.

'Get out of my way, Paul. I want to see Bianca. Now.'

She brushed past the two men and rushed into the treat-ment room, pulling back the curtain in the first cubicle. A farmer was bent over the examining table, his trousers down by his ankles, with a nurse trying to remove a splinter from his behind.

'Do you mind?' the nurse said, annoyed at the intrusion.

'Oh, I'm so sorry.'

Denise stopped dead in her tracks, allowing Paul to swoop in and take her to one side. He guided her back out to the waiting area, where she took a seat, chastened and embarrassed by what she'd just done.

'Got it,' came the nurse's voice from beyond the curtain.

Cory chanced some humor. 'At least there's some good news—that farmer will be able to get his plowing finished this afternoon.'

There was a moment of quivering silence, then Denise laughed, more out of a sense of release than the quality of the joke.

'Bianca is fine,' Cory reassured her. 'She'll be out in a minute, you'll see for yourself.'

The farmer emerged from the cubicle, a broad smile across his face.

'I'm so sorry for intruding,' Denise said, standing up.

'It's no problem,' the farmer replied. 'When you work with animals like I do, you spend your day looking at rear ends. I hope it doesn't spoil your dinner.'

He smiled and walked off. Moments later, Bianca emerged, a neat bandage now covering her stitches. The nurse had done a tidy job. Cory was relieved Denise hadn't seen the wound before it was dressed. He imagined it would have taken more than a farmer with a splinter in his butt to defuse that situation.

Bianca made light of her injuries as best she could, and it played well with her parents.

'You should keep an eye on her for the next 24-48 hours,' the nurse said, and then reeled off the same list of things to look out for in case of concussion that Cory had been given after his own incident.

Denise examined the wound carefully and satisfied herself that all was well.

'Right, let's get you home, Bianca,' she announced. 'It's an afternoon in front of the TV for you—you need to rest and recover, just like the nurse said.'

'Will Bianca be able to continue working at the paper?' Cory asked. She seemed more level-headed now that she'd seen her daughter with her own eyes, so he felt it was a good time to ask.

Denise looked at Paul, who made a noncommittal face at her.

'We'll have to discuss it as a family when we're all back at home this evening, Mr. Miles. I'm so angry about what has happened. We'll talk about it when we've all had time to calm down. I have to be honest with you: my vote at this time is to end it now and find something a little less dangerous for Bianca to get involved in.'

Bianca drew breath with what looked like an incoming protest, but Cory raised his eyebrows.

'If you allow her to stay on,' Cory said, 'I promise there'll be no more drama, just good, old-fashioned, small town newspaper reporting. See you later, Bianca. I'll check in and see how you are.'

Denise gave her husband a terse kiss on the cheek, and he and Cory watched as she led Bianca through the double swinging doors at the end of the long corridor.

'Are you in a rush?' Cory asked.

'No, why?' Paul replied. 'I've got half an hour until my next appointment.'

'How about grabbing a coffee in the cafeteria? I'd like to speak a little more about Councilor Ingram, if that's okay?'

'Sure, I'd like to find out more myself. I can't believe he's dead.'

The two men followed the signs to the cafeteria, Cory bought the coffees, and they took a seat.

'So, suicide,' Paul began. 'Do they know why?'

'It's not confirmed as a suicide,' Cory reminded him, 'but I don't have any more details than that. You know you mentioned the other day about some big plans for the town? He wasn't involved in that work, was he?'

'Funny you should ask,' Paul replied, his brain clearly working overtime. 'This all feels very close to me now. I'm shaken by what you've told me, if I'm being completely honest with you. Councilor Ingram was my liaison with the town council; I dealt directly with him. I had no idea he was struggling with his mental health. It's almost impossible to believe that he'd kill himself like that.'

'What work were you doing with Councilor Ingram? I assume it was planning related?'

'Yes, it was all fairly routine stuff. He'd asked me to go through a process of finding suitable locations for a massive new supermarket in the town. He was sure it was going to bring lots of new jobs and a considerable investment. I was commissioned to do a study of potential sites.'

'Did you come up with any?' Cory asked.

'No, I failed, as it happens. His clients—the grocery chain—had some very exacting requirements. I looked at existing industrial locations and disused sites, but none of them matched the criteria. So my report said that there was no suitable location within existing commercial zoning areas. I think he took it back to the council to discuss, but I lost track of it after that. I can tell you, though, somebody is going to make a lot of money out of this deal when it goes through. We're talking millions of dollars in investment.'

Cory's phone buzzed, but he ignored it, keen to find out if Paul Williams knew any more.

'Are the plans going ahead?' Cory asked. 'Did they find a solution?'

'I think they found their ideal plot, but it comes with some issues. I can't tell you where it is, but I do know that certain people in this town very much want that grocery store built and open by this time next year.'

Cory had a good idea where that land might be, but he kept it to himself. His phone buzzed a second time. He checked the number calling in. It was Nadia, and it was highly unusual for her to be calling at that time of day.

'Please excuse me,' he said to Paul, 'I need to check this.'

He answered.

'Nadia, it's Cory, what's up?'

'I need you over here right away, Cory. There's been an incident at school with Zach. It's urgent. You have to come right now.'

'I've got to go,' Cory said to Paul Williams. 'Thanks for the chat; I'll check in on Bianca later.'

He navigated his way out of the hospital, following the exit signs as if finding his way out of a maze.

His phone buzzed as he rushed across the parking lot and back to his car. He answered as he walked. It was Louise.

'There was no dress.'

'What?' Cory replied. 'I saw it with my own eyes, Louise.'

'The officers searched the entire area, there was nothing there. Are you sure you didn't imagine it?'

'Louise, I'm telling you, I saw it.'

'Bianca was pretty shaken when she came out of the woods. Might she have imagined it?'

'Officer Po-- Louise... I can't believe we're even having this conversation. I saw it. It was there.'

'I just got my head torn off by Cabera, Cory. I had to sit through a dressing down about sending valuable officers on a wild goose chase and putting the investigation in jeopardy.'

Cory juggled the phone as he reached the car, got in, and started the engine. Under normal circumstances, he'd have wound up the call, but he was in a rush and he decided to chance it. He moved the car out of the parking lot, with one hand on the wheel and the other on his phone.

'I'm sorry if it put you in a difficult position, Louise, but I swear to God it was there.'

'But you didn't take a photo?'

'No, I told you, it didn't seem right.'

'Did Bianca?'

'No, not that I know of.'

Cory was getting wound up. Louise Powell was supposed to be an ally; this was not playing out well.

'Look, I'm sorry, Cory, but they called off the dog search because of it. I'm not in Cabera's good books—I need to keep my head down for a while.'

'The officers found the campfire, right? They must have seen where Bianca fell.'

Cory was nearing the end of the town now. As he passed Reece's trailer, he felt relief that the body wasn't Poppy's. But he'd seen the discarded dress for himself, whatever Louise was telling him. It was possible that Poppy might be better off dead.

'Yeah, they found the fire. So what? There are lots of fires in those woods. It'll just be some vagrant passing through, minding his own business. It doesn't warrant calling out the SWAT squad.'

Cory hadn't heard her like this before. He could sense she was angry with him; fair enough, when she'd taken a hit for it. So where was the dress?

'Could an animal have taken the dress?'

'Cory, listen to yourself! You're just reaching--'

'Oh, shit.'

'Are you okay, Cory?'

He'd just come to the curved road at the falls and with only one hand available for steering, the car had veered wide and he'd almost gone careening through the parking lot where several police vehicles were still parked. Cory dropped the phone onto the floor, put both hands on the wheel and pulled the car over. He'd narrowly avoided shooting straight over the edge where Xander's parents had met their end. He slammed on the brakes and screeched to a halt in the middle of the parking lot.

The officers who were gathered on the other side of the crime scene tape looked up. Cabera was still there; recognizing Cory, he began to walk over. Cory wound down the window. He'd have to suck this up.

'Mr. Miles,' he said, positioning his head directly at Cory's level. 'I seem to be very aware of you today,' he said. 'And not in a good way. How the hell did you manage to do that? Driving too fast to find a dress that isn't there?'

That stung, but Cory kept his mouth shut.

'Just distracted by all the activity,' Cory began.

'Cory? Cory? Are you okay?'

Louise's voice could be heard clearly coming from the phone in the foot well.

'Louise, end the call,' Cabera shouted. Cory almost jumped out of his skin. He saw Louise just across the parking lot. Her back had been to them, but she turned around with a look of horror on her face. Cory imagined she'd just figured out what happened.

'Last warning, Cory. You're seriously beginning to piss me off. Chief Tarrant has also had words with me about you. Now I'm going to suggest very politely that you stick to reporting the news and stop trying to make the headlines. And I'm watching you and Louise; if I get a whiff of her leaking information to you--'

'She hasn't,' Cory insisted. 'Louise has been completely professional.'

'Did she know you were driving when you were speaking on the phone to her just then?'

Cory didn't know what to say. He dropped his head in submission and waited for Cabera to dismiss him.

'Get on your way, Cory. Take my advice, leave the detective work to the police.'

'I will.'

Once Cabera had moved away from the car, Cory retrieved the cell phone. He'd gotten a text from Nadia telling him to meet her at the house. She'd be getting angry with him.

Carefully and cautiously, Cory pulled out of the parking lot and re-joined the road. He saw a couple of the officers laughing at him; they of all people would know what it was like to be on the receiving end of a thrashing from Cabera.

Cory didn't tempt fate a second time; he drove as swiftly as he could to Nadia's without breaking any speed limits and with both hands firmly on the wheel. As he turned into Nadia's road, he saw a Westview police car parked on the street outside the house. He swung the car over to the curb and got out as fast as he could, without switching off the engine. Cory ran up the driveway and burst into the house, not bothering to announce himself or ring the doorbell.

'Where's Zach?' he asked. 'What happened?'

Nadia was sitting on the sofa with two police officers,

one of them female. They always use women to deliver the bad news, Cory thought.

Nadia had been crying and her hair was a mess. The body language from the police officers screamed *delicate situation*.

Nadia wasted no time tearing into him.

'Is this your doing?' she shouted at him. 'It's not enough that you can't even look after your own son properly—now you're actually putting him in harm's way.'

'I think it would be helpful if we all calmed down, Mrs. Miles.'

'It's Ms. Hadfield, if you must know,' she seethed at the female officer. 'We were husband and wife, but not for much longer after this. It's the final straw, Cory. I really can't take any more of your bullshit.'

Cory was stunned by the ferocity of her attack, but he was also desperate to know about Zach.

'Look, just tell me what happened to Zach,' he pleaded. 'Is he okay?'

'Yes, he's okay, but no thanks to you,' Nadia yelled at him. 'He was accosted by a man on the school playground today. It frightened the life out of him.'

'Was he hurt?' What happened?'

'He's fine,' the female police officer said calmly. She wasn't the only one who wanted to take the heat out of the situation. 'He's upstairs in his bedroom, resting. He was just a bit upset at the time. The man wasn't very pleasant, and he was scared, that's all.'

'Where were the teachers when this happened?' Cory asked, indignant now. 'Did they get a look at this man? Who was he?'

'It was over in a couple of minutes, Mr. Miles,' the male officer said, speaking for the first time. 'The man moved away quickly as soon as the duty teacher saw him and came to check on Zach.'

'Did the teacher get a look at him?' Cory persisted. 'Will you be able to make an arrest?'

'Unfortunately, Mr. Miles, we only got a basic description. It won't be enough to get an identification. All we got from Zach was that he was an old man who wasn't very nice. Oh, and the teacher thought he looked drunk.'

THIRTY-FIVE

The conversation with Nadia had gone from bad to worse. She was tense and angry with him, blaming his work on the newspaper for what had happened at school.

'All this business with the missing child and you being in the public eye brings unwelcome attention to our family,' she'd told him, as the two officers squirmed uncomfortably in their seats. 'Who knows what this man might have done to Zach? He could have ended up as the next Poppy Norman. It might well have been our child's face on those *missing* posters, Cory.'

'My work is no worse than yours,' he tried to explain in as non-confrontational a tone as he could manage. 'You deal with suspects and guilty parties in court all day. That also exposes him in a way that a job at the grocery store wouldn't...'

He should have known better.

'Are you really suggesting I work at the grocery store to keep our son safe?' she asked. 'Besides, your name and photo are plastered all over the newspaper, in every edition.

It's like advertising who our child is. It would be better if he took my maiden name.'

'Well, if it really concerns you--'

'I don't mean as a temporary measure, I mean permanently.'

Cory looked at her. She was dead serious. She was really suggesting divorce.

The male police officer swallowed hard and stood up like somebody had just lit a fire underneath him.

'I think that now Zach is back home safely, we'd better get going.'

Cory saw the two officers out of the house. Nadia looked like she wanted to be left alone.

'Did you mean that?' Cory asked after the officers had gone.

'Yes,' she answered quietly. 'Things haven't been right between us for some time. I've been thinking about it a lot recently. I think it may be time.'

'Well, if my vote counts for anything, I'd really like to give it a second try. For Zach's sake more than anything. Things used to be good between us, Nadia. We could get back there again. Counseling would help.'

Nadia had been cold with him for so long that Cory wondered why he was even making the suggestion. But they had to try, didn't they? For Zach's sake, if nothing else.

'I'm not sure I care enough anymore,' Nadia answered. Cory struggled to remember the last time she'd shown any warmth toward him.

That hurt, but he decided to leave it. It had been a tense afternoon for everybody, and there was no point discussing the matter while emotions were running so high.

'May I go upstairs to kiss Zach?'

Nadia nodded.

Zach was asleep, exhausted by all the drama, no doubt. Cory knelt down at his bedside and brushed his son's hair away from his forehead. He kissed Zach gently, wondering if he would forget him if he and Nadia went their separate ways. Would he be able to remain a meaningful part of Zach's life? He'd already felt it slipping away from him in the months they'd been separated. He could only hope that Nadia would cool off after he'd gone and arrive at the same conclusion that he had.

'I'll give you a call later on,' he said as he came down the stairs. 'Zach's fast asleep. I know you're angry with me, Nadia, but please think about Zach before you do anything hasty.'

She seemed unwilling to say anything more about the matter, so Cory let himself out of the house. At least the car was working properly now. Something was going according to plan in his life.

The officers had tuned off the engine, removed the keys, left them on the driver's seat and closed the door; he'd forgotten he had left it running out there. Strictly speaking, it was probably an offense to leave a car idling like that in the road, but the two officers probably didn't relish their chances of navigating the frosty situation they'd just escaped from back at the house.

Cory started up the car and made his way slowly toward the exit to Shallow Falls. Already it felt strange without Bianca in the passenger seat. He'd worked alone for some time, but he enjoyed her company. For such an unusual age pairing, it worked well.

As the car neared the *You are now leaving Westview* sign, Cory's phone buzzed. He pulled over at the side of the road, having learned his lesson from the near-miss earlier that day. It was from Bianca.

Things haven't gone well with Mom. She wants me to finish at the paper.

That wasn't a good start. Cory had hoped Paul Williams would be able to sway her. He'd seen for himself how protective Nadia was with Zach, so he could hardly blame Denise Williams. He hadn't exactly given her much basis for placing her trust in him.

I got a message from Xander. I told him to contact me if he needs me. He was in a panic. I'm walking over to his house if you want to pick me up.

A third message arrived on Cory's cell phone.

Damn! Mom won't let me leave the house!

Cory waited a few moments, but no more messages arrived. He was better off in Shallow Falls. From the tone of Bianca's messages, it sounded like a friendly house visit with a bunch of flowers and a box of chocolates might be timely.

Cory resisted the temptation to drive fast back to the falls. He noticed that the police presence had been substantially reduced since the morning, so he pulled over in the parking lot to take a look at the scene. There were no officers that he recognized there now, but he managed to establish that the body had been removed from the scene. That meant they'd get an official identification and formal announcement of the name very soon.

As Cory drove back past Reece's trailer, he felt a pang of guilt that he and Bianca hadn't stopped in on her: they'd been so busy and caught up in the day's events. He didn't want her to feel like she'd been abandoned; he'd get over there as soon as possible.

Cory scanned the streets for Bianca as he drove carefully through the town, but he saw no sign of her. He'd half expected her to have managed to convince her mom to let her out, but it looked like the lockdown was being enforced.

He pulled off onto the main street to buy some flowers and chocolates at the grocery. As he handed over his change to the cashier, he wondered what Shallow Falls would be like with a huge store. It would certainly attract the folks from Westview. They had a supermarket, but it was a chain that had seen better days—and those better days had been way back in the seventies.

Cory peeled off the price stickers as he sat in the car, then circled round by Xander's house one more time, just to be sure Bianca hadn't managed to sweet talk her way out of her incarceration. There was no sign of her, so he headed back to her house, hopeful that a man bearing gifts might make Denise Williams reconsider her position.

Denise was quick to answer the door when he called. He could tell from her face that she wasn't going to go in for the kill, so he greeted her in as friendly a manner as he could muster.

'Hello, Mrs. Williams, how are you? I just wanted to drop these flowers by for Bianca. I also bought these chocolates for you by way of apology for the panic I caused you today. I'm so sorry, I really am. I promise it won't happen again.'

'Thank you, Cory; the gifts are very much appreciated. However, we still need to have a proper discussion about Bianca's future over the weekend. We'll let you know on Monday morning if she's continuing with her internship.'

'May I speak briefly to Bianca, just to wish her well?'

'Do you know she was trying to leave the house ten minutes ago to see that boy, Xander Griffen? She's not very happy with me, because I told her she had to stay at home and get some rest. I'll get her. Bianca? Bianca, it's Mr. Miles.'

There was no reply.

'She's probably got headphones on.' Cory smiled.

'I'll go and get her—one moment.'

Denise Williams went up the stairs, returning seconds later wearing the same facial expression as she had when she'd been marching along the hospital corridor earlier.

'The little devil, she climbed out her bedroom window and she's gone!'

'Oh—that doesn't sound like Bianca,' Cory said, a little taken aback by the information. 'That's more like something a fifteen-year-old might do. It sounds very out of character.'

'I'm furious with her—I strictly forbade her to leave the house after her accident.'

'Look, she won't have gone far. I'll drive over to Xander's and bring her back home. You stay here, in case she comes back. I know she was anxious about Xander when she texted me. I'll bring her back home, don't worry.'

Bianca was behaving like some petulant schoolkid, but this was the adult world of work; she couldn't go around behaving like that. He got in the car and retraced his steps. There was a chance she'd been walking along one of the cut-throughs, or he might have missed her while he was in the grocery store.

Cory drove along the route she was most likely to have taken. It wasn't too long before he saw her walking briskly along the street. He pulled into the curb, lowered his window, and called over to her.

'Bianca—hey, Bianca.'

She was in a world of her own, taking a few moments to respond. She looked agitated when she came over, like something was bothering her.

'You all right?' he asked. 'You look like you had a fright.'

'Just that dick Dean Tarrant driving by and shouting abuse at me,' she replied, her voice faltering as if she was holding back tears.

'We're going to have to do something about him, Bianca. We can't let this go on.'

'Yeah, I know. But I have to get over to Xander. He sounded like he was going crazy when he texted me.'

'No, you're going home right now,' Cory said. He felt like her dad when he said it.

'I can't—Xander needs me.'

'Bianca, you can't go climbing out of your bedroom window against your mom's wishes. And particularly not when you're representing the newspaper. You need to go home, apologize to her, and do your best to convince her to allow you to carry on working with us at the newspaper.'

'But Xander—I promised him--'

'I'll go and see Xander now. Text him on your way home and tell him I'm coming. I'll sort it out for you, Bianca. Get yourself home to your mom—that's the best place you can be right now.'

THIRTY-SIX

Cory scanned the road for Dean Tarrant's car as he drove over to Xander's, but he hadn't a clue what the kid drove, so he may well have driven past him. He wanted to punch the jerk—he'd have grown up knowing that he was protected by his father. The idiot was all but untouchable.

He was still fuming with Bianca, too; is this what parenting a teenage Zach would be like, he wondered?

Cory didn't want to be wound up when he spoke to Xander; it wouldn't help. He took a couple of minutes to do some deep breathing before he walked up to the door. If it worked for the yoga gurus, why not for him?

The door knocker felt like it had rusted even more since their last visit. It would have been easier to use his fist. Xander opened up immediately, looking terrified, and checked that the coast was clear before he fully opened the door.

'Hi, Xander, do you remember me? I'm Cory Miles, from the local newspaper. Did Bianca tell you I was on my way?'

Xander's blank expression gave him his answer.

'That's unusual,' Cory said, speaking to himself as much as anything. 'She said she'd text you.'

'Have they found Poppy yet?' Xander asked.

'Not yet, Xander, but I'm sure they will.'

Cory walked through into the main room. The takeout boxes and soda cans that they'd cleared up previously had been replaced by fresh rubbish. There was some paperwork laid out on the coffee table.

'Bianca said you were scared,' Cory said, trying to speak in a reassuring tone. 'Is there anything I can do to help?'

'Those men came again,' Xander said.

'Which men?'

'They had suits on. They scared me—they say things I don't understand. Mr. Jones sent them.'

'What did they say to you?' Cory asked, trying to get a good look at the paperwork, which was upside down.

'They wanted me to sign stuff.'

'What stuff?' Cory asked, concerned now.

Xander pointed to the paperwork.

'Did you sign it?' Cory asked, trying to conceal the worry in his voice.

Xander nodded.

'May I?' Cory asked, his hands poised to pick up the papers.

'Yes.'

Cory scanned them quickly. It was legal documentation related to the land and house. Much of it was in legal jargon, but he got the gist of it. Xander had just agreed to sell his property and land for an amount which even Cory could tell was well below market value. And he had a damn good idea why the land had been bought.

'What did the men tell you?' Cory asked. 'Did they say anything about the house?'

'They said I had money to buy lots of pizzas now. They said they'll be in touch.'

Cory continued to scan the paperwork. They'd be in touch, all right. Xander was expected to vacate the property within one month or he'd be forcibly evicted.

In spite of the gravity of what had happened, Cory stayed calm. He didn't know much about the legal processes, but he was certain that he'd be able to get the contract rescinded on some basis or another. Surely there was no way a bunch of sharks could prey on a vulnerable guy like Xander Griffen and just help themselves to his house. The newspaper gave him access to legal support, and he'd use it on Xander's behalf.

The signatures of the purchasing party were made on behalf of a company which Cory had never heard of. It had an unusual, noncommittal name. Fenton-Aylesbury Associates. That made him smell a rat, for starters. Everything about this situation screamed double-dealing and corruption.

'Mind if I take some photographs of the contract with my cell phone?' Cory asked. 'I'll just get this paperwork checked out for you. It'll help put your mind at rest.'

Xander gave him the go-ahead.

Attached to the legal paperwork was a boundary map which clearly showed the perimeter of Xander's and Reece's land. This was where the supermarket was going, only it would appear that Xander and Reece were being cut out of the negotiations. For a moment, Cory considered the possibility that Poppy's disappearance was somehow linked to the property situation. But he couldn't find the link. He had to accept that they were just two different things. Talk about unlucky; Reece was experiencing enough misfortune to last a lifetime.

'Thanks for this, Xander. Do you mind if I take a look out the back and just walk the boundary of your property? It'll help me understand this paperwork a little better.'

'Yes, no problem,' Xander said. 'And say hello to Bianca next time you see her.'

Cory let himself out the front door and gave Xander a wave as he passed the window just to be sure he'd grasped that he was going for a look around.

The entire house and outbuildings were in desperate need of some love. The woodwork was thirsty for paint, like a lost man might crave water in a scorching desert. The garden was overgrown, as if the apocalypse had used Xander's land as a tryout before it scorched the remainder of the planet. Weeds and grass grew waist-high, brambles pushed through where shrubs had once grown, and what was left of an old vegetable plot made a sickly protest about the carnage going on around it. It would soon become completely overrun and there would be no evidence left of it.

Cory stood at the boundary of the garden, which was marked only by the rotten remains of a decayed wooden fence, the slats from it crunching underfoot. He scanned the land at the back of the property. It went way back to the trees, a massive plot of a couple of field lengths. It was the perfect location for a modern supermarket.

It was tough walking through the weeds and high grass, but Cory was keen to see how the land bordered onto Reece's property. He could see her trailer in the distance, a police car still parked outside and her own car nearby. The trailer and playing area that the kids used took up very little of the space. Just like Xander's, her land went right back. Plenty of room for a large supermarket, loading bays and a good deal of parking. Cory could see how that would be good for the town; but would it bring benefits to Reece and Xander? He thought not.

He looked over at Reece's land again, comparing the boundaries marked on the documentation shown on his phone to the real-life woods and land in front of him. They'd need Reece's land, too, for the supermarket plan to work. There was a natural space there, bounded by the trees. Xander's land alone wouldn't be sufficient—the two plots had to come as a package. So, would they be applying the pressure to Reece, too? With a 24/7 police presence, that was going to be difficult. He'd need to get over to see Reece; the pieces were beginning to form a picture, but there were still some confusing gaps.

His phone buzzed. He navigated away from the image on his screen and checked the caller. The exchange was Shallow Falls, but he didn't recognize the number. He answered.

'Hi, Cory Miles? It's Bianca's mom, Denise. I got your phone number from the newspaper. Is she with you?'

'No, why do you ask? I saw her a couple of minutes after we spoke and sent her back home. Is she not there?'

'I've been waiting for her all this time. I've been getting angrier and angrier, thinking she probably went over to Xander's place anyway.'

'I'm here right now,' Cory replied, wondering what had happened. He replayed the sequence of events in his head. 'She's definitely not here. Have you checked her room? If she climbed out of the house once, maybe she climbed back in to avoid making a scene?'

Cory could hear as Denise walked upstairs to check Bianca's room.

'There's no sign of her, Mr. Miles. Where did you say you saw her?'

'She was five minutes' walk from your house. She promised me she'd walk straight back. There was no argument—she didn't make me think that she would do anything but what we agreed. Have you tried her cell phone?'

'Yes, she's not picking up. I'm feeling quite concerned. The nurse at the hospital said she might have a concussion. What if she's lying out there in the street?'

'Why don't you walk up your road and check? Go as far as the corner where your cul-de-sac merges with the main road. If you don't see her there, she must have gone on somewhere else. Are you certain she's not in the house? It seems so unlike Bianca to behave like this.'

'She's not here, Mr. Miles. I'm going to put my phone down and check along the street. If you're at Xander's, will you drive over here and watch out for her? I'll meet you back at the house.'

'I'll be right there,' said Cory, ending the call. He'd told a white lie—he wasn't going directly to the Williams' house. He had a stupid jerk to check in on first. He had a feeling that same jerk might have an idea where Bianca had gotten to.

THIRTY-SEVEN

As a local reporter, Cory made it his business to know where the movers and shakers lived in Shallow Falls. So, after his call with Denise Williams, he knew exactly where he was heading.

If he'd been a powder keg about to go off when Bianca told him how Dean Tarrant had harangued her from his car, he was now that same powder keg exploding in slow motion, furious and ready to pick a fight, come what may. He slammed the car door shut, started the car, and over-revved the engine, then slammed it into gear and drove off down the road much more aggressively than he should have done in a residential area.

Chief Tarrant lived in the same part of town as Bianca, though it was in a completely different neighborhood, so in terms of approaching it by road, they were separated entirely. As Cory pulled out into the main road which connected the two residential areas, he ran through the possible scenarios in his mind.

Had Bianca been foolish enough to accept a lift from Dean

Tarrant? Surely not—she had much too sensible a head on her shoulders. If he had enticed her into his vehicle on some false pretense, what might he have done? Abandoned her somewhere and forced her to walk home? Might he have coerced her into his car? The thought of it made Cory shudder; he wouldn't get away with something like that even if he was the chief's son.

Then there was the possibility that Bianca might have gone with him voluntarily. Cory scolded himself for even going there. No way was this some kind of screwed-up courtship. He'd seen Bianca's face; she genuinely hated the guy.

By the time he pulled up at the curb in front of Tarrant's house, he had worked himself up into a frenzy of dark possibilities. He was convinced that Bianca was in danger and he had every intention of putting a stop to it. There was a car pulled up in the driveway, the sort of vehicle a young jerk might drive: black with red trim, double exhausts and alloy wheels.

What was of even more interest to Cory were the two realtor signs outside the house. He knew from previous experience that two signs usually meant somebody was having difficulty selling a house. So why was Chief Tarrant selling? Was he moving up in the world?

The house itself was fairly large, middle-class, and well-kept. The yard was what Cory would have described as low-maintenance if he'd been writing a newspaper feature about it: gravel in place of grass, pots instead of flower beds and hanging baskets that were so neat that they must have been purchased ready-made from a nearby store. The house itself was well-maintained but without customizations or adornments. The paintwork would need a touch-up in the next year, but there was nothing decaying or disorderly about it. It was more a case of make-do maintenance than pride-and-joy decoration.

Chief Tarrant would be too busy to spend much time tending to his property. Its appearance was probably more indicative of the lack of time in his life than an absence of inclination.

Cory stormed up to the door, certain that his number one target was at home. He ignored the knocker entirely, opting for the more assertive option of banging several times with his fist to raise Dean's attention. He followed up the first three bangs with another four—it was the kind of knock which established right from the get-go that this was a no-nonsense house call.

Cory heard movement from inside, so he followed up with another three sharp taps.

'Come on, open up! I know you're in there.'

He was just waiting for that door to open. The moment it did, he'd tear into the idiot and give him a piece of his mind.

He heard the key being turned on the inside, saw the door handle being twisted, and the door began to open. Even before it was fully open, he began to let rip with his angry tirade.

'Get out here and show your face, you little jerk! What the f--'

As the door opened, Cory stopped dead at the sight of an elderly woman with white hair. She was just like anybody's grandma: silver-rimmed bifocals, hair in a bun, a floral dress, and furry slippers. She steadied herself with a cane.

Cory thanked his lucky stars that his last swear word had not been delivered. Subduing his anger, he immediately slipped back into *nice, well brought-up son* mode and changed his tone to deferential politeness.

'Oh, hello. You're not who I was expecting to answer the door. Is this Chief Tarrant's house?'

The old lady seemed to be a little deaf, so he hoped she'd missed his first angry words. At least the heavy knocking hadn't been wasted.

'Hello, my dear, how can I help you? What? Yes, this is Chief Tarrant's house. He's not in, I'm afraid. Would you like to come in for a drink?'

Cory felt his attitude adjust from 110mph to a steady 10mph with speed bumps.

'I'd better not come in, but thank you very much for the offer.'

'Would you like to come in for a drink, my dear? The children are all here drinking orange soda.'

Cory looked closely at her. She wasn't deaf; it looked like she might have dementia or something similar. There were no children, and she seemed a little confused. He despised himself for going in all guns blazing. He needed to be slow and gentle.

'I won't take up any of your time. Is this Chief Tarrant's house?'

She seemed to be drifting in and out of clarity.

'Yes, my dear. Chief Tarrant and his little boy, Dean... they live here. Imagine my son Lance becoming a chief. I'm so proud. But now we'll have to sell the house.'

'Why is the house for sale?' Cory asked, softly. 'Chief Tarrant has lived here for years, hasn't he?'

'I'm just a silly old woman who costs too much to care for. That's what Dean says. You should hear his language! He's only five years old, too.'

Cory wondered how much of what she was telling him

was true and how much was confused memories. He noticed a package of something on the key table just inside the door. It looked like a box of drugs delivered by the pharmacy. He was no expert, but he was pretty sure Namenda was used for memory loss, dementia; the bogeyman that frightened the life out of everybody over the age of fifty.

'Is Dean at home?' Cory asked.

She flinched when he said his name.

'Keep that nasty piece of work away from me,' she replied, suddenly seeming fully aware of what she was saying. 'I'll be safer when I'm in assisted living, away from that spiteful little brat.'

Cory looked at her arms. They were covered by her dress. Was she trying to tell him that Dean was hurting her?

'What's the old lady telling you now?' came a voice from within the house. It was Dean Tarrant. He walked toward the door, gyrating his finger by his head in a dismissive display to convey that she had lost her mind. Cory felt his anger rising once again.

Dean walked up to the open door and swept the old lady away with his arm. She stumbled a little, then steadied herself with her stick.

'Out of the way, old lady, go and take some medication —it might help you to talk some sense.'

He picked up one of the boxes of pills from the side table and threw them at her. She moved out of his way, speaking to herself. 'He used to be such a lovely young boy, but now, I just keep out of his way. Never been the same, not since his mother died.'

'Is that how you always behave with your elders?' Cory asked, trying to control himself. He'd never wanted to lay into a person quite as much as he did with Dean Tarrant right at that moment.

'She'll be dead soon enough,' Dean sneered. 'She's just a damn nuisance. I could get a pool table in that room of hers, yet still she insists on taking up valuable space. And she smells.'

'You really are a nasty piece of work, aren't you?' Cory said.

'Well, just so you know, my dad's on his way here right now. I told him you've been harassing me and that you're now shouting abuse at his mom on the doorstep. What a rude little man you are, I heard everything you said—*urine-soaked old lady, smelly witch, and psycho grandma*—you really need to mind your manners around seniors, Mr. Miles.'

Cory heard the car approaching even as the words left Dean's lips, but he could contain himself no longer. Dean gave him a push as he finished his list of abusive phrases and he responded immediately, pushing back as he tried to steady himself on his feet.

Dean was solidly built and immovable. Cory felt like an annoying fly, unable to rustle up any more than a mild irritation. He ran at Dean a second time, but an impregnable and muscular arm brushed him aside and he stumbled and fell, right into a pot of purple pansies. In a misguided effort to create some form of offensive action, he pulled out one of the plants from between his legs and threw it at Dean.

Cory could hear that the old lady was becoming distressed inside the house. One part of him needed to get his message over to Dean Tarrant, but the other hated himself for upsetting or confusing the old lady.

'Dad, Dad, look, he's attacking me.'

'That's enough, Cory.'

Chief Tarrant's voice boomed from the end of the driveway, stopping Cory dead in his tracks.

'Go and see to Grandma,' Tarrant said to Dean. 'Make sure she's taken her pills and try and calm her down.'

'Yes, Dad. I was scared for our lives—this man's a maniac.'

Then, before Chief Tarrant had reached them, he added something extra for Cory's benefit. 'Whoops! Looks like you're in trouble with the police, Mr. Miles. That's what comes of bullying vulnerable old ladies.'

'Dean, go and help Grandma,' came Tarrant's voice again.

'Yes, Dad. I just wanted to make sure Mr. Miles wasn't going to hurt us again.'

Chief Tarrant stormed up to Cory as he attempted to pull himself out of the plant pot.

'That's enough now, Cory, you've gone too far. This all ends here and now.'

THIRTY-EIGHT

That's all Cory needed as a companion in his cell: Spencer Jones. And he was sobering up. If it had been a nightmare, his imagination couldn't have found a worse cellmate. Spencer smelled of booze and was ranting wildly at Chief Tarrant for placing him there in the first place.

Cory could not recall a time when he'd felt more humiliated. Tarrant had cuffed him in the front yard, soil still caked around the rear of his pants, and driven him in the back of his own car to the police station. And as he was doing so, Dean Tarrant was escorting his grandma into the yard, talking to her about the lovely flowers, holding her arm to support her and looking like the best grandson an elderly lady could have.

As Chief Tarrant turned his back to guide Cory into the back of the car, Dean stuck one finger up at him and ruffled his grandma's hair contemptuously. Cory flexed his body in an automatic response, but Tarrant was onto him right away, giving him a push into the car.

The chief had dropped him off at the desk, still in handcuffs, for processing.

'Stick him in a cell for now, while I think about what we do with him. I'll be on my phone if you need me—I need to check that my mom is fine back home.'

That felt like a final twist of the knife for Cory; he knew he'd got too fired up and he felt terrible about upsetting a senior, particularly one who appeared to have enough problems of her own.

The cells were very basic and smelled of urine. Cory had never been anywhere near this end of the police station before, and he was pleased about that. There were just a couple of wooden benches, heavily vandalized with names, curses, and carvings. He was grateful for one small mercy; Spencer had now fallen asleep and was snoring loudly on one of the benches, sprawled out longways with seemingly not a care in the world.

Cory wondered how long he'd be left in there. Chief Tarrant would be justified if he pressed charges—he knew he'd crossed the line. But his thoughts were about Bianca, not himself. Whatever action Chief Tarrant took, it wouldn't involve jail time or a judge.

The most pressing issue was Bianca's welfare. The contents of his pockets—cell phone included—had been taken at the desk, so there was no chance of getting a message out. What would Denise Williams think of him? He'd abandoned her midway through a search for her daughter. If she wasn't resolved to stop her daughter working at the newspaper beforehand, she would be now.

Spencer Jones stirred and snorted on the opposite bench. He was mumbling something to himself.

'I was doing you a favor... you pull me over like that... only a couple of darn drinks...'

There was one small consolation for Cory in all of this, and that was that there was no way Dean Tarrant was with

Bianca. She had to have walked home a different route, maybe needing to cool off or something like that. But Dean Tarrant wasn't with her, and for that he had to be grateful.

Cory heard a rattle of the door and a police officer walked in. It was Louise.

'Damn, Cory, what the hell have you done?'

'The chief and I appear to have had a little falling out.' Cory smiled at her. He didn't feel much like smiling, though; he was ashamed.

'Look, I shouldn't really be down here speaking to you, but Lorna on the desk tipped me off that you'd been brought in. The chief's pissed with you, so they've been told to hold you here for a couple of hours, then let you go.'

'Well, that's a relief, at least. I was going to ask you to smuggle in a file so I could break out.'

She kept a straight face, conveying mild annoyance as far as Cory could tell.

'Look, Louise, I need to ask you a favor. If you can't help me, that's fine. But it's sort of a police matter, too.'

'Go on, what is it? I'm still furious with you over Poppy Norman's nonexistent dress...'

'It was there, Louise, I promise you.'

'I believe you, Cory, but you try explaining it to three hardened cops and a deputy who's under intense pressure to get some results on three very challenging cases.'

'I'm just trying to help. Like everybody else, I want Poppy back safe and well with her family.'

'We all do, Cory.'

'I know you're annoyed with me, but please, will you speak to Bianca's mum and let her know I got held up? Also, I'm really worried about Bianca—I need to know she's back home okay.'

Louise looked at him for a few seconds, then nodded.

'What's Spencer Jones doing in here?' Cory asked, happy now that he could at least get a check on Bianca. 'Surely snoring isn't an offense yet?'

'Ha! No, he was pulled over by one of the officers at Shallow Falls. He'd just come back from Westview and was weaving all over the road. The man's had far too much to drink to be at the wheel of a car.'

'Westview, you say? Any idea where he'd been?'

'No idea,' Louise replied. 'I know that they've impounded his car. The chief wants him to sleep it off, then he'll call him in for a personal chat later, when he's sober again.'

Cory had a good idea where Spencer Jones might have been, bearing in mind the timings of everything—but why?

'I've gotta go,' Louise said. 'I'll check up on Bianca and let you know what's happening.'

She left him in the cell, the heavy door echoing behind her as she was let out by the supervising officer. The sound of the door made Spencer Jones stir on the bench.

'Ah, Cory Miles,' he said, opening his eyes and clearly trying to figure out where the hell he was.

'Hello again, Spencer,' Cory said curtly, keen to avoid entering into conversation with him while he was drunk.

'How did I get here? I really can't recall...'

'You might want to lay off the booze,' Cory advised. 'You're a respected man about this town, Mr. Jones, but if you carry on like this, you're going to kill yourself in a car accident.'

Spencer sat up on the bench, struggling to orientate himself.

'Well, some of us carry heavy burdens, Mr. Miles. A beer here and there helps to oil the wheels.'

Cory decided to come right out with it.

'What were you doing at Westview today, Spencer?' He wanted to know; had Spencer Jones been the one intimidating Zach in the schoolyard?

Spencer began to speak, then seemed to sober up suddenly, like a switch had just been flicked in his head.

'I was out getting groceries, where else would I have been?'

'Oh, I don't know—maybe paying a visit to one of the elementary schools?'

Cory saw it, but only for a moment. It was a flash of fear in Spencer's eyes, caught in a lie and then swiftly recovering.

'I don't know what you're talking about,' Spencer replied. 'I bought my groceries, had a couple of beers and came straight back to Shallow Falls. And they throw me in jail just because I drive a little wide at Devil's Corner, damn cops. And Chief Tarrant's involved, too, he owes me one--'

Spencer stopped mid-sentence, closing his eyes and drifting off to a snooze like nothing had happened.

'Spencer,' Cory said, trying his best to rouse him back to consciousness.

His eyes opened once again, after some struggle, and he was back in the room with Cory.

'You're still here?' he said, slurring his words. 'What are you doing here?'

'I got into trouble with the chief, just like you,' Cory replied, a little more conversational in his tone now. He wanted to see if he could get Spencer talking, now he was a captive audience.

'What's Tarrant been up to now?' Spencer said. 'You'd think he'd be a bit more grateful when you do the man a favor.'

'And what favors have you been doing for Chief Tarrant?' Cory asked.

'Who said anything about chief--'

The switch seemed to go off in Spencer's head once again, like he had some kind of trigger pin response any time Cory got a whiff of a sensitive issue.

'How was Westview Elementary?' Cory pushed, trying to disorientate the man. He saw that flash in Spencer's eyes once again, the sort of expression that would have created a short spike in a lie detector test.

'Don't know what yer talking about.' Spencer maintained his innocence in the matter. 'Beer and groceries, that's all Westview is good for.'

There was a rattling of keys once again at the entrance to the cells. It was Louise Powell back already. And Cory could see by the expression on her face that she didn't come bearing good news.

THIRTY-NINE

'This looks like bad news,' Cory said, searching for a clue in Louise's face. She waited for the door to be closed behind her.

'Spencer, we're letting you out of here. The chief will catch up with you tomorrow. Go straight home and don't call into Lacey's—then this might blow over for you. They're expecting you at the desk with your belongings. Don't let me see you back here again.'

Louise unlocked the cell. Spencer Jones looked like he couldn't believe his luck.

'What, now?' he asked.

'Go,' Louise said, 'Before I change my mind.'

Cory stayed quiet, sensing that the reason Spencer was leaving was so that they could speak alone. It was lucky that Shallow Falls had such a low crime rate; if these police cells were a hotel, they'd have gone out of business years ago. The main door was opened for Spencer and an officer was waiting to accompany him.

'Just a couple of minutes,' Louise said to her colleague at

the door. The door closed, the echo the only sound in the sparse chamber.

'So, what's going on?' Cory asked, the moment the echo had faded. 'Is Bianca safe?'

Louise was silent for a few moments.

'I want you to know that I'm about to place considerable faith in you, Cory Miles. I could lose my job for what I'm about to do. But I'm doing it because I now believe it's the only way we're going to find out what happened to Poppy Norman.'

Cory was stunned. He'd never seen her as earnest as this.

'I'll do anything to get Poppy back home safe to Reece,' Cory said. 'I'd want people to do the same if it were Zach in her place. I promise, Louise, everything I've told you is true. The dress was for real.'

'I know it was—I don't doubt you for a moment. But my colleagues don't see it that way, and that's why I'm about to do something. I mean it—if I've called this wrong, I'll be looking for a new job.'

Cory nodded. He got it, this was serious.

'Bianca has disappeared,' she began.

'How? Has she been taken?' Cory wanted all the answers at once.

'This is between you and me, Cory. What's about to happen is on us. Don't breathe a word of it when we step outside these cells.'

'I won't,' he replied. If he had to sign a document in blood, he'd have done it at that moment.

'I called Bianca's parents. Her mom was unable to find her after she spoke to you. But she found her cell phone on the grass by the highway.'

'Are the police out looking for her?'

'Her mother has received an anonymous text. It said that Bianca would be returned home safely, but only if you back off.'

'You're kidding me. Really?'

'Yes, you specifically, Cory. You appear to have pissed someone off big time. And I don't just mean the obvious suspects like Chief Tarrant, Deputy Cabera, your wife, Mrs. Williams... did I forget anyone?'

Cory felt his cheeks flaring with embarrassment. He had to admit, it was quite a list.

'Anything else?' he asked.

'Yes. No police, except maybe Louise. If the police get involved, it's game over. That's why we have to do this. We have to close this down.'

'Why did Denise Williams speak to you?' Cory wondered.

'Bianca has talked about us at home. It appears that young intern of yours has excellent observational skills. With you out of the picture, Mrs. Williams swore me to secrecy. I feel like I just made a pact with the devil, Cory.'

'What about Spencer Jones? Why let him go?'

The chief put a movable timescale on both of you. He wanted to teach you both a lesson, and I figure you've both had long enough to cool off now. I need to know if you're with me on this, Cory. If I've got this wrong, my head will roll. If any harm comes to Bianca as a result of what we're about to do, we'll never forgive ourselves. But I honestly believe this thing is so screwed up, this is the only way now.'

'Why, what's screwed up?'

'Never tell anybody I told you this, please...'

'I promise, Louise. We're in this together.'

'Councilor Ingram's death was not suicide. It was made to look that way. He was murdered.'

'How do you know that?' Cory asked. It came as a surprise that he wasn't particularly shocked by the information.

'It hasn't been released publicly yet, but it's official. It must have taken two of them to get him up there, but there were all sorts of signs indicating foul play. It wasn't suicide, Cory.'

'So, it has to be linked to Imogen's death, then?'

'Yes. Imogen's death was no accident, too.'

'How long have you known all this?' Cory asked.

'For longer than I'd have liked to, without you knowing about it,' she replied. 'But whatever the nature of our personal relationship, there are some things I just can't tell you, Cory. You know that.'

He nodded. It was an explosive combination for any police chief to have to deal with: an officer and a newspaper journalist who were on friendly terms.

'So somebody trapped Imogen in that shelving?'

'Yes, she was crushed in there. There's no way she could have done it to herself and the handles on those shelves have safety locks on them. The library volunteers are all trained in their correct use. Imogen Franklin was murdered.'

'When does the rest of the world get to know about this?' Cory asked.

'Tomorrow morning. A Saturday, too. Chief Tarrant will be out of bed early for a press conference. The big guns are getting called in, so it's likely to pass out of Tarrant's direct control now.'

'I can't believe all this,' Cory said, taking a moment to think it through. 'Is it linked? Are the deaths linked to Poppy's disappearance?'

'I just don't know,' Louise replied. 'But I know that the

answers probably lie out there in those woods. That's where you found Poppy's dress. Those officers laughed in my face when they came back empty-handed from the woods. But you saw a dress out there, and so did Bianca. I believe both of you. So, if my fellow officers won't take action, I will.'

'Even if it means losing your job? I think we may have an intern's position free after all this is over--' Cory stopped speaking. He'd meant it as a joke, but realized that if they messed this up, that position might be vacant for another reason altogether. 'I shouldn't have said that, I'm sorry.'

'We're going out into the woods, Cory. That's where I think Bianca is. That's where I think Poppy was taken. We can't sit on this if Poppy's dead. God forbid that's the case—but if she is, Bianca is in extreme danger. We can't leave her or trust the assurances in that anonymous text message to her parents. We have to find her. And if there's still some small chance that Poppy's alive, we have to rescue her.'

'You won't regret this,' Cory said. 'Sometimes you have to act on a hunch, even if you might end up in a pile of crap as a result. And Bianca's just a kid—she'll be terrified. What's the plan?'

'Well, I take it your car is still parked outside Chief Tarrant's house?'

'Um, yeah, probably.'

'We're going back to my house to pick up a couple of flashlights, then we're heading out to the woods. It'll be almost dark out there now. Not a word when I get you checked out of the Hotel Shallow Falls at the desk, okay? Just look like you learned your lesson in here, pick up your stuff, and meet me by my car in the lot. Okay?'

Cory nodded and Louise tapped on the metal door. Her colleague on the other side opened it up. As they were walking up the stairs, Cory stopped to ask a question.

'When Poppy was taken, was there any sign of a struggle? Was there anything that suggested she'd been abducted?'

'Why do you ask?'

'Just a feeling,' Cory said.

'No, there wasn't. That's what's so infuriating about this case. If she'd been snatched, she'd have screamed or cried out or made some kind of a fuss. That's why we spent so much time figuring that she just wandered off. Somebody would have noticed something if she'd been snatched; it was broad daylight. She seems to have gone like a lamb to the slaughter. Why, have you got a theory?'

'Maybe, maybe not,' Cory replied. 'There's just a few things about all this that have been bothering me. I can't see how the deaths of Imogen Franklin and Councilor Ingram fit in with Poppy's disappearance. And now Bianca, too. It's become a nightmare. They wouldn't have warned us off if we didn't have their scent. So what the hell can't I see here, Louise? How does this all piece together?'

She stopped on the staircase and turned to look at him.

'Shallow Falls Police can't figure it out either, Cory— that's why they're bringing in the big guns. We're out of our league. Tarrant's not happy about it, but he loses the entire case tomorrow. We've hit a dead end with all leads, they go nowhere. But I'll tell you one thing for sure. If there's any chance of finding Poppy Norman and Bianca Williams, I'll bet my job as a Shallow Falls police officer that we'll find it in those woods.'

FORTY

While Louise buckled up and started her engine, Cory tested the flashlights in the passenger seat of the car. They'd need them to see out there in the fast-failing light. He'd lost track of time in the cells.

'Both working—this second one is a bit dull, but they'll do the job,' he said, as he placed them both in the cup holders.

'Officially, I'm on my evening break,' Louise said, 'so it's best I use my own car rather than a police vehicle. It might help reduce the trouble I get into if all of this goes pear-shaped.'

'You know, you don't have to do this,' Cory said. 'I'll go alone and sort it out myself, if it's going to get you into big trouble.'

'Let's put it this way—we have the duration of my break to find out something solid about Poppy or Bianca. If we do, you call it in as an anonymous tip-off. If we don't, then we have to discuss overriding the Williams' wishes and getting Shallow Falls Police involved.'

'If we can keep Tarrant out of it, we should. He won't

listen to me after what happened at his house earlier. And Deputy Cabera is pissed with me, too. We've got to find something out in those woods, Louise—all paths seem to lead there.'

She looked at the time on her phone and drove the car out of the parking lot. They made their way steadily through the town, eventually reaching the road which took them to the falls area.

'It's getting dark; those woods are a bear to navigate when you can hardly see where you're going.' Cory thought back to the last time he and Bianca were in among the trees. He still had the scratches as unwelcome souvenirs.

As they neared Xander Griffen's house, they suddenly became aware of a flaring light up ahead.

'What the hell-- pull over, Louise—pull the car over!'

Reece's trailer was on fire, and there was no sign of the children outside, or the officer assigned to look after the family. Reece's car was parked in front, as was a second police vehicle. The flames were roaring against the trailer's two doors, making it impossible for anyone to get out, and flames were beginning to spread across the roof.

Louise swung the car across the road, bringing it to an abrupt halt to the side of Reece's vehicle. The moment Cory opened his door, he could hear the screams from inside.

'Damn it, Louise, they're all in there—the doors are blocked off.'

'Any windows accessible?'

'None.'

'Is there any water around? A hose or something like that?'

'I can't see anything—we've got to get them out of there. The trailer will go up completely in no time.'

Cory ran up to the main door, darting his hand through

the flames to try to grab the metal handle. In the split second that he managed to reach through the fire and touch it, he could sense the intense heat that was coming off it.

'Officer down over here,' Louise shouted. Cory ran over to the other door of the trailer. The screams from inside had now been replaced by coughing; they didn't have long to act. Lying just underneath the trailer, her trouser leg on fire and her head gashed, was Officer Ambrose, one of the personnel assigned to liaise with Reece over the search for Poppy.

'She's alive—just,' Louise shouted, patting out the flame on Officer Ambrose's burned leg.

'Here, help me pull her away.'

They took an arm and a leg each and placed her well away from the trailer.

'The gas cylinders,' Cory said, realizing that there was an even worse hazard at the back of the trailer.

'We can't fight it, I have to call the fire department.'

'OK, do it. But Reece and the kids will be dead by the time they get here. I'm going to get them out.'

'Cory, no—you'll suffocate in there with them.'

'Call the fire department, Louise. It might be too late for Poppy already, but I'm not letting two more children perish.'

He ran off, shocked by the height of the flames and the force of the fire. There was no way Reece and the kids could escape through the doors, and if those gas cylinders blew, they'd all be dead. He ran to the back of the trailer, and spotted the propane tanks mounted at the side, just below a window. Light flames were already licking their way around the containers. Above him, the flames on the roof were intensifying. Testing the heat levels as he moved cautiously toward the trailer, he figured if he darted in fast enough, he'd be able to release the cylinders one at a time.

He watched the movement of the flames in the breeze, making sure that he wouldn't be caught. It didn't matter anyway—he had to move them, or they were going to explode. Cory picked the left-hand tank and ran toward it, trying to figure out how to release the mechanism which transported the gas into the trailer. He put his hand on the metal lever, pulled it over 180 degrees, twisted it and pulled off the valve. As he did so, a face appeared at the window. It was Reece Norman, terror and desperation in her eyes.

'Can you open the windows?' Cory shouted at her.

'They're all either sealed off or they only open a small way,' she screamed, coughing. 'The girls... they're unconscious. We can't get out, Cory, the ceiling's beginning to melt—it's coming down onto the floor.'

'Get the girls by the window, Reece... quickly.'

He picked up the gas tank and ran away from the trailer, dropping it at a safe distance. There was a half brick discarded on the ground, one from the remains of the old house; he picked it up and ran in for the second canister. He could barely make out Reece; it was all but dark now and the smoke inside the trailer was dense and enveloping. The paint on the outside of the gas canister was now beginning to peel and curl as light flames began to lick round it.

Cory pulled down the sleeves of his shirt to give his hands as much protection from the hot metal as he could manage. He unclipped the valve mechanism, releasing the canister. Cory picked it up, but it was heavier than the other, still full of the liquid gas. There was a burst of flame as he saw that he'd not quite released the valve correctly and a small jet of gas had been released at the top.

'Goddammit,' he cursed, as Reece banged desperately at the glass, screaming for him to get them out.

'I can't break the glass,' she shouted, 'I can't reach anything heavy enough.'

He had to move the canister first, otherwise they'd all get caught in the explosion. Cory heaved it up and moved as fast as he could, well away from the trailer. The leak in the valve persisted in shooting out a flame at the side and the flames appeared to have taken hold at the far end. Cory moved it as far as he dared, then threw it away from his body as the heat became too intense. As it landed on the ground, the container struck a brick and the side ruptured.

Cory dove to the ground amid a fierce bang. There was a furious roar of flames as the gas inside exploded. His ears rang with the sound, as if a powerful gun had gone off at his side. The explosion settled quickly and as he looked up to check that he was clear to move again, he spotted Louise coming over to his aid.

'Are you okay, Cory?'

'I'm fine, but they're still in there. I'm going in; I need you to drag the kids clear of the trailer, okay?'

Cory ran up to where the tanks had been, picking up the half brick and standing on the bottle mounts to gain the height he needed. He couldn't see Reece. As he smashed the glass with the brick, the sudden rush of air made the flames inside the trailer roar with a new and deadly power. He moved the brick around the metal frame as quickly as he could, clearing as much of the glass as possible, then pulled himself up through the opening and rolled down onto the floor.

The living area, where only days previously Toni and Megan had been coloring with Bianca, was now a fiery inferno, the table all but destroyed. On the floor was Reece, with Megan at her side, both still, their faces blackened with soot. Cory picked up Megan and moved her toward the window, where Louise was waiting.

'Where are those damn fire engines?' he cursed, as he passed Megan through the window.

'They have to come from Westview—ten minutes, maybe,' she answered.

Moving Reece was not as difficult as Cory had feared; her body was gaunt and limp. He picked her up and maneuvered her towards the window. She began to cough and splutter as she inhaled the fresh air.

'Toni,' she gasped, 'Toni is in the back bedroom.'

'I'll get her,' Cory promised. 'Can you walk? Can you climb through that window frame if Louise helps you?'

Reece nodded and began to move through with Louise's encouragement. Behind Cory, a section of roof fell in where the table had been. The flames were beginning to rip through the fabric of the trailer now; there might not be much for the firefighters to save by the time they finally arrived.

To reach the bedrooms at the rear of the trailer, Cory had to navigate a length of corridor which was engulfed in flames. He looked around. In the sink was a bowl full of water where a couple of cups had been left to soak. In the kitchen area, there was a fire blanket, wrapped up neatly and fixed to the wall, where it had probably sat for years, unnoticed. Cory removed the cups and tipped the bowl of water down his clothes, then unwrapped the fire blanket and pulled it over his head.

'Toni,' he shouted. 'Can you hear me?'

He had one chance to get it right, but there were three bedroom doors. His plan was to dart along the corridor and burst through the door. If he got the wrong bedroom, he might not get a second try.

'Help, I'm scared,' came a small voice. 'Mom! Mom! I can't get out.'

Cory followed the voice to the far bedroom. He worked out his route and took a deep, smoke-laden breath. Then he sped through the flames and crashed into the bedroom door. The room was filling with smoke and the roar of the flames on the roof above was deafening. Toni jumped at the sight of him; he probably looked like a ghost with the fire blanket over him.

'It's Cory Miles, the man from the paper—Bianca's friend. Remember me?'

Toni nodded, coughing at the sudden cloud of smoke.

'We're going to have to climb out the window, Toni. Can you be really grown-up for a few minutes, while I get you out of here?'

She nodded, her eyes widening in panic.

Cory threw the fire blanket onto the floor and moved toward the window. They were more like portholes than windows. Cory cursed the old-fashioned fire regulations that deemed such an old trailer acceptable as living quarters.

He needed to smash the glass, but there was nothing to break it with. He'd use his hand or elbow as a last resort, but he didn't want to cut himself in the process. As he looked around for something to use to smash his way through, there was a deafening crack and a gust of flames. A section of roof had just fallen in, separating him from the terrified child caught in a circle of fire in the corner of her bedroom.

FORTY-ONE

'Toni, stay still,' Cory called out. He could sense movement outside the bedroom window, but if he didn't move fast, Toni would be cut off. The corridor beyond her bedroom already resembled a tunnel of flames.

'I'm scared, I want to get out! I want my mom.'

She was becoming hysterical; Cory feared she might do something stupid. He turned suddenly as the glass behind him shattered. It was Xander Griffen, working with Louise to get them out of there. Xander was raking the shattered glass fragments out of the frame, clearing the way for Cory.

He had his way out now, if he could just reach Toni. The flames were becoming oppressive beyond the bedroom, the smoke getting denser by the second. He spotted the discarded fire blanket at Toni's side.

'Wrap that blanket around you,' Cory called out. Visibly shaking, Toni did as she was told. Cory felt his clothing; it had partially dried out with the intensity of the heat, but it was still damp. He closed his eyes and dived across the burning shard of twisted metal that had crashed into the room. He landed heavily on the floor at Toni's side and patted himself down to put out the flames that were licking the edge of his pants. He got up quickly and put his arms tightly around Toni to give her comfort and reassurance.

'I need you to be really brave now,' he said, looking directly into her eyes and hoping that she could find the strength to get through the next few moments. 'Can you do that?' he asked.

Toni nodded, her tears making tracks through the soot on her blackened face.

'Trust me, Toni—you're going to see your mom in just a few seconds.'

He wrapped the fire blanket tightly around her, making sure her head was covered, then picked her up, cradling her in his arms. He stood on the bed and leapt across the room, over the flames, falling badly on the far side and rolling into the wall, to avoid crushing her under the weight of his body. He scooped her up and passed her over to Xander, who took her into his arms like a magpie seizing its most precious gift and ran away from the burning trailer.

Another chunk of the roof crashed down into the far side of the room, the place where only seconds previously, Cory had promised he would get Toni out of there. He could see that beyond the broken window, Louise was urging him to hurry. Judging by the look of concern on her face, the trailer must be almost entirely engulfed now.

Estimating he only had seconds, Cory clambered through the small opening, guided by Louise. As they landed in the overgrown grass, clear of the burning trailer, Cory turned to take a look at what he'd just escaped from. The living area had already been reduced to a burning metal frame, the bedroom end was ablaze with a bright orange flare, and a deep, black smoke was coming off the entire structure.

'They're out, we got them all out safely,' Louise said, gasping for breath.

Cory coughed, trying to clear the smoke from his lungs. The fresh air was like an elixir, nourishing and replenishing at the same time.

'What the hell happened? That was no accident.' Cory fought to find his voice, hoarse from the effects of the smoke.

'The men turned up and overpowered Officer Ambrose, then tried to make Reece sign some documents. When she refused to sign, they locked them in there and set fire to the doors. These people are animals, Cory.'

The sound of fire engine sirens could be heard far off in the distance.

'A bit late,' Cory cursed. 'There's no way they could have saved Reece and the kids, having to come from Westview.'

'They cut our local firefighting team—that's how it is now,' Louise answered.

'I have to find Bianca,' Cory said, realizing what this meant for his young companion. 'If they think nothing of killing two young children to get what they want, they won't think twice about disposing of Bianca. I'm going out to the woods.'

'You can't, Cory, we have to wait for the police to arrive now.'

'Maybe you do, Louise, but I don't. There's no way I'm waiting to go through the motions with the cops. I need to take your car—can I have the keys?'

Louise looked at him.

'These people are dangerous,' she warned. 'You're out of your depth out there.'

'Give me your gun then.'

'Cory, you know I can't. It's bad enough that we've taken matters into our own hands already.'

'We just saved three innocent lives.'

'Look, take my car and go,' she said, handing him the keys. 'I'll take over here and make sure they're all safe, then I'll follow you. But I can't promise not to come with my colleagues. Just see if she's out there, Cory, and don't engage them if she is. Don't get yourself hurt.'

She wrapped her arms around him and kissed him on the cheek. He looked her in the eyes, trying to convey that he felt the same way. Xander approached them, holding Toni's hand. She looked like she'd recovered well.

'You did well out there, Xander. You're a hero! Thank you.'

Xander smiled like he'd just been paid the biggest compliment of his life.

'I'm out of here,' Cory said, 'before we get overwhelmed with cops and firefighters.'

As he ran over to where the cars were parked, he saw Reece holding Megan, the two of them coughing fiercely, but relieved that they'd escaped with their lives.

'Thank you, Mr. Miles,' Reece said as he hurried by them. 'We needed a friend today.'

Cory nodded and ran on. Officer Ambrose was still lying motionless where they'd left her. He hoped they wouldn't have another body to count. The doors to Louise's car were open, just as they'd left them. He closed the passenger door, climbed into the driver's seat and got ready to drive off. He hesitated for a moment, then realized the switch for the lights was on the opposite side to his vehicle.

There was no time to mess around; he screeched away from Reece's land just as the first fire truck emerged from the wooded area by the road, its red lights flashing. He floored the accelerator while messing with the lights to avoid blinding the other trucks that would be coming from Westview. The only thing he cared about as he roared along the road was getting to the woods and finding Bianca.

As Cory approached the deadly bend of Devil's Corner, he caught sight of a flashing light and headlights approaching from the opposite direction. It would be a second fire truck, or maybe even an ambulance, if it was approaching from that direction.

As he began to drive into the curve of the road, his hand fumbled on the buttons of the car as he tried to dim the high beams. He screwed it up, turning off the car's lights entirely, and making himself all but invisible in the pitch blackness created by the overhanging trees.

The ambulance coming toward him took the corner wide, then swerved as the headlights picked up Cory's car. Cory jerked the steering wheel to avoid a collision, sending his vehicle careening off the road, screeching across the parking lot as he applied the brakes. The car flipped over and smashed through the wooden fence at the edge of the parking lot, rolling several times before coming to rest at the same spot where Xander Griffen's parents had lost their lives.

FORTY-TWO

Cory just wanted the shaking to stop. He'd closed his eyes when the car went smashing through the wooden barrier, starting a series of rolls down the side of the hill that seemed neverending. With each roll, his head jerked violently, as if it was being torn off his shoulders. The flashlights from the cup holders crashed against the windshield and his cell phone dropped out of his pocket, becoming part of the debris as if he was trapped in some deadly, spinning washing machine.

His head was spinning, pounding, and thumping like a sinister metronome, counting him down to the final smash. It came as the car roof crunched against the large rock at the side of the falls.

Cory heard the sound of running water as the final small rocks followed him down the hillside and banged against the underneath of the car as it rested prone, like an upside-down tortoise. Airbags had inflated all around him, and he thanked his luck for Louise's head rests and safety options; he would not have fared quite so well in his own old car.

He could smell something—fuel. He was hanging upside down in his seat, secured by the seatbelt, with his cell phone, the two flashlights, and various other bits of car debris resting directly below him. The drip of the fuel caught his attention. Could the car go up in flames? He wasn't certain, but he didn't want to stick around to find out.

Not the first time that week, Cory carried out a quick check to make sure everything was still intact. The force of gravity on his body was formidable, as if his entire weight was about to push down on his head. His hair was hanging down toward the roof of the car. He found it strangely annoying, desperate to brush it back so it fell flat.

Surely the team in the ambulance would stop to help him? Or would they rush to their first call and alert the police to what had happened on Devil's Corner? He wasn't really sure, but he did know that help would be arriving soon, in one form or another. And he wanted to be gone by the time it arrived.

His hand moved to the seatbelt buckle, but it was jammed. He pushed his fingers into it, trying to activate it, but it was locked tight, and the strap was too taut across his lower body for him to wriggle free.

He tried reaching for his phone, but couldn't quite touch it. He swung his hand slightly, managing to catch the handle of a flashlight which he used to move the phone nearer to him. With a stretch, he managed to activate the screen with a fingertip. There was a Facebook message waiting for him from Nadia. It must have come in while he was fighting the fire at Reece's. It wasn't helpful being in a cell phone dead zone. If only Nadia could see where he was at that very moment.

He stretched out his finger, desperate to open up the message, like it was the most important thing in the world, in spite of his present predicament. He managed to touch the small circular icon with Nadia's profile picture in it, and the message opened. He didn't understand why he couldn't focus on the text; then he realized his vision was blurred. Blinking, he tried to make it out.

I tried to call but there was no answer. I'm sorry, Cory, but I wanted you to know I'm filing for divorce. It's been a long time coming. If we can work through this together, Zach will be fine, he'll adjust. I'm sorry it's come to this. You'll get the papers tomorrow, I wanted you to know beforehand. Nx

Cory thought it ironic that she'd left the *x* on the message. It was force of habit more than anything else. He thought about how much Zach meant to him. Where had it all gone wrong for him and Nadia? They seemed to have lost hold of their relationship like the string on a balloon might slip through a child's fingers.

Was it all his fault? Should he have spoken up when Nadia took the job? Might things have worked out better if he'd taken a better-paying job, freeing up his wife to spend more time as a mom and less as the primary wage earner? It was all water under the bridge now, the woman he'd loved— the woman he still loved—had called time on their relationship. It would soon be over.

A tear splashed down onto the screen of Cory's phone as he thought of his precious son growing up without his father constantly by his side; even worse, he might gain a stepfather, probably a man who Cory would despise. It burned inside him like a self-devouring virus.

As he blamed himself for his failure in their relationship, he thought, too, of Bianca and Poppy Norman. He'd let them both down in his impetuousness. How many times had he been on Devil's Corner? It wasn't dangerous if you didn't approach it like a maniac, but that's exactly what he'd done. And now Poppy was probably dead already and Bianca was scared out of her wits—if she was even still alive after what had happened at Reece's trailer.

As he hung upside-down, the dripping of the fuel still insistent, he considered his options. His life had suddenly turned to crap. He'd placed his intern in danger, let down his son, failed Reece and Poppy Norman, and been unable to salvage his marriage. For a moment, he wondered if it might have been better for all parties if that final crash into the rock had finished him.

Then he was roused out of his self-pity by the sight of a flame outside, reflected in the car window. Suddenly it leapt higher. The fuel must be leaking from somewhere—a torn hose perhaps.

He felt a sudden urgency and anger. Dean Tarrant and those men in suits who'd been intimidating Reece and Xander—they were a bunch of bullies. Imogen Franklin, who never hurt a soul in her life, murdered by the same people most likely. And the one unforgivable thing was threatening children like Poppy, Toni, and Megan. Damn it, they'd even tried to scare him through Zach. It was all connected, and he was beginning to see how.

The flames were blazing even more fiercely outside. Where were those ambulance workers? Somebody ought to be here by now. Cory didn't want to die in that confined space, strapped tight to a seat, upside down and unable to move. How long until it blew? Weren't fuel tanks made better these days to prevent that very thing from happening? He didn't know.

He looked around at what had fallen onto the roof area: two flashlights, his phone, a packet of tissues and a pair of sunglasses. Nothing that he could use to cut his way out.

There *had* to be something. Then he saw it; he'd been looking for the wrong thing.

A fair-size shard of glass had fallen into the car as it had rolled down the hill. He stretched out his arms, then reached with his fingers as far as he could. No, it was just too far away. He grasped at one of the flashlights again and managed to pull it closer to him. Again, he stretched, fumbling to get a grip on the shard. He got it. He maneuvered it into a firmer grip, then moved it up toward his seatbelt.

A flare of fire to his side startled him and he let the shard slip, but managed to grab it before it tumbled down to the roof of the car. The sharp, pointed end cut through the flesh on his hand. He flinched but ignored it—he didn't have much time left now.

The blaze was becoming so fierce now that no amount of safety features would prevent the whole vehicle from turning into a ball of flame. As Cory began to saw at his seatbelt with the piece of shattered glass, he knew that it was only a matter of time before Louise's vehicle would become a deadly coffin.

FORTY-THREE

Flashing blue lights in the distance told Cory that help was on the way. But he'd be engulfed by flames by the time anybody reached him. If he couldn't get himself out, nobody else would manage it.

The shard of glass had cut his flesh with ease, yet he was getting nowhere as he used it to saw through the fabric of the seatbelt. The fire had surrounded the outside of the vehicle and the metal of the hood was making metallic clanging noises as it heated and expanded.

At last, he pierced a tear in the edge of the belt and, with his weight bearing down upon it, it became easier to make progress. As he cut, his weight tore it a little further, until he reached the final threads. He knew when he sliced through those, he'd go crashing head-first into the roof space. He had no choice. He was on borrowed time; the gas tank might explode at any moment.

Here we go, he thought, bracing for the impact. Cory made the final cut, then crumpled into the roof space like a bag of bricks and with the same amount of grace. Through the windshield, he could see the beams of flashlights from whoever was coming to assist him. He wanted to avoid them if he could; he wanted to find Bianca, preferably without the police. That's what the text to Bianca's parents had said —*no police*—and they'd only screw everything up if they piled into the woods with barking dogs and armed teams.

Cory managed to flip himself over, found his phone and a flashlight, then kicked at the glass on the opposite side from the rescue crew. The windshield was partially broken already, so with a couple of good kicks, he was through. Like a tunneler in a cave, he pulled his body through the small opening, out onto the grass, flames licking around him, scorching his skin. He rolled down the grassy bank into the shallows of the river.

As he splashed into the water, there was a sudden burst of flames as the fuel tank exploded. He heard the gasps of the rescue team on the far side of the vehicle. In spite of their panic, expecting someone to be in there, they'd figure it out soon enough. It would give him time to find Bianca.

Cory kept low as the light from the flames lit up the river, pulling himself along in the water to avoid being seen by the rescuers. There were two paths down to the river. He'd have to move along to the far path in order to avoid detection. Movement was easy downstream, and the cool water was a blessed relief on his skin after the near-cremation he'd just experienced—twice in one day.

When he was well away from the blazing car, and almost level with the far set of steps up to the parking lot, Cory pulled himself out of the water. Above him, he could see an ambulance, a fire engine, and two patrol cars. He'd need to circle around them, cross the road, and head for the far side of the woods.

He looked at his phone. It was dead, flooded by the water. He tried the flashlight, pointing it toward his body so it wouldn't be seen by the rescuers. It was rubber, the heavy-duty variety, so it still worked. He placed his phone on a nearby rock. What was he going to do with it in a cell phone dead zone, anyway—take a selfie when he rescued Bianca?

Keeping low, Cory skirted around the far end of the picnic area, then made his way up the small steps built into the hill. He reached the top, checked that the coast was clear, and darted across to the opposite side of the road. He wanted to work his way around Devil's Corner to the place where he and Bianca had stopped in the dark when she'd spotted the campfire. It was away from the emergency services, too. They'd figure it out soon enough, but he wanted a head start.

As he walked around the bend of Devil's Corner, he thought about Reece Norman and the fire at her trailer. And the more he worked through the permutations, he decided they'd all missed the one piece that connected everything. In Cory's mind, there was only one person who could be responsible for bringing this all together. If he'd guessed right, he'd have to proceed with great care.

As he neared the last bend at Devil's Corner, the beams from a car's headlights appeared behind him and he heard the roar of an engine approaching at some speed. Cory moved off the asphalt and onto the small grass verge to duck out of the way. The car passed clear of the parking lot then pulled over to the left side of the road, about two hundred yards ahead of Cory. The driver had dimmed the headlights passing the falls, quick to kill the engine and turn off the lights once he was off the road.

Cory got closer so he could take a look at the driver, but he knew who it was before the door even opened. Even though it was dark, he could see its red trim and had heard the distinctive growl of the double exhausts. It was Dean Tarrant.

He got out of the car and pulled out two bags which Cory could see were packed to the brim with groceries. As he moved to cross over the road, Cory stood on a twig. The snapping of wood sounded like a cymbal crashing in the silence of the woodland.

'Who's there?' Tarrant called out. 'Is that you, Shannon?'

Cory stood still. He gulped, loud enough in the silence to wake up the dead.

'I know there's someone there,' Dean said, placing the bags at the road side and readying his fists.

'The game's up, Dean,' Cory said, deciding to chance it. 'I know you've got Bianca out here. I know this is where Poppy is.'

'Cory Miles... or Mr. Scoop, as I like to call you...'

Dean walked over to where Cory was standing, arms flexed and fists clenched, ready for a fight.

Cory stood firm.

'Well, it looks like I just got my front-page story. *Police Chief's son abducts teenage girl.* I bet that'll sell a few newspapers.'

'You know what, Mr. Scoop? You're a pain in the ass. You don't have a clue what's going on right under your own nose. And you don't take warnings very well, either, do you? A brick through the window, a visit to your boy on the playground--'

'Was that you, you prick?'

'Yes and no. It was Shallow Fall's favorite drunk, Spencer Jones. But yes, I sent him out there. Amazing what a man like Spencer Jones will do for a free beer.'

Cory felt his anger rising once again. This young idiot

had threatened his son and sent a brick hurtling through his window. There were no witnesses; it was Tarrant's word against his. It was time his ass got a kicking.

But Tarrant was rushing right at him, eyes blazing with fury. He raised his right arm and pounded his fist into the side of Cory's head as if he was a punching bag. It floored Cory immediately, and he crashed onto the asphalt.

Dean swung back his foot, and Cory convulsed in pain as the heavy boot smacked into his body three times.

'You're too old for it, Mr. Scoop, you should stick to frightening old ladies.'

Dean readied his foot for another blow. Cory knew he had to be quick this time; if he couldn't get Dean down on the ground, he'd never stand a chance of overcoming him. As Dean's foot came toward him, Cory caught it with his hands, twisting it hard. Dean howled in agony and crashed to the ground. Cory was about to leap at him when a car's headlights reared up from the direction of Westview.

The driver only just registered them in time, swerving at the last minute and screeching to a stop just in front of them. It was a female driver. She was sufficiently angry to shout abuse at them, but not so stupid as to get out of her car to deliver her message.

'You damn morons,' she cursed. 'Get out the road and back into the woods with the animals, where you belong.'

She roared off into the night, leaving Dean nursing his twisted ankle in the middle of the road and Cory desperately trying to catch his breath, having been winded by the violent kicks.

Dean was up on his feet too soon, limping badly but still approaching with the force of a rhino, ready to finish him off. Cory was still down on the ground, retreating fast, backing up along the road to buy enough time to get back on his feet. He reached the two bags that Dean had abandoned at the roadside. Unable to find the momentum to get on his feet, Cory knew he had to do something. Dean was charging at him now, a twisted ankle barely reducing his speed.

In desperation, Cory fumbled in the shopping bags for something to throw. His hand found a large can and as Dean moved up close to pound his fists into Cory's head, he smashed the edge of the can against his knee. Dean crumpled, howling with pain.

That was Cory's moment. If he didn't strike now, he'd never take Dean down. He lifted up the now-dented can as high as he could and crashed it against the side of Dean's skull, watching as he dropped to the ground. Cory waited to make sure he was down.

Without warning, Dean raised his head off the asphalt as if he was just about to get up. Cory lifted the can one last time and threw it at Dean's head. It bounced right off and Dean's head dropped flat to the ground. He was completely still.

Cory moved off the road and onto the grass strip that bordered the woodland. He rested for a moment, looking out into the darkness of the trees. And then he saw it; a single flame, the light of a campfire. If his hunch was right, that's where he'd find Bianca. And if he was lucky, Poppy would be there, too.

FORTY-FOUR

When he'd finally managed to drag himself back up to his feet, Cory walked over to Dean, who was motionless and out cold. He felt for a pulse; he was still alive. That was a relief; he'd meant to stop Tarrant, but he had no intention of killing him.

He took Dean's limp arms and pulled him over onto the roadside, well clear of any danger from passing vehicles. He hadn't a clue how long he would stay down, and he wasn't going to hang around long enough to find out. He rushed off into the woods, losing his grip on the flashlight and dropping it, making directly for the flames.

The scratches from the low branches were a minor annoyance now, compared to the searing pain he felt in his head and rib cage. Dean Tarrant could pack some punch. Slowly and quietly, he made his way towards the campfire. As he drew closer, Cory thought about how Bianca must have startled whoever was out there. He had to take care not to do the same. He decided to pull himself along the ground slowly, staying low, taking his time.

Soon, he was only yards away from where the camp had been set up. He almost gasped when he saw who was there.

Tied to a tree, blindfolded, and with gray tape tying her hands and covering her mouth, was Bianca. Her hair was disheveled, and her clothes were soiled and torn, but she was alive. At a safe distance from the campfire was a tent, and somebody was inside. They were singing, as if in a world of their own. It was a child's voice: Poppy!

So, he'd been right in his hunch. Cory couldn't figure out how the planning issues were caught up with Poppy's disappearance. But then he'd realized how when he was quizzing Louise on the stairs to the cells.

The reason nobody knew who'd snatched Poppy was because she hadn't made a fuss. There was no screaming, no violence, no scene. She'd just walked off perfectly happily, disappearing without a trace. He'd been worrying at the problem constantly all week: who would a child walk off with like that?

Now, the answer was sitting on a camping stool right in front of him. It was Poppy's father, Reece Norman's ex-partner. The soldier who'd gone AWOL. Walking up those stairs from the cell, he'd known—it had to be Harry Shannon, the only man who could take a small deaf child into the woods so that she was comfortable enough around him to play happily in a two-person tent with her new doll, thinking the entire experience was one big adventure.

And there was Dean Tarrant, bringing in supplies. Of course—he would know Harry Shannon; they were both young men on the way up, seeing their opportunity with Reece's land. He hadn't quite figured out how it all linked in, but he was right—Harry Shannon had taken Poppy. Even more important, she was alive.

Shannon had given the game away with the dress. It

hadn't been abandoned—it had been drying on the tree. When it had mysteriously disappeared after Louise dispatched the officers to retrieve it, that was just Harry covering his tracks. Cory had got a grasp of it now. All he had to do was to figure out how to get Poppy and Bianca out safely.

He was lying flat behind a bush, watching. Bianca was intently rubbing her bindings against the side of the tree. Good for her—she was still putting up a fight. After thinking it through, Cory could come up with no better option than letting the police deal with it. He knew where they were and that they were safe. If the police took it carefully and didn't spook Harry Shannon, this could all end well. Then his great plan got screwed.

'You've gotta get out of here.'

Cory stayed low behind the bush, recognizing the voice. It was Dean Tarrant, come back to screw him up some more.

Harry Shannon jumped up. Poppy carried on playing, unable to hear the sound. Cory had to remind himself that she wouldn't be able to work out what was going on if things kicked off. She'd scare easily.

'What the hell?' Shannon said.

'There's some dick of a reporter causing trouble out here.'

'Damn man, did he do that to your head?'

Cory watched as Bianca began to struggle. She'd heard Tarrant's voice. That was her own bogeyman, come to get her.

'We have to finish the girl,' Tarrant said.

Harry Shannon was startled.

'Hey, you said nobody would get hurt.'

'What the hell did you think would happen?' Dean

snapped at him. 'You want to make that amount of money, you do whatever it takes. I did all the dirty work: Imogen Franklin, Councilor Ingram, plus a bit of arson here and there. Oh, and I'd have taken care of Mr. Scoop if he didn't keep getting away from me. Now Bianca has to go, and you need some skin in the game.'

'No way,' Harry Shannon shouted. 'You said I only had to take Poppy for a while and apply a bit of pressure on Reece to get her to sign off the land. I'm no killer, man. I ain't killing the girl.'

'You damn pussy. You want your share of the million dollars, you need to get your hands dirty,' Dean seethed at him. He stormed toward Bianca, grabbed her arms, and pulled her to her feet.

Cory had to intervene *now*.

'That's enough, Dean! It's over.'

As Cory stood up, he heard a click from Harry Shannon's direction. Harry was pointing a pistol at him with a shaky hand.

'Step back,' he shouted at Cory. 'And you, Dean, leave the girl. I said you shouldn't have brought her here. What the hell were you thinking?'

'Man up, Harry,' Dean shouted.

Cory stood still, trying to get the measure of Harry Shannon. He seemed unstable and erratic.

Poppy had come out of the tent now, getting upset at what was going on. Harry signed some words to her, and she began to walk over to him. Dean moved fast and with the ease of a giant, he grabbed Poppy by her waist and moved her to stand directly in front of him. He placed his hands around her neck and began to squeeze. Poppy started to struggle, but he held his hands firm so that she couldn't move.

Harry Shannon panicked.

'You leave her alone—keep her out of this,' he screamed, waving the gun around.

'You kill the girl and finish Mr. Scoop over there. Then you get to keep your daughter. You don't get your hands on Reece's land without dancing with the devil.'

Harry Shannon looked like a man having a breakdown. He moved the gun, waving it back and forth between Bianca and Cory. By the time his finger began to squeeze the trigger, he was pointing the weapon directly at Bianca.

'No,' Cory shouted.

Harry pivoted and aimed the gun directly at Dean's chest. He fired, and Dean released Poppy instantly, rearing back and crumpling to the ground.

Poppy ran to Harry, who put his spare arm around her.

'Get Tarrant's car keys,' Harry ordered Cory.

'You can still walk away from this, Harry,' Cory told him. He watched as Bianca struggled to free herself. It must have been petrifying, hearing it all play out without being able to see what was happening.

'Do it,' Harry commanded.

Cory walked over to Tarrant, found his keys, and threw them over to Harry.

'Now listen to me,' Harry shouted, like a man struggling to control himself. 'I'm taking Poppy and we're driving away from here...'

'Did you know he torched Reece's trailer?' Cory said.

'What?' Harry seemed confused.

'Dean Tarrant, or his henchmen, at least, tried to murder Reece Norman and her other children tonight. Are you that desperate to get your hands on her money, Harry?'

'What? No... it wasn't supposed to play out like this. Take Poppy, Reece caves and signs the documents, and we'll get the money, that's what he said. You're lying. You're trying to get inside my head.'

Harry was waving the gun at him, his finger tensing on the trigger again. The gun went off. Cory heard the sound but didn't realize the bullet had hit him until he fell to the ground, crashing down onto the leaf-covered soil as everything went silent.

FORTY-FIVE

It took Cory a couple of minutes to regain consciousness.
The pain at the side of his arm was intense, his blood-soaked
sleeve signalling the site of the gunshot wound. His head
felt heavy and his stomach was sore from the kicking he'd
endured.

Fragment by fragment, Cory's mind focused on the situation. He could still move his hand; it hurt like hell, but it
wasn't going to take him down. Dean Tarrant was still flat
out on the ground, possibly dead. And Bianca was still
blindfolded and tied to the tree.

Cory opened his eyes and lifted his head. Harry
Shannon had taken Poppy and they were running through
the woods, making for Dean's car. He didn't know how long
he'd been out. A few seconds? Minutes? It could be half an
hour as far as he knew. No, the fire hadn't gone down, so
Harry didn't have that much of a head start.

Although Harry Shannon appeared to have no love of
Army life, he'd certainly managed to pick up some core
skills while he was serving. He knew how to survive and

stay low, for instance, already showing himself adept at avoiding detection in the woods. It appeared he also had a good relationship with his daughter: Cory had seen him signing with her and she'd appeared quite comfortable in the tent, until things had started to go south when Dean arrived.

If Harry took Dean's car, he'd have an advantage over the police. Would he disappear into the night again, taking Poppy with him this time? Cory couldn't allow that.

He pushed himself up, slowly and awkwardly. His legs were still working, but he was severely bruised from the fight and the pain was intense.

Cory rushed over to Bianca, who flinched when she heard the sound of movement immediately to her side.

'Bianca, it's me. I'm getting you out of here.'

Cory removed the covering from her head and saw the look of relief on her face at being able to see at last. With her eyes, she urged him to remove the tape from her mouth.

'I'm going to pull it off as slowly as I can, but this will hurt.'

Cory began to peel the tape. Bianca started to speak before it was even fully off.

'Where's Poppy, Cory—is she safe?'

'She's with Harry—they've gone running off into the woods. Are you okay, Bianca? Your wrists are chafed from the tape.'

'I'm fine—quick, get it off.'

Cory moved his fingers as fast as he could, tearing at the tape and ripping it away to free her hands.

Bianca looked into his eyes.

'We need to be careful—Chief Tarrant is in on this, too.'

'You're kidding me? How?'

'Money problems. Something to do with his mom needing care. That's what this is all about. Harry and Dean seem to know each other from when Harry was living with Reece. They're former drinking buddies, as far as I can tell, with Spencer Jones. They've been working on this for some time. Councilor Ingram was in on it, too, but he was having conscience issues from what I heard—he was going to blow the entire plot wide open.'

'I can't believe this is happening in Shallow Falls. It's a sleepy American town, for God's sake. Things like this don't happen here.'

'Harry's no killer. He's actually a pretty good dad with Poppy—she likes him.'

'Tell that to Dean Tarrant,' Cory said, indicating his body on the far side of the fire. As if taking his cue, Tarrant began to stir.

'I have to get to Poppy. Can you get Dean secured with these ropes before he comes around? Move fast, Bianca— he's strong as an ox.'

'I will. And you take care. If Chief Tarrant has Harry Shannon shot, he can pin this entire thing on him. He and Dean can cover it up and make Harry the scapegoat. Harry needs to stay alive—don't let them shoot him as a fugitive.'

'I have to go,' Cory said, looking over at Dean, worrying that he might be putting Bianca in danger. He looked like he was still dazed and no immediate danger to her.

But Bianca was right. Harry looked like he was in over his head. And with the cops at Chief Tarrant's beck and call, he'd be able to pin everything on Harry Shannon. Even Spencer Jones would be easy to stitch up if they needed to finger the brains behind the entire scam. But for Poppy's sake, too, he needed to make sure that she grew up with her father around as much as possible.

Harry was armed and he'd snatched his child. If the police thought there was any danger of him shooting or harming her, they'd take him out in the blink of an eye. He had to get to Harry, to reason with him that it was time to give himself up.

'Get Dean secured, Bianca. Do it now, before he moves more. Then I want you to make your way back to the parking lot. There's an ambulance crew there. Get some help, to make sure he lives. I want that jerk to go to prison.'

Bianca gathered the ropes and moved toward Dean. Cory gave him one more check to be certain he was still out enough from his wound that Bianca would have time to safely secure him.

'Take care, Bianca,' he said, moving off toward the road.

Harry Shannon was navigating his way through the dark woods with Poppy. Even though he was behaving like a scared animal, he'd shown Cory already that he was a different kind of father than Jerry Hunter. He seemed to care for his child, even if he'd been completely misguided taking her from the school and hiding with her in the woods.

Cory ignored the scraping of the low branches. He had to get to Harry and Poppy before it was too late. He moved as fast as he could, his chest, arm and stomach raw with pain, thinking only of getting to Poppy, returning her safe to Reece.

Sooner than he'd expected, Cory burst through the trees and into the road. He hadn't quite got it right—he was a hundred yards or so in the wrong direction from Dean's car. The sign on the road pinpointed his location, warning of the deadly bends up ahead from the Westview direction.

Cory began to jog, passing Dean's car. Harry hadn't made it that far; like Cory, he must have come out wide of it when he exited the woods. He ran past the shopping bags with their contents half-spilled into the road. It looked to Cory like they'd been investigated by inquisitive animals already.

Then he stopped dead in the road. There was a gunshot —then a second. The sounds lingered in the air like a wisp of smoke taking its time.

Cory began running, forgetting any potential hazard on the winding road, intent on reaching the falls as soon as possible. As he came around the bend and reached the Westview end of the parking lot, he was distressed to see the scene at the top of the falls. An officer's gun was pointing straight at him.

'Whoa, stop there.'

'It's me, Cory Miles, from The Shallow Falls Tribune.'

'Damn, Cory, what are you doing here? Stay back, this nutjob is armed. He has the child.'

Another officer was shining the beam from a flashlight directly at Harry, who looked like a startled deer in head-lights. He was holding Poppy over the edge of the falls. She looked out of her mind with fear.

The police officers were the ones he'd bought coffee for at Lacey's. Cory had to try to take the heat out of the situation. Harry was panicking now; if Poppy got hurt, he'd never forgive himself.

'Cory? Thank God, I thought you'd died in the car fire.'

It was Louise's voice. She was walking over from the parking lot, coming to give the officers backup. Her gun was poised, ready for action.

'Louise, I'm fine. I want to talk to Harry.'

'That's Harry Shannon?' she replied.

'Trust me, Louise. Can I move in to speak with him?

He's not dangerous. Do you hear what I'm saying? Trust me.'

The three officers looked at each other. Far in the distance, the sound of police sirens could be heard. This was all going to play out within minutes. Backup would arrive and Harry would be taken out. If Poppy made it out alive, she'd be without a father.

'Harry, it's Cory Miles, the man in the woods. I don't have a weapon. I know Reece well, and I know the other children--'

'Keep away from me, or I'll drop her in the falls,' Harry shouted. 'You make a move and I drop her. You hear me? She's going in! I want Tarrant's car. I get to walk away from this.'

In the distance, Cory was aware of the police cars arriving in the parking lot. He also heard a shout, far off, that said Chief Tarrant had arrived. It was in Tarrant's interests to have Harry Shannon shot dead. Harry was armed and threatening a child. Chief Tarrant could give the command the moment the child was out of danger.

'Trust me, Louise, and be ready.' Cory said. 'Harry, I'm going to step over the police tape and walk very slowly so you can see me. I won't move in close and I'm not armed. You can hear the police now, Harry. I want to help you and Poppy. I want to get you out of here alive.'

'You come too close, I'll drop her into the falls.'

As Cory got closer, he had a better view. Harry was right at the top of the falls, holding Poppy under her armpits, moving her toward the edge whenever he felt threatened. On the other side of the police tape, which was still there after the killing of Councilor Ingram, were three officers, including Louise, their weapons trained on Harry, waiting to take their shot the moment they could bring him down without harming the child.

Cory heard Chief Tarrant's voice barking instructions in the distance.

'The moment you get a clean shot, take him down.'

Harry heard it, too, and he moved Poppy over the edge of the falls again. The child was terrified, screaming and kicking now. Cory saw the impact that had on Harry, but he was a scared man, cornered, terrified for his life. Cory could see he was expecting a bullet any moment.

'Harry, it doesn't have to end this way. Let me take Poppy. Put your gun on the ground—you can walk away from this. You can still be a father to Poppy. You haven't killed anyone. Dean Tarrant is still alive. This doesn't have to end badly.'

Cory spoke gently and calmly, aware that all around him, armed officers were moving into place. He was also moving in, closer and closer to Harry.

'You get a shot, take him out.'

Tarrant was covering his ass; he needed this man dead.

'Be ready, Louise,' Cory said quietly. She was to his left side, just beyond the police tape, watching like a hawk.

'That's far enough,' Harry shouted. He now had one arm around Poppy's waist and was pointing the gun randomly toward the officers who had their own weapons trained on him. Harry was desperately looking for a way out, but it was clear to Cory that he wasn't going to find it.

'You're basically a good man, Harry, and you love your daughter. You haven't killed anybody. Please, trust me.'

Harry held up the gun toward Cory, about to shoot. As he did so, he had to pull Poppy around, so that she was no longer dangling over the falls.

'Now, Louise,' Cory shouted.

A shot rang out and Harry Shannon fell to the ground. As Louise fired, Cory dived down and rolled toward him, snatching Poppy as she fell. The two of them rolled off the edge, toward the rocks, the crashing of the water from the falls roaring below.

EPILOGUE

For the first time in 97 years, The Shallow Falls Tribune came out two days late that week. Never in its history had it been published on a Sunday. It was a bumper issue, too, and every copy sold out. The entire town simply couldn't wait to get chapter and verse on what had happened at the falls that night. There were rumors and speculation, but only the local newspaper would carry the truth. And the entire town was desperate to hear it.

'That's a piece of history there,' Bianca smiled. 'And I was part of it. Not bad for a first week as an intern.'

Cory laughed, but winced as he did so. He was more comfortable now, propped up in a hospital bed, his wound treated and bandaged, but it would take some time for all of him to heal properly. He didn't care; they'd saved Poppy.

'Who drew the picture?' Bianca asked, looking at a hand-drawn card, showing a man holding a child's hand. She picked it up and looked inside.

To Cory, thank you for helping me, love Poppy

'That's lovely,' she said, placing it back on Cory's bedside table. 'I heard that Reece and her kids are staying at Xander's house while they get back on their feet, or as much as they ever were. It makes sense. I'll bet Xander will be glad of the company. There certainly are enough rooms in that house of his.'

Louise Powell entered the room, wearing her civilian clothing and clutching a bunch of flowers.

'For the patient,' she smiled. 'I figure they'll brighten things up a bit around here. How are you doing, Bianca?'

Bianca rubbed her wrists and held up her hands.

'Still sore, but I got off lightly, if you ask me. And Mom and Dad think I'm some kind of hero. They won't even hear about me leaving the paper now. They've completely changed their tune. Hey, Cory, I didn't tell you—the school may be reversing their punishments. It looks like I might make it to the yearbook after all. They said they'd await the outcome of the trial, but it was looking pretty likely. I might even get a full apology.'

'Nice one, Bianca—you deserve nothing less,' Cory said. 'And I'll be honored to work with you as an intern; journalism needs more young people like you.'

'Did you hear about the chief yet?' Louise asked.

'I don't hear anything stuck in here,' Cory told her.

'Well, the good news is, he's been arrested,' she continued. 'He fought it, but that delightful son of his told them everything from his hospital bed. The kid's a weasel, trying to save his own ass while dropping his father right in it. Spencer Jones, too—he'll be spending more than a night in jail after this. The five of them were in it together: Chief Tarrant, Dean, Harry Shannon, Councilor Ingram, and Spencer Jones. I'm not certain we'll get the people they were working with to secure the land—that's all tied up in crooked, arms-length companies and the like. What a mess!

Those were some moves you pulled out there, by the way. I didn't know you had it in you.'

'He's been all cagey about his heroic rescue,' Bianca teased. 'Can you tell me what happened?'

'It was a bit of a team effort, actually.'

Louise looked at Cory and he smiled as she explained.

'I shot Harry Shannon in his shin on Cory's mark. Neither of us could be sure that the other officers wouldn't shoot, so Cory had it all worked out. He rolled with Poppy over the edge, but he knew how the rocks lay. It was the perfect move, they dropped onto the small ledge above the falls so Poppy was perfectly safe if the guns started going off.'

'Wow, it sounds amazing,' Bianca said, clearly gripped by the tale.

'It was damn scary to be honest with you,' Cory replied. 'I hear you're a bit of a hero, too, Bianca?'

'If you mean I gave Dean a kick in the balls when he started getting feisty with me, then, yes, I'm a hero. I never thought tying up a jerk would give me so much pleasure.'

Cory laughed.

'How is Poppy?' he asked Louise.

'Oh, you know kids,' she said. 'She's happy to be back with her mom and sisters. I'm so pleased for Reece; that poor woman deserves a break. And Poppy still has her father. There's no way he won't serve time, of course, but at least we got him out of there alive. We make a great team, Cory.'

As if right on cue, Zach ran into the room, jumped on Cory's bed, and gave his dad a hug. Cory winced with pain as Zach landed right on his rib cage, but he was so ecstatic to see his son, he didn't care.

Nadia followed immediately afterward, registering Louise and Bianca, visibly uneasy about being in the room.

'Hi, Nadia,' Cory said. 'Thanks so much for bringing Zach in to see me.'

'I know we have our problems, Cory, but don't think I'm not proud of you for what you did to save that child. You're a good dad, Cory—the best. I won't ever take that away from you.'

'Thank you, Nadia. I can't tell you how much I appreciate that,' Cory replied, choked up by her words. He was beginning to accept that it was over. She didn't love him, but they didn't have to be enemies. It could work like this, putting Zach first and placing aside their differences.

'I got you that information you wanted,' Nadia continued. 'Xander Griffen's contract won't stand up in court, it was signed under coercion, and he should have had a designated proxy to act on his behalf anyway, what with his learning difficulties. He's getting signed up with social services to get the help he needs. Both he and Reece are potentially sitting on decent pots of cash. Oh, and it looks like Jerry Hunter swindled Reece out of her insurance money on the house. The whole thing is a very sorry affair.'

'Well, it helps having direct access to legal professionals through your wife,' Cory said.

He felt a sense of relief. They'd returned Poppy safely to her mother, and his own son was delighted to see him, sitting next to Cory on the bed, cuddled in hard. It was the best feeling in the world. He couldn't even begin to think how much better Reece Norman was feeling at that moment, with all three of her children safe and Poppy back where she belonged.

He'd known he was taking a risk when he took a chance on Louise knowing what his intentions were at the top of the falls. But he couldn't see any way out of it; if he didn't do something fast, Harry Shannon would be shot and Poppy's life would be in extreme peril.

As he looked around the room at the faces of his friends and family, Cory knew that he would do exactly the same thing in an instant. To save the life of a child, he was prepared to risk everything.

If you enjoyed this book, you'll love the Morecambe Bay series of psychological thrillers. Nine books and non-stop suspense. Available in paperback and e-book formats.

AUTHOR NOTES

Now You See Her is the first psychological thriller I've located in the USA. Usually my books are set in the United Kingdom and have a distinctly British feel to them.

I've been to New York twice, but I consume American TV more than I watch UK television shows, so most of my knowledge is based on fictional situations.

To make sure I got the language right, I teamed up with an author friend called Bill Cokas—who also writes mysteries—and he ran through the book for me, making sure I didn't mess anything up.

Bill listens to my podcast for authors at Self-Publishing-Journeys.com which has listeners from all over the world. That can be very handy at times, when you need to make sure you're getting things right in your book.

I read a lot of Linwood Barclay novels—he's one of my favorite authors, alongside Harlan Coben.

Most of the time I'd say my books were more like Harlan Coben's standalone thrillers. *Now You See Her* is very much in the style of a Linwood Barclay story, with its local police department, small town setting, and local characters.

As a former journalist, I often choose reporters as my main characters because I know their world so well. I spent 18 years of my working life at the BBC, most of that time as a radio presenter and journalist. You get a lot of access to the police and senior figures in the community as a reporter, so it makes a good job for a character to have in a thriller.

A lot of my books are drawn from personal experience. Lacey's Diner is very much modeled on the diner I ate breakfast in when I first visited New York to attend an awards ceremony with the BBC. By the way, Prince appeared live on stage that night—can you imagine how pleased I was?

Poor old Imogen Franklin gets killed off in the library stacks and this is another potential murder location I spotted some time ago. My wife works in our local library and on the top floor, they keep their archives in these stacks. They can be quite dangerous if staff don't follow the correct protocols.

At my wife's place of work, she always places a chair between the shelves, just in case. That gave me a great idea for a way to dispatch one of my characters when she told me about it. Sorry, Imogen, it's nothing personal!

When I was a lot younger and had to buy old cars that were very cheap, I'd go to junkyards with my dad, scavenging for parts and spares. I don't see as many around these days in the UK; I guess that's because cars are so complicated these days that most of us take them to dealers to get fixed rather than patching them up ourselves.

When you're a thriller writer, you spend a lot of time thinking how you can place your characters in danger. It struck me some time ago that a junkyard is a great place to do this, hence Cory's rather thrilling attempt to get his hands on a starter motor.

I hope you enjoyed reading *Now You See Her* as much as I enjoyed writing it.

If you liked this story and want to stay in touch, I'd be delighted if you registered for my email updates at https://paulteague.net/thrillers, as that's where I share news of what I'm writing and tell you about any reader discounts and freebies that are available.

Paul Teague

Sunday 00:23

There was a heavy thud against the bonnet of the car. Something – or someone – had emerged from the woodland, out of the fog and the darkness, onto the road in front of them.

Lucy cried out, abruptly woken from her doze.

'What the hell was that?'

It was late and, bored of chatting through the day's events with Jack, she'd been half asleep.

'Shit!' he cursed, slamming on the brakes. The car swerved onto the muddy verge. They veered too far to the left, running into a shallow ditch, the wing striking a tree. Whatever it was, it had shattered the glass of the windscreen and Jack had lost what little visibility he'd had.

'That must have been a deer. It was huge.'

Jack pulled on the handbrake and put the gear stick into neutral. As if it mattered, they weren't going anywhere.

'What lights have we got in this bloody thing?'

He scanned the control panel of the car looking for the

interior light. Damn hire cars, he could never find the right switch without fiddling around for five minutes. It was cheaper to hire than it was to get the clutch changed in theirs. When he found the light switch they gasped as they saw what was splashed across the windscreen. Blood. A lot of it.

Lucy began to panic.

'Look at the mess on the window. What would do that?'

'Keep calm, Luce. I'm going out to take a look. You coming?'

'No thanks, I'll stay here. Put the headlights on full beam, you won't be able to see a thing out there. Take your phone too, you can use the torch.'

'Good idea,' said Jack, retrieving his phone from the glove compartment and opening the door.

'Christ, it's cold! Pass me my top, will you?'

Lucy reached over to grab his tracksuit top from the back seat. It was still wet. She handed it to him and then felt her ankle to see if her sprain from earlier was any better. It had been some run. They'd both done well to finish. And now it was a long drive home in the dead of night. They wanted to get back for Hamish, to be there before he woke up

'Be careful out there. It's muddy.'

'No phone signal,' Jack said as he stepped out of the car and looked at his screen. 'The car is fucked. This thing is going on a tow truck. Who knows where the nearest phone box will be, if there even is one ...'

His voice trailed off as he moved to the front of the car.

'Don't you think you should close your door?' Lucy called after him, but he didn't hear her. She tried to lean over to close it herself, but she felt a twinge of pain in her leg. A half-marathon, the first in quite some time too. Of course she was aching all over.

Jack continued to inspect the damage to the car. Lucy lowered her window as he came round to update her.

'It was big and heavy, whatever it was. There's blood on the bumper and all over the bonnet. It's made a right mess of the front. You did remove the insurance excess when you booked the car, didn't you?'

'Yes, it's fine, there's no excess. We can blame the bump in the car park on this too. It'll be less embarrassing than admitting we didn't see that low wall.'

'There's something moving over there. Please don't tell me it's still alive. I don't want to have to finish it off.'

'Is there a wheel wrench in the boot?' Lucy suggested. 'You could kill it with that. Is it cruelty to animals if you put something out of its misery?'

'Press that button next to your knee and open up the boot. I'll see if there's anything heavy in there. I can't see a bloody thing in this fog.'

Jack walked off, holding his phone out for light, for what little good it did him. Lucy gently stretched her legs, testing for pain and strains. She was stiff, but everything was moving fine. Carefully she eased herself out of the car. It was on a slope and she was getting out into a low ditch. As she took her weight on her injured ankle she became more confident realising that nothing seemed to be too badly damaged. She leant back into the footwell, fumbled around for the boot switch and heard the click as it opened. Jack was cursing several feet away. They might be needing that wrench.

Jack appeared out of the gloom. She saw the light from his phone first, then the fluorescent strips on his top. He was pale with shock, she couldn't remember when she'd seen him look like that. She immediately knew it wasn't good.

'What happened? What is it?'

Jack lurched to the side and threw up onto the muddy verge.

'It's a man,' he said, wiping his mouth with a tissue. 'We hit a man.'

'Oh, my God. Is he alive?'

'He's alive. I don't know what to do. He's barely conscious. Can you get a phone signal? Is there a first aid kit in the car?'

'Damn it, Jack. Where did he come from? We're in the middle of nowhere. How can we hit a man out here?'

'Check your phone, Luce, see if we can get some help.'

'No signal. Nothing. My battery's almost gone too. Where is he? You haven't left him in the road, have you?'

'What else could I do?'

There was a feeble moan up ahead.

They turned and walked to the front of the car.

'Jesus Christ, Jack.'

Lucy surveyed the bloody mess on the road. It was a man, forties she thought, his dark hair was greying. He wasn't dressed for the outdoors, he looked like he'd just left the office. He was wearing a shirt, no tie, and dark trousers. His right eye was blackened and bruised, his face scratched and bleeding. His leg was bent back awkwardly, exactly as he'd fallen after being struck. Bone was sticking through his torn trouser leg. His thick glasses were damaged.

This time it was Lucy who threw up. She'd seen things like that on TV, but with a real person lying there, crying with pain, it got the better of her. She wiped her face, as Jack had done, and walked back over to him to try and figure out what to do next. She struck something with her foot and knelt down to inspect it. It hadn't felt like a stone or a stick. It was the man's wallet. She picked it up, they'd need it for identification when help came.

'What shall we do?' Jack asked. 'I don't know whether we should move him or leave him here. We might do more harm than good if we carry him to the car.'

'What's your name?' Lucy asked, finding the courage to bend down and get closer to the man. He was struggling not to pass out, muttering urgently. She put her hands on his head to try to make him more comfortable, but he flinched.

'Careful, Lucy, he might have broken his spine. We can't just move him, we'll need to get some help.

'What the fuck am I supposed to do? He's in pain, he could be dying. I wasn't the dickhead who hit him anyway!'

And there it was again. Her rage could surface at a moment's notice.

'Look, Luce, we're going to have to go for help. One of us will have to stay with him. We'll need to find the emergency triangle in the back of the car and set up some sort of cordon or warning in case another car comes along the road. There's nothing else we can do.'

She knew that he was right. And it made sense for her to stay with the man. Her ankle was not as bad as she'd thought it was, but who knew how far it was to the next village? Jack would have to go.

'You get off, try and find some help. I'll make it as safe as I can here. Put your running bib on, you'll light up better if any cars come. In fact, get mine out of the car too, it'll make us both more visible.'

In silence they put on the safety gear that they'd used during the race only hours before. Jack moved to kiss Lucy, but she was in no mood for it.

'Be as fast as you can, Jack. I don't want to be left alone here with him.'

He touched her arm and jogged off into the thickening fog. The man became agitated. At first Lucy thought it was the pain, but he was desperately trying to get her attention.

'What? What is it? What's the matter?'

She leant in closer, his voice was so weak.

'Run ...' he said, his hand reaching up to hold her arm, 'run ... for your life!'

From nowhere came headlights on full beam, a vehicle revving hard, speeding towards them. Lucy flung herself out of the way. It struck the man, spinning his body with the force of the blow. Lucy gasped.

'Jack!' she screamed, but he didn't hear her, he was too far along the road.

The vehicle stopped beyond their own car, and she heard the change of gears as it started to reverse. The passenger door opened. She saw a hand, it was holding something. It was a gun. She saw the light as it fired, the bullet hitting the injured man's head, its impact spattering her with blood.

Lucy watched as the shooter fired a second bullet into the body and then levelled up his weapon to aim at her. She'd seen all she needed to. Still clutching the wallet, she turned towards the trees and did exactly what the man had told her to do.

She was running for her life.

Dead of Night is available as a paperback or e-book.

ALSO BY PAUL J. TEAGUE

Morecambe Bay Trilogy 1

Book 1 - Left For Dead

Book 2 - Circle of Lies

Book 3 - Truth Be Told

Morecambe Bay Trilogy 2

Book 4 - Trust Me Once

Book 5 - Fall From Grace

Book 6 - Bound By Blood

Morecambe Bay Trilogy 3

Book 7 - First To Die

Book 8 - Nothing To Lose

Book 9 - Last To Tell

Note: The Morecambe Bay trilogies are best read in the order shown above.

Don't Tell Meg Trilogy

Features DCI Kate Summers and Steven Terry.

Book 1 - Don't Tell Meg

Book 2 - The Murder Place

Book 3 - The Forgotten Children

Standalone Thrillers

Dead of Night

One Last Chance

No More Secrets

So Many Lies

Two Years After

Friends Who Lie

ABOUT THE AUTHOR

Hi, I'm Paul Teague, the author of the Morecambe Bay series and the Don't Tell Meg trilogy, as well as several other standalone psychological thrillers such as One Last Chance, Dead of Night and No More Secrets.

I'm a former broadcaster and journalist with the BBC, but I have also worked as a primary school teacher, a disc jockey, a shopkeeper, a waiter and a sales rep.

I've read thrillers all my life, starting with Enid Blyton's Famous Five series as a child, then graduating to James Hadley Chase, Harlan Coben, Linwood Barclay and Mark Edwards.

Let's get connected!
https://paulteague.net

www.ingramcontent.com/pod-product-compliance
Lightning Source LLC
Chambersburg PA
CBHW060903190726
48286CB00002B/352